THE GOOD LUCK OF RIGHT NOW

ALSO BY MATTHEW QUICK

Forgive Me, Leonard Peacock

The Silver Linings Playbook

Boy21

Sorta Like a Rock Star

THE GOOD LUCK OF RIGHT NOW

A NOVEL

FROM THE BESTSELLING AUTHOR OF THE SILVER LININGS PLAYBOOK

MATTHEW

HARPER

www.harpercollins.com

This novel is a work of fiction. Any references to real people, events, quotations, establishments, organizations, or locales are intended only to give the fiction a sense of reality and authenticity, and are used fictitiously. All other names, characters, and places, and all dialogue and incidents portrayed in this book, are the product of the author's imagination.

HarperCollins books may be purchased for educational, business, or sales promotional use. For information, please e-mail the Special Markets Department at SPsales@harpercollins.com.

FIRST EDITION

Designed by William Ruoto
Illustration by Jarrod Taylor

Library of Congress Cataloging-in-Publication Data
Quick, Matthew, 1973–
The good luck of right now / Matthew Quick.
pages cm
ISBN 978-0-06-228553-9
ISBN 978-0-06-231669-1 (Signed Edition)
ISBN 978-0-06-232632-4 (International Edition)
1. Family life—Fiction. I. Title.
PS3617.U535G66 2014
813'.6—dc23 2013026035

---

14 15 16 17 18 OV/RRD 10 9 8 7 6 5 4 3 2 1

FOR MY FAMILY—DAD, MOM, MEGAN & MICAH

If you want others to be happy, practice compassion. If you want to be happy, practice compassion.

—The Dalai Lama

Certainly there have been better actors than me who have had no careers. Why? I don't know.

—Richard Gere

THE GOOD LUCK
OF RIGHT NOW

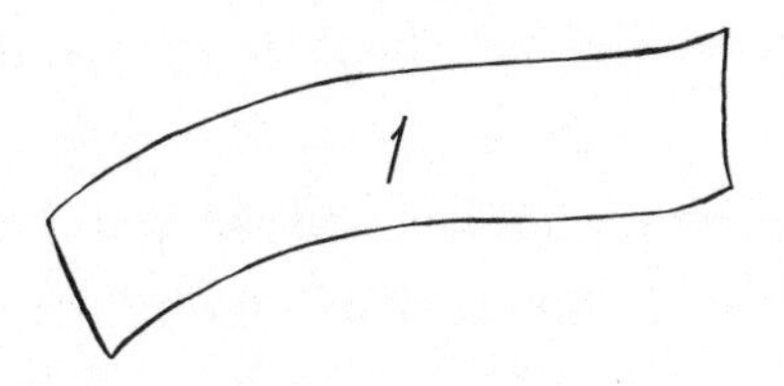

THE YOU-ME RICHARD GERE OF PRETENDING

Dear Mr. Richard Gere,

In Mom's underwear drawer—as I was separating her "personal" clothes from the "lightly used" articles I could donate to the local thrift shop—I found a letter you wrote.

As you will recall, your letter was about the 2008 Olympics held in Beijing, China—you were advocating for a boycott because of the crimes and atrocities the Chinese government committed against Tibet.

Don't worry.

I'm not one of those "crazy types."

I immediately realized that this was a form letter you sent out to millions of people through your charitable organization, but Mom was a good enough pretender to believe you had personally signed the letter specifically to her, which is most likely why she saved it—believing you had touched the paper with your hands, licked the envelope with your tongue—imagining the paper represented a tangible link to you . . . that maybe a few of your cells, microscopic bits of your DNA, were with her whenever she held the letter and envelope.

Mom was your biggest fan, and a seasoned pretender.

"There's his name written in cursive," I remember her saying to me, poking the paper with her index finger. "From Richard Gere! Movie star *RICHARD GERE!*"

Mom liked to celebrate the little things. Like finding a forgotten wrinkled dollar in a lint-ridden coat pocket, or when there was no line at the post office and the stamp sellers were up for smiles and polite conversation, or when it was cool enough to sit out back during a hot summer—when the temperature dips dramatically at night even though the weatherman has predicted unbearable humidity and heat, and therefore the evening becomes an unexpected gift.

"Come enjoy the strange cool air, Bartholomew," Mom would say, and we'd sit outside and smile at each other like we'd won the lottery.

Mom could make small things seem miraculous. That was her talent.

Richard Gere, perhaps you have already labeled Mom as weird, pixilated—most people did.

Before she got sick, she never gained or lost weight; she never purchased new clothes for herself, and therefore was perpetually stuck in mideighties fashions; she smelled like the mothballs she kept in her drawers and closet, and her hair was usually flattened on the side she rested against her pillow (almost always the left).

Mom didn't know that computer printers could easily reproduce signatures, because she was too old to have ever employed modern technology. Toward the end, she used to say that "computers were condemned by the Book of Revelations," but Father McNamee told me it's not true, although we could let Mom believe it was.

I'd never seen her so happy as she was the day your letter arrived.

As you might have gathered, Mom wasn't all there during the last few years of her life, and by the very end extreme dementia had set in, which made it hard to distinguish the pretending of her final days from the real world.

Everything blurred over time.

During her good moments—if you can believe it—she actually used to think (pretend?) that I was you, that Richard Gere was living with her, taking care of her, which must have been a welcome alternative to the truth: that her ordinary unaccomplished son was her primary caregiver.

"What will we be having for dinner tonight, Richard?" she'd say. "Such a pleasure to finally spend so much time with you, Richard."

It was like when I was a boy and we'd pretend we were eating dinner with a famous guest—Ronald Reagan, Saint Francis, Mickey Mouse, Ed McMahon, Mary Lou Retton—occupying one of the two seats in the kitchen that were always empty, except when Father McNamee visited.

As I previously stated, Mom was quite a fan of yours—you probably visited our kitchen table before, but to be honest, I don't remember a specific Richard Gere visit from childhood. Regardless, I indulged her and played my role, so you were manifested through me, even though I'm not as handsome, and therefore made a poor stand-in. I hope you don't mind my having invoked you without your permission. It was a simple thing that gave Mom great pleasure. Her face lit up like the Wanamaker's Christmas Light Show every time you came to visit. And after the failed chemo and brain surgery, and the awful sick, retching aftermath, it was hard to get her to smile or be happy about anything, which is why I went along with the game of you and me becoming we.

It started one night after we watched our well-worn VCR copy of *Pretty Woman*, one of Mom's favorite movies.

As the end credits rolled, she patted my arm and said, "I'm going to bed now, Richard."

I looked at her, and she smiled almost mischievously—like I'd seen the sexy fast girls do with their shiny painted lips back when I was in high school. That salacious smile made me feel nauseated, because I knew it meant trouble. It was so unlike Mom too. It was the beginning of living with a stranger.

I said, "Why did you call me *Richard*?"

She laid her hand gently on my thigh, and in this very flirtatious girlish voice, while batting her eyelids, she said, "Because that's your name, silly."

During the thirty-eight years we had known each other, Mom had never once before called me "silly."

The tiny angry man in my stomach pounded my liver with his fists.

I knew we were in trouble.

"Mom, it's me—Bartholomew. Your only son."

When I looked into her eyes, she didn't seem to see me. It was like she was having a vision—seeing what I could not.

It made me wonder if Mom had used some sort of womanly witchcraft and turned me into you somehow.

That we—you and me—had become one in her mind.

Richard Gere.

Bartholomew Neil.

We.

Mom took her hand off my thigh and said, "You're a handsome man, Richard, the love of my life even, but I'm not going to make the same mistake twice. You made your choice, so you'll just have to sleep on the couch. See you in the morning." Then she floated up the stairs, moving quicker than she had in months.

She looked ecstatic.

Like the haloed saints depicted in stained glass at Saint Gabriel's, Mom seemed to be guided by divinity. Her madness appeared holy. She was bathed in light.

As uncomfortable as that exchange was, I liked seeing Mom lit up. Happy. And pretending has always been easy for me. I have pretended my entire life. Plus there was the game from my childhood, so I had certainly practiced.

Somehow—because who can say exactly how these things come to be—over many days and weeks, Mom and I slipped into a routine.

We both began pretending.

She pretended I was you, Richard Gere.

I pretended Mom wasn't losing her mind.

I pretended she wasn't going to die.

I pretended I wouldn't have to figure out life without her.

Things escalated, as they say.

By the time she was confined to the pullout bed in the living room with a morphine pain pump spiking her arm, I was playing you twenty-four hours a day, even when Mom was unconscious, because it helped me, as I faithfully pushed the button every time she grimaced.

To her I was no longer Bartholomew, but Richard.

So I decided I would indeed be Richard and give Bartholomew some well-deserved time off, if that makes any sense to you, Mr. Gere. Bartholomew had been working overtime as his mother's son for almost four decades. Bartholomew had been emotionally skinned alive, beheaded, and crucified upside down, just like his apostle namesake, according to various legends, only metaphorically—and in the modern world of today and right now.

Being Richard Gere was like pushing my own mental morphine pain pump.

I was a better man when I was you—more confident, more in control, surer of myself than I have ever been.

The hospice workers went along with my ruse. I firmly instructed them to call me Richard whenever we were in the room with Mom. They looked at me like I was crazy, but they did as I asked, because they were hired help.

Hospice workers took care of Mom only because they were being paid. I wasn't under any illusion that these people cared about us. They glanced at their cell phone clocks fifty times an hour and always looked so relieved when they put on their coats at the end of their shifts—like departing from us was akin to attending a wonderful party, like walking out of a morgue and into the Oscars.

When Mom was sleeping, the hospice workers sometimes called me Mr. Neil, but whenever she was awake I was you, Richard, and they were doing as I asked because of the money they were being paid by the insurance company. They even used a very formal, reverent tone when they addressed us. "Can we do anything to make your mother more comfortable, Richard?" they'd say whenever she was awake, although they never once called me Mr. Gere, which was okay with me, since you and Mom were on a first-name basis from the start.

I want you to know that Mom truly loved watching the Olympics. She never missed the games—she used to watch with her mother too—and watching gave her such great pleasure, maybe because she never left the Philadelphia area during her seventy-one years on earth. She used to say that watching the Olympics was like taking a foreign vacation every four years, even after they switched the winter and summer games to different years, and therefore the Olympics occurred every two years, which I'm sure you know already.

(Sorry for being redundant, but I am writing to you as Bartholomew Neil—unlike you in every way imaginable. I hope you will bear with me and forgive me my commonness. I am not pretending to be Richard Gere at the time of writing. I am much more eloquent when I am you. MUCH. Bartholomew Neil is no movie star; Bartholomew Neil has never had sex with a supermodel; Bartholomew Neil never even escaped the city in which you and I were born, Richard Gere, the City of Brotherly Love; Bartholomew Neil is sadly intimate with these facts. And Bartholomew Neil is not much of a writer either, which you have already surmised.)

Mom loved gymnastics, especially the triangle-torsoed men, who "moved like warrior angels." She clapped until her palms were pink whenever someone did the iron cross on the rings. That was her favorite. "Strong as Jesus on his worst day," she'd say. And she even watched the opening and closing ceremonies—every second. Every Olympic event they televised, Mom watched.

But when she received your letter—the one I mentioned earlier, outlining the atrocities committed against Tibet by the Chinese government—she decided not to watch the Olympics set in China, which was a great sacrifice for her.

"Richard Gere is right! We should be sending the People's Republic of China a message! Horrible! What they are doing to the Tibetan people. Why doesn't anyone care about basic human rights?" Mom said.

I must admit that—being far more pessimistic, resigned, and apathetic than Mom ever was—I argued futilely *for* watching the Olympics. (Please forgive me, Mr. Gere. I had little faith back then.) I said that our watching or not watching wouldn't even be documented, let alone have any impact on foreign relations whatsoever—"China won't even know we aren't watching! Our boycott will be pointless!" I protested—but Mom believed in you and your cause, Mr. Gere. She did what you asked, because she loved you and had the faith of a child.

This meant I did not get to see the Olympics either, and I was initially perturbed, as this was a traditional mother-son activity in the Neil household, but I got over that long ago. Now I am wondering if Mom's boycott, her death, and my finding the letter you wrote her—maybe these things mean you and I are meant to be linked in some important cosmic way.

Maybe you are meant to help me, Richard Gere, now that Mom is gone.

Maybe this is all part of her vision—her faith coming to fruition.

Maybe you, Richard Gere, are Mom's legacy to me!

Perhaps you and I are truly meant to become WE.

To further prove the synchronicity of all this (have you read Jung? I actually have. Are you surprised?), Mom booed the Chinese unmercifully at the 2010 Vancouver games—even the jumping and pirouetting Chinese figure skaters, who were so graceful—which was just before I began to notice the dementia, if memory serves.

It didn't happen all at once, but started with little things like forgetting names of people we saw on our daily errands, leaving the oven on overnight, forgetting what day it was, getting lost in the neighborhood where she lived her entire life, and misplacing her glasses repetitively, often on the top of her head—small everyday lapses.

(She never forgot you, though, Richard Gere. She talked to you-me daily. Another sign. Never once did she forget the name Richard.)

To be honest, I'm not really sure when her mental decline

began, as I pretended not to notice for a long time. I've never been particularly good with change. And I didn't think of giving in to Mom's madness and being you until much later. I am slow to the dance, always late for the cosmic ball, as wiser people like you undoubtedly say.

The doctors told me that it wasn't our fault, that even if we had brought Mom to them earlier, things would have most likely ended up the same way. They said this to us when we got agitated at the hospital, when they wouldn't let us in to see Mom after her operation and we started yelling. A social worker spoke with us in a private room while we waited for permission to see our mother. And when we saw her, her head bandages made her look mummified and her skin looked sickness yellow and it was just so plain horrible, and—based on the concerned looks the hospital staff were giving us—we were visibly terrified.

On our behalf, the social worker asked the doctors whether we could have done anything more to prevent the cancer from growing—had we been negligent? That's when the doctors told us that it wasn't our fault, even though we'd ignored the symptoms for months, pretending away the problems of our lives.

Even still.

It wasn't our fault.

I hope you will believe me, Richard Gere.

It wasn't my fault, nor was it yours.

You sent only one letter, but you were with Mom to the end—in her underwear drawer, and by her side through me, your medium, your incarnation.

The doctors repeatedly confirmed that fact—that we couldn't have done anything more.

The squidlike brain tumor that had sent its tentacles deep into our mother's mind was not something we could have predicted or defeated, the doctors told us multiple times, in simple straightforward language that even men of lesser intelligence could easily grasp.

It wasn't our fault, Richard Gere.

We did everything we could have done, including the pretending, but some forces are too powerful for mere men, which the social worker at the hospital confirmed with a reluctant and sad nod.

"Not even a famous actor like Richard Gere could have secured better care for his mother," that social worker answered when I brought you up—when I shared my worry of being a failure at life, not even able to take care of his only mother, which was his one job in the world, the only purpose he had ever known.

Miserable failure! the tiny man in my stomach screamed at me. *Retard! Moron!*

The brain-cancer squid ended our mother's life only a few weeks or so ago, a short long blur (that stretches and shrinks in my memory) after surgery and chemo failed to heal her.

The doctors stopped treating her.

They said to us—"This is the end. We are sorry. Try to keep her comfortable. Make the most of your time. Say your good-byes."

"Richard?" Mom whispered to me on the night she died.

That's all.

One.

Single.

Word.

Richard?

The question mark was audible.

The question mark haunts me.

The question mark made me believe that her whole life could be summed up by punctuation.

I wasn't upset, because Mom had said her last word to the you-me Richard Gere of pretending, which included me—her flesh-and-blood son—too.

I was Richard at that moment.

In her mind, and in my own.

Pretending can help in so many ways.

Now we hear birds chirping in the morning when we sit alone in the kitchen drinking coffee, even though it is winter. (These must be either tough, hardy city birds unafraid of low temperatures, or birds too lazy to migrate.) Mom always had the TV blaring because she liked to "listen to people talk," so we never knew about the birds chirping before. Thirty-nine years in this house, and this is the first time we ever heard birds chirping in the morning sunlight while we drank our coffee in the kitchen.

A symphony of birds.

Have you ever really listened to birds chirping—really truly listened?

So pretty it makes your chest ache.

My grief counselor Wendy says I need to work on being more social and forming a "support group" of friends. She was here in my kitchen once when the morning birds were chirping and Wendy paused midsentence, cocked her ear toward the window, squinted her eyes, and wrinkled her nose.

Then she said, "Hear that?"

I nodded.

A cocky smile bloomed just before she said—as only someone so young could—in this upbeat cheerleader voice, "They like being together in a flock. Hear how happy they are? How joyful? You need to find *your* flock now. Finally leave the nest, so to speak. Fly even. *Fly!* There's a lot of sky out there for brave birds. Do you want to fly, Bartholomew? *Do you?*"

She said all of those words quickly, so that she was out of breath by the time she finished her cheery cheer. Her face was flushed robin's-breast red, like it gets whenever she's making what she considers to be a remarkably extraordinary point. She looked at me wide-eyed—"kaleidoscope eyes," the Beatles sing—and I knew the response to her call, what I was supposed to say, what would make her so happy, what would validate her existence in my kitchen and make her feel as though her efforts mattered, but I couldn't say it.

I just couldn't.

It took a lot of effort to remain calm, because part of me—the evil black core of me where the tiny angry man lives—wanted to grab Wendy's birdlike shoulders and shake all of the freckles off her beautiful young face while I screamed at her, yelling with a force mighty enough to blow back her hair, "I am your elder! *Respect me!*"

"Bartholomew?" she said, looking up from under her

thin orange eyebrows, which are the color of crunchy sidewalk leaves.

"I am not a bird," I told her in the calmest voice available to me at that time, and stared fiercely at my brown shoelaces, trying to remain still.

I am not a bird, Richard Gere.

You know this already, I know, because you are a wise man.

Not a bird.

Not a bird.

Not.

A.

Bird.

Your admiring fan,
Bartholomew Neil

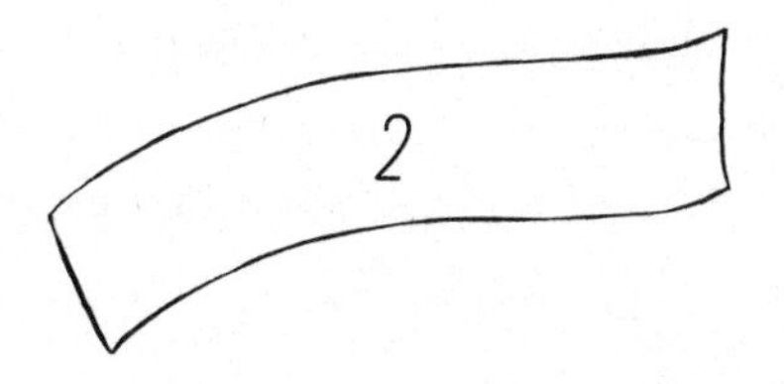

THAT GUY HUNG OUT WITH PROSTITUTES

Dear Mr. Richard Gere,

In order to remedy the gaps in our collective knowledge of each other, I went to the library and googled you on the Internet.

Patrons are permitted to look up anything at the library except pornography. I know because I once saw a man (with gray dreads that made his head look like a dead dusty spider plant) get kicked out for viewing Internet pornography in the library. He was sitting next to me, rubbing his crotch through his filthy, incredibly baggy jeans. On his screen were two naked women on all fours like dogs licking each other's anuses. They kept moaning, "Ewwwww-yeah!" and "Mmmmmm-haaaa-YES!" I remember laughing because it was so ridiculous. The women acting like dogs, not the fact that the man was kicked out.

(Do people really enjoy looking at women behaving in this manner? I find it hard to believe, but if it is on the Internet, there must be a market. And not just crazy library patrons either—but people with computers at home, where such viewing is allowed.)

An older librarian came over and said, "This is not appropriate. Sir, you cannot behave this way here. This is entirely unacceptable! There are rules, sir. Sir, please."

The man yelled at the librarian, refusing to go. He said, "I ain't no sir! I'm a man! M-A-N MAN! H-U-M-A-N HUMAN B-E-I-N-G!" which made the old librarian jump and take a step back. She did not like his spelling at her.

Everyone in the library had turned and was staring by this point.

I was glad The Girlbrarian was not there to see.

(The Girlbrarian would not have been able to deal with such a situation, and I like that about her. She's beautifully slow to take action. She thinks about things a lot before she makes a move. I watched her once as she sorted through books that had been damaged. I don't know for sure, but based on my observations, I guessed it was her job to decide which damaged books should be thrown away and which should be taped together and kept. Most people would have glanced cursorily and quickly tossed each book to its fate one way or the other, right or left, keep or trash, but she examined the books so carefully, turning each over and over like precious dead butterflies that she could maybe open and make fly again if only she were gentle enough. I watched her for three full hours from the other side of the library as I pretended to read the newspaper. It was a miraculous sight to behold, until one of the other librarians came over and yelled at The Girlbrarian for taking so much time. She said, "These aren't gilded in gold, Elizabeth!" The Girlbrarian flinched when the words hit her ears, and she hid in her long brown hair that covers her face like a waterfall can cover the entrance to a mysterious cave. That older librarian sorted through the remaining books in less than five minutes as The Girlbrarian watched through her hair with her shoulders slumped. I saw The Girlbrarian's hands start to reach for several books as they were tossed into the throwaway pile, but she managed to refrain and her fingers never got more than five or so inches from her white-corduroy-covered thighs. You could tell The Girlbrarian wanted to intervene and argue on behalf of many of the books.)

Have you noticed that far too often the best people in the world lack power, Richard Gere?

China has power.

Tibet lacks power.

Are you impressed with my research into and knowledge of your favorite cause?

When the police arrived, the pornography man—who was most likely homeless, because he smelled like fish guts rotting in an old leather boot—shook his head several times, like he was really dismayed, disappointed even, and then he yelled, "I've paid taxes in my life! Dozens of times! Thousands of dollars. I've funded the U.S. government, which is your employer! You! And you! And *you*! All of you are government employees! Public servants. You work for *us*! The people! Not the other way around. I am *your* boss. You! *You! YOU!*" He pointed his index finger at all of the library workers and policemen. "Now I want my representation! This is a free country! If I want to look at porno, I can, because it's my constitutional right as an American citizen. Porno for everyone!" The man ranted for some time about how much American presidents loved sex. Bill Clinton's stained dress. Thomas Jefferson making love to his slaves. JFK and Marilyn Monroe. I wrote most of it down in my notebook immediately, because it was interesting, real, spontaneous, even if it remains unconfirmed, and is most likely an exaggeration.

But I recognized something important that most people do not understand: that homeless man was pretending he had the right to speak openly and freely, and pretending can be more important than settling for what is agreed upon as true—what everyone else is holding up as fact. (In this case, the fact was this: homeless men are not supposed to speak to people with homes—especially in a confident manner.) Facts are not always as important as pretending. Pretending gave that man the power he needed that day to speak his mind. Most of the government employees will never speak their minds, which is why they were so afraid of the homeless man. He disrupted their lives with his pornography and interesting presidential proclamations. If only more people pretended for good causes. If only The Girlbrarian could pretend more effectively—she would accomplish many great things, I am sure of it. The problem is that madmen do all of the pretending and action taking. Have you noticed this?

I always write down interesting important things.

I don't look at pornography because I am a Catholic, and I try not to masturbate, but I'm not always successful with my efforts.

Do you ever masturbate, Richard Gere?

I bet you haven't had to masturbate in a long time—not since you became famous. When you marry a supermodel like Cindy Crawford, you probably don't ever have to masturbate again. (I know you are no longer married to Cindy Crawford, but Carey Lowell. Like I said, I've been researching you.) Why would you even need pornography, with such beautiful women in your home?

Is it wrong for Buddhists to masturbate?

I used to tie my hands to my bedposts—you can do this without help if you practice enough times to master the art of making effective wrist nooses—in an effort to keep from masturbating as I fell asleep at night. But then Mom—who seemed never to tire of liberating me in the a.m., whenever I called out for freedom—reluctantly told me it was better to masturbate than have sex with strange women who have diseases like AIDS and herpes and the flu. She said you can even get the flu from having sex with strangers, and that many people die from the flu every year, which is why we got flu shots at Rite Aid every September.

But Mom also said, if I needed gratification, I should take care of it myself. She said that to me when I was in my twenties and was arrested for trying to solicit a prostitute who was an undercover cop.

Father McNamee arranged for a lawyer to help me and took me to the thrift store to shop for a suit. The men working at the thrift shop were homosexuals, and were—according to Father McNamee—therefore well versed in fashion. They were nice and helped me find the perfect courtroom outfit. "How does he look?" Father McNamee asked them when I came out of the dressing room. "Innocent," one of the homosexuals said, and then smiled proudly.

"Catholics aren't supposed to approve of homosexuality, right?" I asked Father McNamee when we were walking home.

"Catholics aren't supposed to get arrested for soliciting the services of prostitutes either," he said in this terse, almost mean way, even though he knew I was (and even looked) innocent.

"I liked the homosexuals who helped me find my suit. Is that wrong according to the Catholic Church?" I asked. "I just want a definitive answer."

"Between you and me only—off the record—it's not wrong," Father McNamee said. "I liked them too. I've known Harvey for thirty years."

"Who's Harvey?"

"The owner of the store—and my friend."

"So you have homosexual friends?"

"*Of course*," he said, but he sort of whispered it fast.

During a dinner at our home, Mom once said to Father McNamee, "Seventy-five percent of all priests are gay. That's why the church makes homosexuality a sin. Every rectory would be an all-out Roman orgy if they didn't."

They both laughed so hard at that one, maybe because they had been drinking bottles of wine.

When I went to court the judge said it was entrapment, because the cop—who was dressed up in a pink wig and a leather miniskirt and pointy cone bra and the highest heels you have ever seen—had stopped me on my way home from the library and rubbed up against my leg, calling me "Big Baby Daddy" (which was confusing, because how can you simultaneously be a baby *and* a daddy?) and asking me for money.

I asked how much she needed, and she said, "Twenty for head. Sixty for anything you want." (I wrote that down later in my Interesting Things I Have Heard notebook.) No one had *ever* rubbed up against my leg like that before—it felt like I was frozen in time and space, like an ancient caveman trapped in ice or amber maybe—like it was a moment, and so I agreed to give the pink-haired woman some money with a nod, mostly because I thought it would make her happy, and my mouth was too dry to speak.

To be honest, I thought it would make her keep rubbing against my leg too, and that felt really, really good—like I was a stack of pancakes and she was the butter melting on top of me, sliding down. And I also did this because she had hypnotized me with her lips and eyes and mind and her makeup and her smell and her sweat—I wanted her to rub up against my thigh forever.

Pancakes and butter.

It all felt very lucky, like I had won a prize.

But just as soon as I pulled money out of my wallet, all of these men jumped out from behind trees and trash cans—pointing guns and flashing badges and screaming for me to get down on my knees and put my hands behind my head. They had a bullhorn that hurt my ears and made me feel like there were angry wasps tunneling through my mind.

When they handcuffed my wrists behind my back, I was so afraid, I peed my pants and the cops yelled at me because they didn't want "the piss" to get on the seat of their cruiser. One of them called me "a fucking retard," I remember, because I wrote that down later in my notebook too—and also, I don't like to be called a retard, but have often been called one, which is unfair and maybe even cruel.

He said, "Another fucking retard. He pissed himself. *Look!*"

The men laughed and the woman dressed in the pink wig lit up a cigarette as she rolled her eyes at me and shook her head.

"We should put this pathetic sack of shit out of his misery," said a short cop. He was dressed like a bum, but his badge was hanging around his neck. It shimmered under the streetlights. He had a compact modern pistol in his hand, like what cops on TV carry. I worried that he was really going to shoot me between the eyes, because he looked at me like he didn't believe I should exist, and all he had to do was pull a trigger to make me disappear forever. He had the power.

"I'm sorry," I said, and meant it. I didn't want to be the root of so much trouble. I was starting to believe that the angry cop was right about me. "I didn't mean to cause any inconvenience."

He shook his head disgustedly—like I was dog dirt he had just accidentally stepped in—and then he walked away, scraping me off on the rough cold sidewalk until his sole was completely clean of me.

I hope you have surmised by now that I am not a retard, Richard Gere.

I am "above average intelligence."

Mom always told me that, anyway. She said I scored remarkably high on an unconventional IQ test my elementary school required its students to take, but that the world doesn't always measure intelligence the right way.

"The world likes money better than truth," Mom also used to say. "So we're screwed!"

She used to laugh so hard whenever she said that.

"And you're just a little off," Mom would say. "Off in the *best* of ways. Perfect the way you are. My beautiful son. Bartholomew Neil. I love you so much."

My young grief counselor Wendy says I am "emotionally disturbed" and "developmentally stunted" from having lived in a "codependent relationship" with my mother for so many years.

I don't think Wendy likes Mom very much.

She once said Mom fed off me, which made my mother sound like a cannibal with a bone through her nose, stirring me up in some giant cauldron perched upon a pile of flaming wood.

Mom wasn't like that at all; she was no cannibal.

This all went into my notebook.

Wendy told me I was "emotionally disturbed" and "developmentally stunted" when I asked why I needed a grief counselor, since I wasn't really sad anymore that Mom had died—when I told her I had made peace and didn't cry at night or anything like that. I had no grief to manage. She was wasting her time.

"She died peacefully because of the morphine," I said. "And I'll see Mom again in heaven."

Wendy the grief counselor ignored my mention of heaven. She said, "You say you haven't even cried yet. *Yet.* You are most likely repressing many emotions."

"Do birds repress things?" I said, as a joke, keeping my eyes on my shoelaces, and Wendy laughed in a good way that made me feel like I had stumped her with her own metaphor, and was therefore not a retard.

But as I was saying before, Mom had to come get me out of jail, and it took so long that my pants were dry by the time she got there, but my thighs had chapped from rubbing against wet jeans because I was pacing while incarcerated.

There was this interesting Puerto Rican man in my cell wearing makeup and he kept blowing kisses at me and saying he wanted to "cut me gently" whenever the cops weren't around. I know he was Puerto Rican because he had on a T-shirt that read PUERTO RICANS FUCK BETTER. Although maybe he could have been a non–Puerto Rican who just liked to have sex with Puerto Ricans, I suppose. Regardless, it was interesting and unusual, so I wrote it in my notebook.

That night, after she bailed me out of jail and took me home, Mom told me that self-gratification—while it was technically a sin in the Catholic Church, sometimes referred to as the sin of Onan—was probably the path for me. She wasn't really mad at me for getting arrested, especially after I told her what had happened—how the pink-haired woman had basically jumped out of an alley and began to rub against my leg before I could say or do anything. Mom nodded and said she wished she had told me about self-gratification before all of this happened, but such talks were usually the job of the father, and my father had died far before I was old enough for sex talks, so Mom really isn't to be blamed.

That night Mom came into my room, sat on the edge of my bed like she used to when I was a boy, pointed above my headboard to the crucifix—her gift to me when I was confirmed—and she said, "That guy hung out with prostitutes. He got arrested too. So you're in good company, Bartholomew. Don't let this rip you apart inside, okay?" When I didn't respond, Mom said, "I wish you had run into a Vivian Ward instead of an undercover cop." She was referencing Julia Roberts's character in *Pretty Woman*, which I don't have to tell you. "I want more. I want the fairy tale," Mom said, just like Julia Roberts said to you in the movie. "I want the fairy tale for you, Bartholomew. If I couldn't have it, I want it for you. So keep believing in fairy tales, okay? Keep believing that even some prostitutes are good-hearted women. Believe. Pretend even!" I don't know why—maybe because Mom was always so hopeful for me, and I never could manage to confirm her wild suspicions about her only son—but I had to turn my face away from her. I felt the tears coming, the pressure building up behind my eyes. Mom ran her fingers through my hair for a few minutes, like she did when I was a boy. Even though I was too old to be tucked in like that, I was glad she did what she did. It made the angry man in my stomach fall asleep. It was like her hand was able to perform a miracle that night. "I want the fairy tale for you, my sweet, sweet trusting boy," she said once more before she turned out the lights and exited my bedroom.

My father was most likely murdered by Catholic-hating Ku Klux Klan members, and I therefore have no memory of him. People forget that the KKK hated Catholics just as much as they hated Blacks and Jews, once upon a time. Mom said no one cares if you hate Catholics anymore because of all the pedophile priests, which is why people forget that the KKK probably still hates Catholics. (Mom also said if priests keep molesting little boys, the KKK would soon have a higher approval rating than the Catholic Church.) This is also why my father's killer was never brought to justice, according to Mom, nor did any newspapers cover the murder, which is maybe why I couldn't find any record of it at the library.

"It was once very hard for Catholics in this country," Mom used to say when I was a boy. "Your father—a good Catholic man—went out for a pack of cigarettes and never was seen again. The police say he left us for another family up in Montreal, where he was originally from, but we know better."

So Mom did her best and can't really be blamed for my arrest. I once asked her if my father was also a good pretender, and she said he was. Apparently, he was a lot like me.

Why didn't my father get to give Mom the fairy tale?

Why do most people fail to give each other the fairy tale?

Do you know why, Richard Gere?

Has your moviemaking taught you this?

Your admiring fan,
Bartholomew Neil

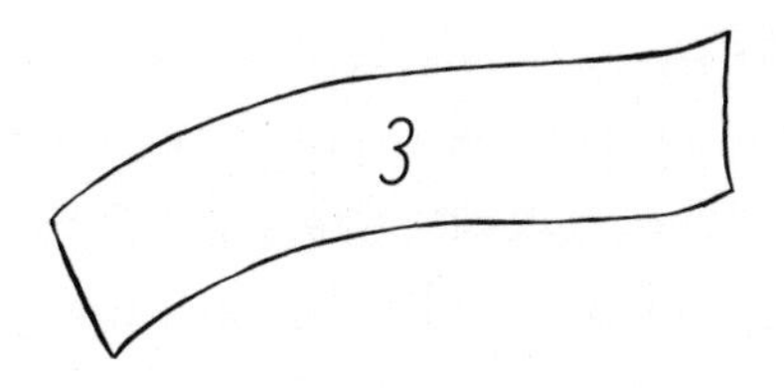

SADLY, I DO NOT THINK I AM TELEPATHIC

Dear Mr. Richard Gere,

I woke up this morning, put on coffee, and tried to listen to the tough (or lazy) morning birds, but the tiny angry man in my stomach was raging, screaming, *Idiot! Neanderthal! Stupid!*

It was quite disconcerting because I had no idea why he was upset. Usually I know right away what's bothering him, because it's usually what's bothering me.

I racked my brain, but I couldn't remember.

I fixed my coffee, and when I took my first sip—it came to me.

I had completely forgotten the point of my last letter, going on and on about unrelated past things. I didn't even tell you the most important part about yesterday's trip to the library, which makes me feel that I am indeed a gigantic emphatic moron.

(I get sidetracked easily by interesting things, and for this reason, people often find it hard to converse with me, which is why I don't talk very much to strangers and much prefer writing letters, in which there is room to record everything, unlike real-life conversations where you have to fight and fight to fit in your words and almost always lose.)

At the library, I found an article on the *Huffington Post* that said you "received blessings from the Dalai Lama at Mahabodhi temple in Bodh Gaya." It was dated March 18, 2010. There were pictures of you bowing to the Dalai Lama and him reaching down, touching your forehead with his hands in prayer position. There was also a photo of you praying with your eyes open while wearing expensive-looking Bose headphones. I wondered what you were listening to. On your left wrist were wooden beads, and on your right an old leather watchband. Judging by your eyes, you were enraptured.

Do you remember that day?

Have you seen this photo?

Being blessed by the Dalai Lama must have been a great honor, and I want to congratulate you right away, even though this event happened almost two years ago. I guess this is your equivalent of meeting the pope. I'd be very excited if I met the pope—even this new pope who is German. Mom never liked Germans, because her father was killed in World War II. (I have nothing against Germans.)

Then I found an article from the *Syracuse Buddhism Examiner.* It read "A TIME magazine survey on a wide-ranging list of the highs and lows of the past 12 months has listed the 'Self-Immolation of Tibetan Monks' as the number one 'underreported story' for the year 2011." There was a picture of a monk on fire. He looked like a pillar of flaming lava. It was hard to believe that the photo was an actual man burning alive because the reddish orange color almost looked beautiful and the man was perfectly still.

(Also, I thought about how it is okay to look at a man on fire on the Free Library's Internet, but not two naked women licking each other. Who makes the rules? Death is okay. Sex is bad. Mothers must die. Cancer comes when you least expect it.)

I looked at the man on fire for a long time, but couldn't make my mind believe it was a person. Not that I doubted or mistrusted the caption. It was just very hard to believe that such things actually happen. That people on the other side of the world care enough about *anything* to set themselves aflame.

From what I understood, these monks performed the self-immolation in order to attract attention to your mutual cause—returning the Dalai Lama to Tibet.

The article went on later to say "TIME magazine has conceded that it generally takes a U.S. President aggravating Beijing by meeting with the Dalai Lama, or a high-profile celebrity Richard Gere fundraiser to get Tibet into the news these days."

When I read that statement, it hit me—you, *my* friend, Richard Gere, are more powerful than a U.S. president, because the president wasn't even named, and yet you were.

How does it feel to be more famous and powerful and iconic than Barack Obama?

I also understood that you can do more for the Dalai

Lama by hosting a dinner party than Buddhist monks willing to burn themselves to death. Their sacrifice hardly makes the news—they go unnamed—but your being blessed by the Dalai Lama was in the *Huffington Post*.

You are a powerful man, Richard Gere.

I'm glad that I chose you to confide in during this difficult period in my life. The more I learn about you, the more I realize that Mom was right to keep your letter in her underwear drawer—that maybe she knew I would need your counsel after she was gone, and left your letter behind for me to find as a clue. It's almost like she's still helping me by making sure you and I are corresponding.

On a website called Tibet Sun, I read (and copied into my Interesting Things I Have Heard notebook) this: "A former Buddhist monk, who burnt himself last week in protest against the Chinese rule in Tibet, has reportedly died from burns. He was the twelfth Tibetan to have burned themselves in Tibet since March this year in protest against Beijing's rule in Tibet. Seven of them are reported to have died."

Twelve monks have lit themselves on fire trying to accomplish what you are trying to accomplish.

This, of course, reminded me of the twelve disciples of Jesus Christ, including Bartholomew (sometimes referred to as Nathaniel), who is my namesake.

I wondered if you, Richard Gere, were not the modern-day Jesus Christ of Buddhism.

It made me wonder if you ever thought about lighting yourself on fire, since you are also a Buddhist. Imagine how much news coverage that would demand. Everyone around the world would be transfixed if famous Hollywood actor and humanitarian Richard Gere performed a self-immolation.

Imagine it—the power!

Your greatest role!

I sincerely hope you will not light yourself on fire, because I have only just begun writing you. I would like to continue this conversation, so please do not go the way of these Tibetan monks. I believe you can accomplish much more alive than dead, and it doesn't seem like their sacrifices are doing much to weaken China. Also, there is the clue—what I found in Mom's underwear drawer—and perhaps you are meant to help not only the Dalai Lama but also me, Bartholomew Neil. Your self-immolation would not help me at all at this juncture, or at least I cannot see how.

No one in the United States even knows that these monks are making such a huge sacrifice, which makes me feel very disheartened for them.

"Life is shit," my young redheaded grief counselor Wendy says whenever we reach an impasse in our conversation.

It is her default platitude.

Her words of wisdom for me.

"Life is shit."

When Wendy says that, it's like she's pretending we are not bound together by her job, but really truly are friends. It's like we're having a beer at the bar, like friends on TV do.

"Life is shit."

She whispers it even. Like she's not supposed to say that

to me, but wants me to know that her happy talk and positivity are part of her pretending game.

Just like being a bird.

And I'll try to connect the freckles on her face to make pictures—like new constellations—and I can make a heart when I try really hard.

Her face is an oval.

Her eyes are sometimes the color of a May sky at 2:00 p.m. on a Saturday, and sometimes they are the color of polar bear ice.

She's beautiful in a little-sister way.

But back to the monks—I'm not sure I would light myself on fire for any cause whatsoever, and sometimes I worry that I just don't believe enough in any one thing to make a significant contribution to the world, now that I no longer have to care for Mom.

Sometimes I wish I felt the passion and purpose you must feel for returning the Dalai Lama to Tibet, but I've never experienced such intense feelings.

Mostly I've just been content to spend time with my mother, and she said that our spending time together was fine by her.

She said she needed me, and it was nice to be needed.

She never made me feel as though I should be doing more with my life—like making money and having beers at the bar with friends—and I sometimes worry that her lax attitude was a mistake, especially while raising a fatherless boy.

Now that Mom is no longer with us, I've been wondering if it's time for me to find something to be passionate about.

Perhaps before I turn forty. I'd like to have a beer with a friend at the bar—at least once.

I'd like to take The Girlbrarian somewhere nice—perhaps the Water Works behind the art museum, where you can listen to the river flow.

Wendy says that the "next phase of my life" could be my best. I want to believe her, but she is only a young girl who has not experienced much thus far in life. I like her, but I do not consider her a confidant.

You are my confidant.

I would like to have a beer with you at the bar, Richard Gere.

What do you think?

I would gladly heed your advice.

Do you think I should become passionate about something?

The more I research on the Internet, the more sympathetic I become toward *your* cause, Richard Gere, I must confess.

The Dalai Lama seems like an extraordinarily nice man. I've been reading about him and his philosophies. He says that we must relinquish our sense of I or self.

The Dalai Lama says, "We must recognize that the suffering of one person or one nation is the suffering of humanity. That the happiness of one person or nation is the happiness of humanity."

In the Dalai Lama's book *A Profound Mind*, you wrote in the afterword that our lives are like the beam of light coming out of a movie projector, illuminating the screen, which is emptiness. I liked that. It was good—beautiful.

Is it true?

I will read more about Buddhism.

But regarding my becoming passionate—maybe I should start with something smaller than taking on China.

I can't even speak with The Girlbrarian, and I've been secretly trying to do that for years now. I'm at a disadvantage because I'm not Richard Gere handsome. I'm six foot three inches tall with too much hair on my arms and in my ears, but not enough on the top of my head. Plus I do believe my nose isn't symmetrical, even though no one has ever commented on this or made fun of it. But mirrors don't lie.

Sometimes I send The Girlbrarian messages with my mind, but I do not think she is telepathic. Sadly, I do not think I am telepathic either.

I'd appreciate any input you could offer.

Your admiring fan,
Bartholomew Neil

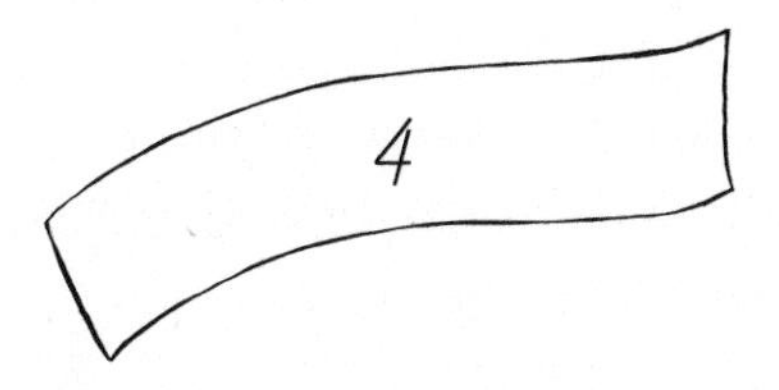

I WOULD EVENTUALLY HAVE TO GO INSIDE OF FATHER MCNAMEE AND TAKE INVENTORY

Dear Mr. Richard Gere,

Father McNamee seemed distracted this past Saturday night.

First, he announced that Mass would be held in Mom's honor, even though I had not requested it, nor had I filled out the required card, nor had I made a donation to the church. What's even stranger: he had already dedicated last week's Mass to Mom. As a Buddhist you probably wouldn't know, but it's not customary to give two masses in one person's honor in such a short period of time.

Then, even though it was not a funeral or Easter or Christmas, Father McNamee insisted on lighting and swinging the incense censer, much to the chagrin of the other priests, who tried to stop him by putting their hands on his shoulder and whispering fiercely, but Father McNamee would not be persuaded otherwise. The other priests stopped whispering fiercely only when Father McNamee's efforts to overcome them sent the incense ball swinging all the way around like a slingshot and flying across the sanctuary. There was a collective gasp as it rocketed toward the stained glass window, but luckily, gravity won out and the censer smashed against the stone wall. A small cloud plumed up before the altar boys were able to extinguish the incense and clean up the mess.

And yet Father McNamee didn't even acknowledge the interruption.

Under normal circumstances, he would have made a joke, perhaps referencing David's victory over Goliath. Father McNamee can be quite funny and is very popular—his spirited bingo calls bring out old women by the hundreds, and he's often raised money for worthy causes by doing stand-up where he combines "homilies with comedy"—but after the incense incident, when he failed to put the congregation's fears at ease, you could feel the tension thickening inside Saint Gabriel's.

Something was wrong.

Everyone knew it.

The other priests kept exchanging glances.

But the Mass continued and the routine settled everyone into the ritual of Saturday-night service—that is, until it was time for Father McNamee to give the homily.

He took the pulpit, lowered his chin, grabbed two fistfuls of wood, leaned out, and glared at us without saying a word.

This went on for a good sixty seconds or so and created more of a stir than the incident with the incense.

"Mmmmmmmmm," he finally said, or rather he moaned.

The noise seemed to bubble up from deep within him like a monstrous belch that had been waiting a long time for the opportune moment to explode.

Then he began to laugh until tears streamed down his face.

When he was done laughing, he stripped off his robe—stood before us in an undershirt and slacks—and said, "I renounce my vows! I am now—at this very moment—officially defrocked!"

There was a great gasp from the congregation.

Then Father McNamee disappeared into the priests' quarters.

Everyone began murmuring and looking at each other, until Father Hachette stood and said, "Let us sing hymn one-seventy-two, 'I Am the Vine.'"

The organ started up, pews creaked as everyone stood in unison, and the congregation happily began to sing, relieved that we were once again on familiar ground.

Standing alone in the last pew, I hid my Interesting Things I Have Heard notebook inside the hymnal and scribbled away.

When we finished, Father Hachette said, "'I am the vine, you are the branches; he who abides in Me, and I in him, he bears much fruit, for apart from Me you can do nothing,' John 15:5. You may be seated." (I also wrote that in my notebook. Accuracy confirmed.)

I don't remember what Father Hachette spoke about during his impromptu homily, because I couldn't stop thinking about Father McNamee. A few times I thought

I might get up and go into the priests' chambers to see if he was okay—to encourage him, to tell him he shouldn't quit being a priest. There was a warm feeling in my chest. It made me feel like I should help in some way—but what could I do?

Father McNamee is an accomplished and trusted priest; he helps many people—like, for example, his famous program where he organizes troubled inner-city youths and "transforms" them into counselors at his summer program for handicapped kids, which makes the local news every July.

He came to visit Mom often when she was sick and arranged for a church member to do all of the legal work required for me to own the house after she died, since she didn't have a very good will. Father McNamee arranged for Wendy to visit once a week at no charge to me, because Mom left me with very little money. He also spoke so beautifully at her funeral, calling her a "Woman of Christ" (I wrote that in my notebook), and—because I have no other living family members—he drove me to the shore afterward and we walked the beach together to "get my mind off" her passing.

"We're just like Jesus and his disciples hanging out by the sea," I said to him while we were strolling past cold whitecaps, and Father McNamee must have got some sand in his eyes because he started to rub them. I heard him whimper in pain as the seagulls screamed above. "Are you okay?"

"Fine," he answered and waved me off.

The wind flicked one of his tears airborne, and it landed on my earlobe.

Then we walked for a long time without saying anything at all.

He spent the first night after Mom's funeral with me too, in our home, and we drank more whiskey than we probably should have—Father McNamee doing three "fingers" for every one of mine got him red and drunk quickly—but it was good to have his company.

Father McNamee has done so much for Mom and me over the years. "God sent him to us," she used to say about Father McNamee. "Father McNamee was truly called."

A few years ago, I finally confessed the sin of masturbation to Father McNamee, and he didn't make me feel shameful about it. He whispered through the confession screen, "God will send you a wife one day, Bartholomew. I am sure of it."

Shortly after that, The Girlbrarian started working at the library, and I have often wondered if this was God's work. Again, we are reminded of Jung's *Synchronicity. Unus mundus.*

Now I pray to God and ask for the courage needed to speak to The Girlbrarian, who always seems to glow in the library the way Mary glows in the stained glass window whenever the sun shines into Saint Gabriel's.

But courage never comes.

I pray for words, and those evaporate instantly whenever I see The Girlbrarian at the library and get so hot, it's like my brain is boiling in my skull.

Perhaps the you-me of pretending would have a better shot, but the thing is, I want The Girlbrarian to fall in love with Bartholomew Neil and not us, Richard Gere. You would win her over with a flash of your smile or a wink—it would be so easy for you. I want to win her affection, but my ways are slower.

From what I have been reading about Buddhism, this desire is what keeps me trapped far away from enlightenment. But then I remind myself that you have a wife, and if Richard Gere the great Buddhist and friend of the Dalai Lama can have such desires, it must be okay for me too. Right?

When this past Saturday's Mass was over, Father Hachette would not let me speak with Father McNamee, nor would he let me into the priests' chambers. "Pray for Father McNamee, Bartholomew. The best thing you can do is pray. Petition the Lord," Father Hachette kept saying over and over as he reached up and patted my chest like he would pat a large pet—perhaps a Great Dane. "Just calm down," he kept saying. "Let's remain calm. All of us—one and all."

Maybe I was more upset than I realized. Although the angry man in my stomach was not trying to destroy my internal organs. It was a different sort of upset. I have a tendency to get agitated when I worry. Regardless, Father Hachette looked scared. People are often afraid of me when I get agitated or angry. But I've never, ever hurt anyone—even in school when people used to shove me and call me a retard.

(The worst day of my life turned into one of the best experiences I ever had in high school, but taken as a whole, it made me feel very much like a retard. This beautiful girl named Tara Wilson came to my locker and in this very sexy voice she asked me to go down into the high school basement during lunch period. I knew this was where students went to have sex during school, and I was excited that one of the most popular girls in my class wanted to take me there. I also knew it was a trick. The angry man in my stomach was cursing and kicking and stomping and telling me not to fall for it. *Don't be their retard!* the little angry man yelled. But I knew it was my only chance with Tara Wilson, and it was just too nice to pretend that she wanted to take me down into the high school basement, even though she looked so nervous and was sweating in December, so the pretending was extra hard. She even held my hand as we walked down the steps, which was wonderful. That brief minute of hand-holding was probably the best part of high school for me. And I still think about Tara Wilson—the way she used to poof her bangs up with hair spray, the three gold rope chains she wore around her neck and the gold dog tag that read T-A-R-A and had a small diamond chip on the lower right corner, how she smoked Marlboro Reds like a movie star on the corner after school, and how she'd throw her head back and blow the smoke straight up at the clouds as she laughed—like a wonderful beautiful kind of smokestack—with her cigarette resting in the crook of a peace sign. Even though she tricked me, I still like her very much to this day and hope that she has a nice family somewhere and is doing well. I hope Tara Wilson is happy. When we made it down into the basement, Tara led me to a dark corner. There were a dozen or so classmates down there—all boys. They circled me and started chanting, "Retard! Retard! Retard!" Before

I knew what was happening so many hands were on me, and then I was alone in a dark supply closet and couldn't get out or see anything. I screamed and banged on the door for hours, but no one came. Eventually, I pretended I was in my bed at home sleeping soundly and dreaming up this awful nightmare. I pretended I would wake up soon, Mom would make breakfast, and that helped for a time. Then the angry man in my stomach became furious, kicking and screaming and commanding me to escape, so I tried to knock down the door with my shoulder, but it felt like trying to move a mountain with my mind—my biceps started to ache and swell—and I eventually slid down into the darkness, wondering if I would die down there. I prayed, asking God to save me, but no one came. The cold set in. I spent the night there shivering on the concrete and Mom worried terribly, even calling the police. When I had given up entirely, the light rushed in and blinded me. "Oh my God. Are you okay?" I heard. It was Tara. And it was the next day, before anyone had arrived at our high school. She handed me a bottle of water and a bag of homemade chocolate chip cookies. I drank the water immediately because I was so thirsty. "I'm sorry," she said. "They made me do it." My eyes adjusted to the light. Her makeup was running down her face, and she looked so apologetic and wretched that I forgave her right away. She told me that this classmate named Carl Lenihan had taken off her clothes when she was passed out drunk at a party, and then he took pictures of her. He was making her do things for him, using the pictures as blackmail. She begged me not to tell anyone that she had let me out. She was crying hysterically as she explained all of this, waving her hands around in the air, saying she thought I might have died from the furnace fumes and she was waiting outside the high school doors when the janitors arrived to open up for the day, and she was so glad I was okay—alive. But then—out of the blue—Tara Wilson did the strangest thing. She hugged me for a long time and cried into my shirt, saying she was sorry so many times. She cried and trembled so hard I thought she was going to die. I didn't know whether she wanted me to hug her back or not, so I just stood there. Then she pulled my head down, kissed my cheek, and ran up the stairs and out of the high school basement. She never spoke to me ever again. When I'd pass her in the hallways, she would look the other way. And I never told anyone that I spent the night in the dark, cold supply closet in my high school's basement. I don't know why. I didn't pretend that it never happened or was only a dream. I kept it to myself. You, Richard Gere, are the first person I have ever told. I told Mom I spent the night behind the art museum looking at the river flow—that the flowing water had hypnotized me and I had forgotten about time. I don't think she believed me, but she didn't call me a liar either, which I appreciated. She just looked into my eyes for a long time and then dropped it. Mom understood that it was better to let some things alone. Words could be used as weapons that do too much damage. All of the popular boys in my high school class called me "Tara" or "Closet Boy" until I graduated. Sometimes they called me "Tara's retard." And Tara never acknowledged me ever again. This is when

I learned that nice people sometimes felt they had to pretend to be mean and awful. Since Tara, I've seen many people pretending to be rude and cruel and thoughtless. Have you noticed this too, Richard Gere? People choosing to pretend for evil rather than good? I don't understand why people do this, but I understand that most choose the way of Tara, and this has often confused me.)

Back at Saint Gabriel's, I said to Father Hachette, "Will you ask Father McNamee to call me this evening?"

"Sure. Sure," Father Hachette said. His narrow face was the color of stop signs, and his few wisps of hair were blowing around under the heat vent on the wall. "Just go home and pray. I'll have Father McNamee call you. Now off you go, Bartholomew. God bless you."

I didn't believe Father Hachette would do as I asked, because Father Hachette was not called by God in the same way that Father McNamee was—you can tell by looking into his eyes and by the fact that he doesn't help as many people in the church; it's not that he's a terrible priest, he's just not "truly called" like Father McNamee, or at least that's what Mom always said—but even though I had that warm God-wants-you-to-do-something feeling in my chest, I went home anyway, figuring that Father McNamee would contact me eventually, because he has always been a regular visitor of Mom's and mine.

When I arrived home, Father McNamee was sitting on the front steps. His white beard looked extra feral and his nose was shiny red. There were two brown paper bags to his left and a pizza to his right.

"Communion," he said. "Will you break bread with me?"

I nodded, but I did not like the wild look in Father McNamee's sky-blue eyes, which sucked at me like powerful whirlpools.

Something was off.

If he were a house, one of the windows would have been smashed and the door would have been ajar. It was like he had been broken into and robbed. I wasn't sure what was missing just yet, and I knew I would eventually have to go inside Father McNamee and take inventory, if that makes any sense. I couldn't imagine Father McNamee ever hurting me in any way, but I also couldn't shake the feeling that something wasn't quite right about him—and that I should be careful. He had been compromised, as they say in spy movies and on TV shows about presidents and prime ministers and secret agents.

We ate and drank in the kitchen.

"The body of Christ," Father McNamee said when he placed a mushroom slice on my plate.

Father McNamee didn't take a slice for himself; he only drank his Jameson.

I tried to eat, but I wasn't very hungry.

I was still trying to figure out what had been stolen from inside Father McNamee.

"The blood of Christ," he said when he poured a finger of whiskey into my glass. "Drink."

I took a sip and felt the burn.

He downed his in one gulp and his face reddened immediately.

Mom would have said he "had the blossom."

"Bartholomew," Father McNamee said. "Now that I've left the church, I need a place to live. I don't even own the clothes on my back, technically. My rather well-to-do childhood friend is sending money, but it's not a fortune. If you take me in, I can also offer you my prayers."

"You're really leaving the church? You're really renouncing your vows?"

He nodded and poured more whiskey.

"Why?"

"Exodus."

"Exodus?"

"Exodus," he said.

"Like Moses?"

"More like Aaron."

Mom had read me biblical stories as a child and I had gone to church every week for my entire life, where I often read the Bible, so I knew that Aaron was Moses's spokesperson when he led the Jews out of Egypt.

"I don't understand what you're telling me," I said.

Father McNamee threw back another three fingers of whiskey and poured himself a fresh glass.

"Do you ever feel as though God speaks to you, Bartholomew?" He searched my eyes until I looked down at my pizza slice. "Has God sent you any messages lately? Do you know what I'm talking about? Are you the answering machine recording God's voice? Can you advise me? What has God told you lately? Has He sent you any messages at all—for me or otherwise?"

I thought about The Girlbrarian first—and then I thought about you, Richard Gere, and the letter Mom left behind for me. I wondered if your letter could have been a message from God, even though you are a Buddhist. (Mysterious ways.) But I didn't say anything about you to Father McNamee. I don't know why. Maybe because he looked like a broken-into house.

"I've watched you grow up," Father McNamee said. "You've always been different. And you've lived the life of a monk, really. Always at the library reading, studying. Living a quiet, simple existence with your mother, and now . . ."

He looked out the kitchen window for a long time, although there wasn't anything to see, except the reflection of the ceiling light that looked like an electric moon.

"Your father—he was a religious man. Did your mother tell you that?"

"Yes," I said. "He was martyred. Killed for the Catholic Church by the Ku Klux Klan."

"The *Ku Klux Klan*?" Father McNamee said.

"According to Mom."

Father McNamee smiled in this very bemused way—almost like he was being tickled.

"What else did she tell you about your father?"

"He was a good man."

"He *was* a good man."

"You knew him?"

Father McNamee nodded solemnly. "He used to confess to me a long time ago. He was deeply religious. Tapped in.

God spoke to him. He had visions. His blood runs through your veins."

"And my mom's blood too," I said, although I'm not sure why.

Father McNamee had never spoken to me like this before, even when he was fall-down drunk. But Mom had often spoken of my father's visions. She once told me that my dad would close his eyes so tightly that all he could see was the color red—and then he would hear the unknowable voices of angels, which he described as the high-pitched noise wind makes when rushing through leafy forests, only more musical and divine—and he could understand the angels.

"She lives on through you," Father McNamee said. "Your mother. That's true."

When it was clear he wasn't going to say anything else, I said, "Do you really want to live with me?"

"I do."

"Why?"

"God told me to do something a long time ago, but I'm only getting around to it now. Mostly because God is giving me the silent treatment at the present moment."

"What?"

"Am I not speaking clearly?"

"No. I mean, yes," I said. This was a lot to take in. "What exactly did God tell you?"

" 'Defrock yourself and live with Bartholomew Neil.' Again, it was a long time ago. I think God is mad at me, because I didn't listen."

I shook my head. God would never speak to Father Mc-Namee about me. What he said was not true. Father Mc-Namee was just trying to make me feel better. Telling white lies. Pretending. Including me in his calling, because he knew I am not called and felt sorry for me.

"You look surprised, Bartholomew. God speaks to people all throughout the Bible. He's always talking to people."

I stared at my mushroom pizza slice and thought about how far Father McNamee had fallen. I began to worry that the squidlike cancer was now attacking his brain too.

"You have nothing to say to me, Bartholomew? No word from God? Nothing?" He looked up at me, raised his whiskey glass, and said, "So?"

"Why would you want to live with me?"

"I think God has a plan for you," Father McNamee said. "Unfortunately, God no longer speaks to me. So I don't know what exactly that plan might be. But the good news is that I'm here to help you carry it out, if you're game." He took another shot of whiskey and said, "So what's the plan, Bartholomew?"

I just looked at him.

"You really don't know, do you?" he said, tilting his head sideways and squinting at me through his bushy white circle of beard and hair. "God hasn't spoken to you lately?"

"I have no idea."

"None at all? Not even a suspicion? An inclination? A feeling? *Nothing?*"

I shook my head and felt embarrassed.

"You've heard no calling?"

"Sorry," I said, because I hadn't heard anything remotely like a calling.

"Then I guess we wait," he said. "And I will pray. God may no longer speak to me, but maybe He's still listening."

"Forgive me, Father, but are you serious about all of this? This isn't a joke?"

"No joke," Father McNamee said.

"Are you really leaving the Catholic Church?"

"I have officially defrocked myself. I'm not leaving—*I've left.*"

"Can I still confess my sins to you?"

"Technically, no. Not as a Catholic. But as a man, certainly."

I didn't know what to say, so I drank my whiskey.

It burned.

Father McNamee drank half the bottle before he passed out on the couch. I sat in the armchair and studied him. His forearms were thick and he had a great belly, but he was solid all over and not jiggly like a fat man. He was like a potato with a head, arms, and legs. His beard made him look like Santa Claus. And his skin was rough and pocked and used-up raw—like he had lived a hard full life of service, gardening in the vast soil of men, harvesting souls.

Potato skin.

A giant potato.

"Irish," Mom had often called him. "Father Irish."

I placed a blanket over Father McNamee, and he began to snore loudly.

Upstairs I wrote as much as I could remember in my notebook, and I wondered if Father McNamee really believed that God had a plan for me now that Mom was gone, or was he only drunk. I stayed up most of the night thinking and wondering.

In the morning I found Father McNamee kneeling in the living room, praying. I didn't want to interrupt, so I put on coffee and fried eggs in butter and hot sauce. I also sliced and fried a few pieces of scrapple, because it's good for hangovers. Father McNamee always ate scrapple after a night of drinking Irish whiskey. I know because he had spent many nights on our couch. Mom used to cook scrapple for him.

"Morning, Bartholomew," he said when he took his place at the kitchen table. "You don't have to cook for me, you know. But thanks."

I served breakfast.

We drank our coffee.

The winter birds sang to us.

"Good eggs," he said.

I nodded.

I wanted to ask him about God's plan for me, but something held me back.

"So what exactly do you do all day around here, Bartholomew?"

"I often go to the library."

"What else?"

"I write in my notebook."

"That's good. What else?"

"I listen to the birds."

"And?"

"I used to take care of my mother."

"Your mother is no longer with us."

"I know that."

"So what will you do *now*? What will we do *today*?"

I hadn't a clue, so I just looked at him, hoping he would tell me. But he only focused on his food, and by the time he was done, his white beard was striped like a candy cane with hot sauce.

"God still hasn't spoken to you yet, has He?"

"I don't think so," I said.

"God can be a bastard like that."

Father McNamee went into the living room and got down on his knees. He stayed that way for hours. I started to worry that maybe he was dead, because he was still as a rock.

I listened for God's voice, but all I heard were the birds.

I wondered if maybe I should tell Father McNamee about you, Richard Gere, but for some reason I didn't—and I'm not going to either.

You are my confidant, Richard Gere, and I'm not about to share my pretending with anyone, because pretending often ends when you allow nonpretenders access to the better, safer worlds you create for yourself.

I'd like for us to be secret friends, Richard Gere.

I think I can learn from both you and Father McNamee, and I'd like to keep those two worlds separate for now. Like church and state. I learned that back in high school in the history class Tara Wilson was also in. Separation of church and state. Not that you are my state, because you are not. And evidently Father McNamee is no longer my church either.

Your admiring fan,
Bartholomew Neil

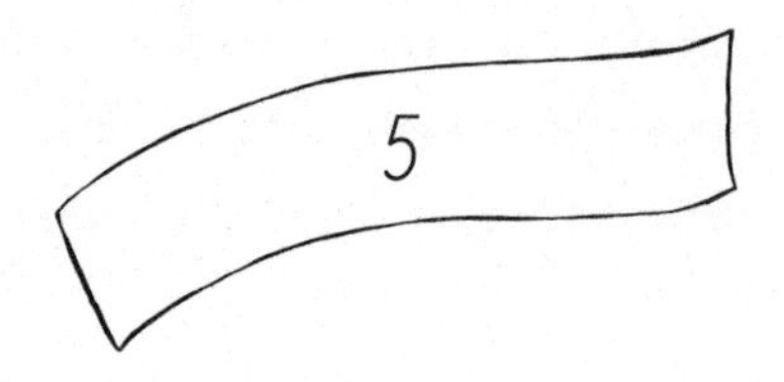

CHARLES J. GUITEAU'S DISSECTED BRAIN

Dear Mr. Richard Gere,

I had the strangest dream last night:

Standing on the Ocean City boardwalk, I watched the sun come up. It was warm, so it must have been summer, but there was no one around for miles and miles, which made me think it wasn't. The sun heated my face to just the right temperature as waves crashed in the distance and seagulls cried up above and even the metal railing I was leaning against was as warm as a woman's arm.

I was feeling so at peace in my dream until I heard Mom's voice yelling, "Richard! Richard, help me! Help me, Richard! I'm going to fall! Help!"

I looked around, but I couldn't see Mom anywhere—or anyone else either.

"Richard!" she cried. "Help me, please! I can't hang on! It hurts! It BURNS!"

Finally, I understood she was under the boardwalk.

I looked for stairs to the beach, but I couldn't find any.

When I looked over the railing, all I saw was the ocean—little bits of sun refracting here and there like a twinkling galaxy.

The beach was gone.

"Richard! Richard! Help me!" she cried.

Even though she was using your name in the dream, I knew she meant me, because of all the pretending we had done before she died.

I dropped to my knees and peered through the cracks in the boardwalk and saw Mom hanging on to a live electrical wire that was sparking and shocking her; beneath her was a large black endless pit. She was young, how she looked when I was a boy—she had long black hair and her face was still smooth and unwrinkled—maybe in my dream she was the same age as I am now.

It didn't make any sense.

Where was the sand?

Where was the ocean?

"Mom!" I yelled as our eyes locked.

For a brief second I could tell she saw me through the cracks between the boards—her pupils focused and a strange, almost horrified look bloomed on her face.

She let go of the wire and began to fall, shrinking farther and farther away. The whole time she was aging too: I could see her hair turning white and getting shorter, the wrinkles sprouting from her eyes, tunneling through her face, shriveling her hands and arms.

In my dream I screamed, "*Mom!*"

"Bartholomew?" I heard a man whisper.

When I opened my eyes, Father McNamee was sitting on the edge of my bed, just like Mom used to do when I was a boy.

I blinked at him.

Only the hall light behind him was on—the lights in my room were still out—so his body was silhouetted. It took a second for me to realize I was no longer dreaming.

"You were yelling in your sleep," he said. "Are you okay?"

"I was having a dream," I said. I wanted to tell him what I was dreaming about, but it sounded too insane at the time, and it takes me a little bit to remember my dreams after I wake up, so I didn't say anything.

"I couldn't sleep either," Father McNamee said. "You want a sandwich?"

"No, thank you," I said, because I wasn't hungry.

"Okay, suit yourself. But maybe you'd want to keep me company while I eat mine?"

"Okay," I said, and then followed Father McNamee down to the kitchen.

I sat at the table as he made himself a ham and Swiss on rye.

"Do you know anything about the twentieth president of the United States?" he said when he sat down. "James A. Garfield?"

I just stared at his chewing face, trying to wake up fully.

He had yellow flecks of mustard in his beard.

"I'm reading this book about him," he said. "It's upstairs on the nightstand."

I nodded.

He gestured with his sandwich, shaking it at me for emphasis, the lettuce hanging on for dear life. "James A. Garfield was indeed the twentieth president of our great country. He seemed like he was a good, noble man. Wanted to advance the civil rights movement. Provide universal education. Make sure all children—black and white—could read."

I wondered why Father McNamee was saying all this to me in the middle of the night, but I didn't ask. I was very sleepy, and the experience was starting to feel more and more like yet another bizarre dream.

"Do you know who Charles J. Guiteau is, Bartholomew?"

I shook my head no.

Father finished chewing a bite, swallowed, and then said, "He shot President Garfield and claimed God made him do it. What's even more eerie is that when Garfield was shot in a Washington train station, supposedly he said, 'My God, what is this?' As if he were questioning God's will. Garfield didn't expect to be shot that day. He thought he was putting good into the world, doing God's work perhaps. But two bullets made him question God. 'What is this?' he said to God."

It was like one of Father McNamee's homilies. He had often made historical allusions in his homilies. But why was he telling me this in the middle of the night? Was it the whiskey?

"Guiteau yelled, 'Arthur is president now!' " A piece of lettuce flew out of Father McNamee's sandwich and onto the table, leaving a mustard smear. "Arthur being the vice president at the time. And then Guiteau demanded to be arrested. He would later claim that God had used him to determine history."

Father McNamee took another huge bite, chewed, and swallowed.

"Are you drunk?" I asked, because this late-night lecture was intense, even for Father McNamee.

"Irish ex-priests don't succumb to drunkenness, we just become more talkative on whiskey," he said, winked, and then continued. "Because they didn't know much about bacteria back then, people stuck their unwashed fingers in the wounds, President Garfield's bullet holes became infected, and he died a long, slow, painful death. They moved him to the Jersey Shore at the end."

This mention of the beach made me think about my dream, seeing Mom disappear into the great hole under the boardwalk.

Synchronicity? I thought.

"And when he finally passed, Garfield's wife supposedly yelled, 'Oh! Why am I made to suffer this cruel wrong?' "

Father McNamee paused to finish the first half of his ham on rye.

He licked mustard off his thumb and said, "During the trial Guiteau cursed at the judges and jury and seemed oblivious to the fact that he was going to be executed. In fact, he thought himself a hero and was sure the new president would grant him a pardon. The lawyers argued whether or not he was sane enough to stand trial. He was clearly insane, but they tried and executed him, anyway."

I nodded, because I understood that this was the end of the story, but I was too tired to say anything.

Father McNamee said, "You don't want to talk, do you?"

I looked at the clock on the microwave and said, "It's three a.m."

He nodded and ate the second half of his sandwich quickly.

I felt like it was rude to leave, so I didn't.

When he finished, he stood, patted my shoulder twice, and said, "Sleep well, Bartholomew."

I listened to him climb the steps, and then I went upstairs too and soon was back in my bed.

I lay there thinking about President Garfield and his assassin, my mother falling into a great pit and aging as she descended, and wondering if there was any connection at all.

When first light poked through my window, I felt the tiredness weighing down my head because I had spent the whole night pondering.

I showered and dressed and made breakfast.

Father McNamee was reluctant to eat the food I prepared, saying he didn't want me waiting on him all the time, and he should be cooking for himself, but I said, "I used to cook for Mom, so I might as well cook for you too—plus cooking makes me miss her less," and he got a very sad look on his face.

"I really appreciate your letting me stay here, Bartholomew."

Then Father McNamee and I ate in silence and the tough

(or lazy) morning birds performed their symphony in the cold outside.

I wanted to ask him if our middle-of-the-night conversation about the twentieth president wasn't a bit insane, but I didn't. Maybe I was afraid I was going mad like Mom and Charles J. Guiteau had. I didn't think I could go through another battle with madness. I also worried that I was going to have to start pretending for Father McNamee now that he was living with me, because he was acting a little peculiar himself.

I don't think I could pretend for someone else's benefit again, because now I need to pretend for me—so that I can keep living post-Mom. But I also worried that Father McNamee was trying to tell me something, and I was too much of a moron to understand.

Don't be Tara's retard again! the angry man in my stomach screamed. *Don't trust anyone, and keep to yourself always!*

When we finished washing and drying the breakfast dishes, Father McNamee said, "Get your coat. I want to show you something."

Without saying a word, we walked for a long time through the winter morning sunshine and traffic toward the center of Philadelphia, ending up on South Twenty-Second Street.

"Here it is," Father McNamee said, and then I followed him through gray columns and heavy wooden doors into a brick building that turned out to be the Mütter Museum.

Inside were various body parts and organs preserved in glass cases, deformed skeletons, surgical tools, and so many other curiosities. I could tell right away that it was a medical museum, but it also felt a bit like stepping into a horror movie.

We stopped in front of a display and Father McNamee said, "Look at that."

It was an old-fashioned jar—the kind that maybe people used to preserve fruit. It was sealed at the top by a metal bar and some wax. Inside was a yellow fluid and what looked like artichokes.

"Charles J. Guiteau's dissected brain," Father McNamee said. "They kept it because of the historical significance and so future generations could learn from it."

"What could they possibly learn?" I asked.

I couldn't make all the pieces inside the jar fit to make an entire human brain—but the museum looked very official, so I knew it must really be Charles J. Guiteau's, just as it was labeled. Still, it didn't look real.

"He was a sick man. Doctors need to study sickness in order to understand it—so they can help other sick people," Father McNamee said.

I didn't like looking at cut-up brains, and as I thought about those parts once being in a skull that saw and heard and breathed and spoke and commanded a body to walk around in this world, I began to feel as though I was going to vomit. Maybe it was because I hadn't slept the night before and was feeling exhausted, but I have never liked thinking about dismemberment.

"Can we leave now?" I asked, wishing Father were wearing his priest collar again instead of the wrinkled red button-up that many washes had faded pink.

Father McNamee looked at me. "This upsets you, doesn't it?"

"A little," I said, thinking, Who wouldn't be freaked out by all this?

"Let's go, then," Father said, and we did.

We walked for a few blocks before I asked if we could sit down for a second.

I sat on the steps of someone's three-level home, which people around here sometimes call trinities.

"Are you okay?" Father McNamee said.

"Why did you wake me up in the middle of the night?"

"You were yelling. You were having a nightmare."

"Why did you show me that cut-up brain?"

"Are you angry with me?" Father asked me.

I didn't want to answer that question, so I remained mute.

I did feel a little angry.

Everything was happening too quickly.

Father McNamee sat down next to me, and we watched the traffic pass for a long time, but I didn't answer his question.

The nausea subsided.

My anger lessened.

We sat so long my backside and thighs began absorbing the concrete's cold.

A man in an expensive-looking overcoat and silk scarf walked up to us and said, "These are my steps, and you are loitering."

Father McNamee nodded and said, "Forgive us."

The man pushed through without saying another word.

His knee hit my shoulder as I was trying to stand, and I said, "I'm sorry," even though it wasn't my fault, and I sort of felt like the man kneed me intentionally—like he wanted to hurt me.

We left.

After fifteen minutes or so of walking, Father McNamee said, "Has God spoken to you yet?"

"No," I said.

"You can bet your ass God didn't speak to Charles J. Guiteau," Father McNamee said.

I didn't say anything.

I didn't want to talk about Charles J. Guiteau anymore.

Mostly I didn't want to think about his dissected brain preserved forever in a jar.

"How am I so sure God didn't tell Guiteau to kill Garfield? Do you want to know?"

I felt Father McNamee's eyes on me, so I nodded. I didn't really want to know, but I knew nodding was the easiest thing to do—what he wanted, and what would end this discussion most quickly.

"God doesn't tell you to do bad things. God doesn't tell you to kill your president. Even when God told Abraham to kill Isaac, he didn't let him do it. He sent his angel to stop him. That was a test. But God has already tested you, Bartholomew—with your mother's sickness—and he has found you to be good, pure of heart. You endured it well."

I didn't like what Father McNamee was saying because it implied that God gave Mom cancer to test me, and if that were true, I don't think I could believe in God anymore.

"Something tells me you're soon going to help others in quiet ways," Father McNamee said.

I thought about how maybe Charles J. Guiteau imagined he was doing what was best for the country when he killed President Garfield—that maybe he really truly believed he was doing the right thing. Or maybe he was just plain crazy. But I didn't want to argue with Father McNamee. He looked so confident—like he had delivered the most important homily of his life. And I was starting to believe that maybe he was going crazy himself.

"God doesn't always use words to speak to us, Bartholomew," he said as we waited for a red light to turn green. "Sometimes we simply get feelings. Hunches. Have you had any of those?"

I shook my head no.

We walked the rest of the way home in silence.

Father knelt down in the living room to give praying a go again, and I walked to the library, enjoying the feeling of being in motion and the cold air in my nose and the warm sun on my face.

The Girlbrarian wasn't working.

I pretended to read current events magazines like *Newsweek* and *Time*, but mostly I thought about my dream—Mom falling into the great black pit under the boardwalk.

When I returned home several hours later, Father McNamee was still praying—eyes smashed shut, fists strangling each other white, lips mouthing words with alarming speed, and temples moist with sweat.

He didn't come to dinner.
He was still on his knees when I went to bed.
I wonder what he says to God for so many hours.

Your admiring fan,
Bartholomew Neil

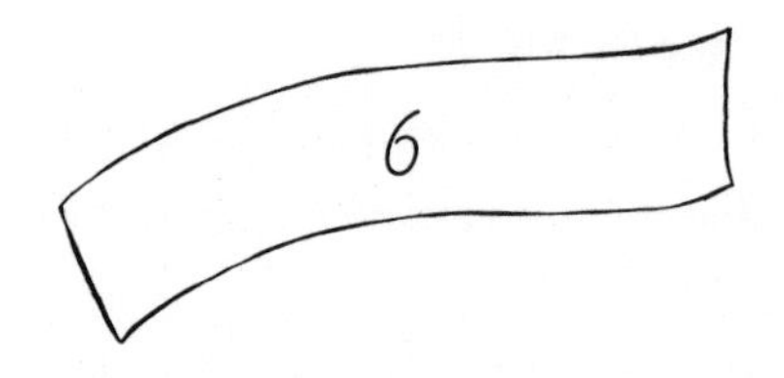

"A SITUATION COMPLICATED BECAUSE OF HIS OPPRESSIVE TENDENCY TO OVER-ANALYSE"

Dear Mr. Richard Gere,

Wendy came to the house for her regular visit while Father McNamee was praying in the living room, like he does for hours and hours, even when I am watching television. Nothing bothers him when he is praying. It's like he goes into a deep trance. You could dump ice water on his head and he wouldn't even flinch.

"What are *you* doing here?" Wendy said to Father McNamee.

"He's praying," I answered when Father McNamee failed to look up. "Let's go into the kitchen."

"Why is he praying in your living room, Bartholomew?"

"He always prays in my living room."

"Since when?"

"Since he moved in with me. He defrocked himself, and now—"

"Father McNamee?" Wendy yelled.

When he didn't respond, she went over and poked his arm three times.

Father McNamee opened one eye—like he'd only been pretending to pray the whole time—and said, "Yes."

"What's going on here?" Wendy said.

"I've moved in with Bartholomew."

"Why?"

"I'm taking care of some old business that doesn't concern you."

"It's a bad idea."

Father McNamee sighed. "You are so young, Wendy. I admire your youth."

"You asked me to help Bartholomew become independent—"

"Your point?" Father McNamee stood, looked up at the ceiling, and said, "Excuse me, God."

"This wasn't part of the deal," Wendy said.

"Let's talk outside, shall we?"

Wendy and Father McNamee went out the front door and talked on the sidewalk. I watched them through the window, but couldn't hear what they were saying. Father McNamee kept nodding confidently. Wendy kept pointing her index finger at Father McNamee's face. This went on for fifteen minutes.

Finally, Father McNamee walked away down the street.

Wendy took a few deep breaths, lifting and dropping her shoulders, before she saw me staring at her through the window. She looked angry for a split second, but then she smiled and walked toward the house.

"Should we sit in the kitchen?" she asked when she entered, and then strode right past me before I could answer, which was unlike her.

She removed her floral-pattern trench coat and hung it on the back of Mom's chair. Then we sat down at the kitchen table, but the birds were not singing, which seemed like a sign of some sort.

"Do you want Father McNamee to live with you?" Wendy said. Her orange eyebrows were scrunched together. Her orange hair was pulled back in a ponytail. The tops of her freckled ears were so full of light they appeared translucent.

"It doesn't bother me."

"That's not an answer," she said.

I shrugged.

"Father McNamee does not seem well. Has he been acting strange?"

I shrugged again, because he had, and I didn't want to say that. Maybe I just didn't want to be alone, and I knew that Father McNamee was likely to leave if I said I didn't want him there. It was confusing, the way I felt, so I went into silent mode.

"I'm going to take that as a yes," Wendy said, misinterpreting my lack of words. "Look, Bartholomew, I know I've been telling you to find a flock and make friends. Remember how we outlined your goal of having a beer at a bar with a peer sometime within the next three months?"

I nodded.

"Well, I think that Father McNamee living here will not help you accomplish that goal."

"Why?" I asked.

"You've spent the first forty years of your life taking care of your mother. You haven't been on your own for two months before a man much older than you moves into your home. *Don't you see a pattern developing?*"

I had no idea what she was talking about, which made me feel like a Neanderthal. I'm sure you, Richard Gere, know exactly what she meant and probably saw the problem two or three letters ago.

"I don't understand," I said.

She bit her lip, looked out the window for a second, and then said, "Did Father McNamee tell you that he expects you to deliver a message from God?"

I knew that telling the truth would not be a good idea, so I said nothing.

"I understand that Father McNamee has been your religious leader for your entire life—that your faith and the Catholic Church are very important to you. I understand that Father McNamee cares about you a great deal. Furthermore, he was the one who put me in touch with—"

"What happened to your wrist?" I said. The words were out of my mouth before I could stop myself from speaking. There was a purple and yellow bruise on her left wrist that looked painful and awful. I saw it jump out of her sleeve when she was motioning with her hands.

"What?" Wendy said, and pulled down her sleeve, covering the bruise.

The look on her face made me wince.

"Oh," she said. Then she looked up and to the left, which

I've read is a classic sign that someone is lying. "I fell Rollerblading. Down on Kelly Drive. Should have worn my wrist protectors. But they are *so* dorky. I'm okay."

I didn't believe her, but I didn't say anything more. Wendy is a terrible liar. She began talking about Father McNamee again, saying something about how she had been contacted by Father Hachette, who is very concerned about Father McNamee. He hadn't told anyone where he was going. He hadn't even said good-bye to anyone. She'd have to report his whereabouts to Father Hachette. I remember hearing the words "mental health" several times, but I can't elaborate more because I was creating scenarios in my mind regarding Wendy's bruise—trying to explain why her wrist was yellow and purple—instead of listening to her rant about Father McNamee. If she had fallen Rollerblading, she might have sprained her wrist or broken it—this was true—but I don't think it would have turned such awful colors, but maybe I was wrong about that. I am no doctor.

I imagined maybe a dog had bitten her, but I hadn't seen any puncture wounds or scabs. Maybe she had a pet snake that had wrapped itself around her wrist too tightly, and she was afraid they'd take her pet away from her if she told the truth?

Maybe.

But I couldn't make any of these scenarios stick. I feared the worst—that something horrible was happening, and Wendy was pretending.

The angry man in my stomach wasn't happy.

"Are you worried about me, Bartholomew?" Wendy said,

and then looked at me the way Mom did when she first started calling me Richard—like the sexually active girls back in high school, tilting her forehead forward, staring up from under her eyebrows. Just like Tara Wilson looked at me before she took me into the high school basement. "You haven't taken your eyes off my wrist."

I looked down at my brown shoelaces.

"How sweet," Wendy said in an almost mean way.

I didn't like what she was doing. Using my concern for her against me. Using her beauty as a weapon.

"Father McNamee is not insane," I said. "He's just . . ."

I thought about telling Wendy about Charles J. Guiteau—that there are good and bad types of crazy—but I knew she wouldn't understand.

Wendy said, "Regardless, I don't think you're emotionally ready for another housemate—especially one who is your mother's age."

"Why do you say that?"

"Because you need to work on making age-appropriate friends. Finding an age-appropriate support group. Finding your own way."

"Being a bird," I said.

"Okay, maybe that was a stupid metaphor. I'll admit it." Wendy watched me stare at my shoelaces for a long time—I could feel her eyes on me—and then she said, "You okay?"

I nodded.

"Have you thought any more about coming to the support group I told you about?"

"I'm still thinking about that."

"Is there anything you'd like to talk about this week?"

"No, thank you."

"What do you and Father McNamee do together?"

"Guy things."

"Guy things?"

"Yes."

"You're not going to tell me?"

"You are not a guy," I said and then smiled, because it felt good to have guy secrets—like I was one step closer to having a beer with a friend at the bar. You would have been proud of me, Richard Gere. Truly.

"I see," Wendy said, and then laughed in a good way. "What have you been reading about at the library this week?"

"The Dalai Lama," I said, because it was true. "And Tibet."

"Interesting. Any particular reason why?"

"Did you know that Tibetan monks have been performing self-immolations to protest China's rule?"

"*Self-immolations*. Like burning themselves to death?"

"Not like. Exactly so."

"I didn't know that."

"Why?"

"What do you mean?"

"Why don't you know about that? Why doesn't *anyone* know about that?"

"I don't know. If it's true, you'd think it would be on the news."

"It *is* true. You can look it up at the library. On the Internet."

"You'd think Richard Gere would be promoting that more," Wendy said, and then laughed. "That's his thing, right? Tibet?"

I couldn't believe that she brought up your name at first, even considering Jung's theory of synchronicity. Her saying those two words stunned me. But then—once her meaning sunk in—the tiny man in my stomach was enraged; he kicked and punched my internal organs.

"You shouldn't make fun of Richard Gere. He's a wise and powerful man," I said. "He's doing good, important work. You wouldn't understand. He's helping people. Many people!"

"Okay, okay," Wendy said and pulled out my binder from her bag. "I didn't know you were such a Richard Gere fan. Jeez Louise."

I wanted to tell her that not merely am I your fan, but you are my confidant. I wanted to tell her about the you-me Richard Gere of pretending, but I knew that it would cause me more trouble than it was worth. Wendy wouldn't understand our correspondence. Wendy wants me to be a bird. And to go to her support group of age-appropriate people. But birds do not befriend famous movie stars and internationally known humanitarians.

Do not hate Wendy.

It's not her fault.

She really does want to help me.

She just doesn't know how, but it's not her fault.

Wendy is only in her midtwenties—the age I was when I was arrested for letting the undercover cop prostitute rub up against my leg. Nobody knows anything when they are in their midtwenties. Think back to when you were that age, Richard Gere. Remember your time in New York and London when you played the lead in *Grease*? Your reviews were sensational—you were much more accomplished than Wendy is now—but could you have been able to advise me back then? No. So cut Wendy some slack. She's just a young woman doing her best.

"Can I level with you?" Wendy said.

I nodded.

"I'm a graduate student."

I blinked at her, waiting for more, and she looked at me like she had said all I needed to understand.

"You know what that means, right?"

I shook my head.

"It means I'm not a licensed therapist yet."

I looked at her.

"I'm practicing on you. That's why I don't charge money."

"Thank you."

Wendy laughed in this very excited and surprised way—like I had told a joke. "Listen, I'm all for being honest with people. Going to group therapy would be good for you. Truly. It would help. You might even make an age-appropriate friend—maybe even have your beer at the bar. I really believe you should go. Truly. Truly. Truly. But I'm also *required* to convince you to go. I'm getting graded on this. All of my classmates have convinced their clients to attend group therapy already, and you're starting to make me look bad. I shouldn't be saying all this to you; I know that. But would you please just go to group therapy for *my* sake? So they don't throw me out of my grad class? Would you do it for me? Please?" Wendy put her hands together like she was begging me. The bruise on her wrist jumped out of her sleeve once more, ugly as a cockroach emerging from under a floorboard. The tiny man delivered a swift kick to my kidney. Then Wendy raised her eyebrows and said, "Pretty please?"

"My going to group therapy would help you do well in grad school?" I asked. This seemed to put the idea in a different light—going to group therapy to help Wendy rather than to help myself. I don't know why this made group therapy more appealing, but it did, maybe because I didn't need help and didn't want to waste my time doing something that wouldn't help anyone.

"It would help *a lot*, actually. More than you realize. I'm not doing very well in school lately."

"If I go to group therapy, will you do something for me?" I asked, because I suddenly had a good idea.

"Sure! Anything!" Wendy said, practically leaping from her chair.

"Would you maybe give me lessons on how to impress a woman?"

Wendy made a lemon face and said, "What do you mean?"

"I want to know how to approach a woman so that she might want to have a beer at the bar with me."

"You're elevating the stakes of your goal, Bartholomew."

"Is that good?"

"It's very good!"

She seemed really happy. She is such a child. So easily pleased.

"Can you help me?" I said.

"Who's the girl?"

"I don't want to tell you."

"Okay," she said, smiling under those thin orange eyebrows. I made the heart constellation out of her freckles once very quickly. "I see how it is."

"I've never been on a date before."

"That's okay."

"You don't think of me as a retard now that I've told you I've never been on a date?"

"I don't think of anyone as a *retard*, because that's a word that shouldn't ever be used."

I smiled.

"It's an age-appropriate goal," Wendy said. "I'm definitely in."

"So?"

"So what?"

"How do I make it happen?"

"Why don't you let me think up a course of action, and we'll talk about it next week. We'll fix you up and do our best to get you the girl, Bartholomew. I promise," Wendy said. She wrote something down on a piece of paper, tore it out, and handed it to me.

Surviving Grief
Monday 8pm
1012 Walnut Street
Third Floor
Tell Arnold I sent you.

"You'll go?" she said.

I looked at the piece of paper.

Surviving Grief

"Okay," I said. "I'll go."

Just then, the front door banged open. Father McNamee was standing there, his face red with cold. "Has our dear Wendy talked you into throwing me out on the streets yet, Bartholomew?" he asked as he charged through the living room.

Wendy took a deep breath—and then she exhaled audibly through her lips. She stood, met Father McNamee at the kitchen entranceway, and said, "Why did you ask me to help Bartholomew if you don't respect my opinion?"

"I respectfully disagree with your opinion," Father McNamee said. "But I still respect it very much."

"I don't understand what type of game you're playing here," Wendy said.

Father McNamee chuckled and winked at me.

"I'm reporting your whereabouts to Father Hachette," Wendy said.

"I no longer answer to the Catholic Church. I defrocked myself."

"I don't understand what's going on, but I don't like it! Not one bit!" Wendy yelled.

She punched her way into her floral-pattern trench coat, grabbed her bag off the kitchen table, and then stormed out of the house, slamming the door behind her.

Father McNamee and I looked at each other.

Then Wendy stormed back into the house and said, "You will be at that meeting, right, Bartholomew?"

"What meeting?" Father McNamee said.

"Bartholomew?" Wendy said, ignoring Father McNamee. "Promise me."

"I promise," I said, but didn't bring up her end of the deal. I didn't want Father McNamee to know I was trying to woo The Girlbrarian. I don't know why.

"Good," Wendy said, and then she stormed out once more.

"She's feisty," Father McNamee said.

He reached up, squeezed my shoulder once, and then went into the living room to continue his praying.

I had no idea why Wendy didn't want Father McNamee to live with me, nor did I understand why Father McNamee had asked Wendy to help me and then blatantly disregarded her opinions.

But I really didn't want to think about any of that.

I sat in the kitchen trying to hear the birds, but they just wouldn't sing on that day.

Wendy's perfume lingered.

Apricot.

Lemon.

Ginger.

What was I going to do next, now that Mom was gone?

I kept thinking about you, Richard Gere.

In the biography that Peter Carrick wrote—on page 17, when he is discussing your relationship with Cindy Crawford, Carrick writes, "He [you, Richard Gere] admitted it was hard for him to make decisions and saw the process as something definite rather than transitory, a situation complicated because of his oppressive tendency to over-analyse."

When I read that, I knew the you-me of pretending was no accident, because I have always been kept paralyzed by my obsessive thinking, which is why I began playing the you-me Richard Gere game when my mother got sick. When I was you, I didn't have to think for myself, and this protected me from making mistakes. I wondered if you have ever played such a game, and then it hit me that you are an actor who plays this game all the time, right?

In his book *A Profound Mind*, the Dalai Lama writes, "To change our lives we must first acknowledge that our present situation is not satisfactory."

It would seem that both Wendy and Father McNamee want me to change my life.

But I wouldn't say that I am unsatisfied at all, especially since I have you, Richard Gere, to advise me.

Your admiring fan,
Bartholomew Neil

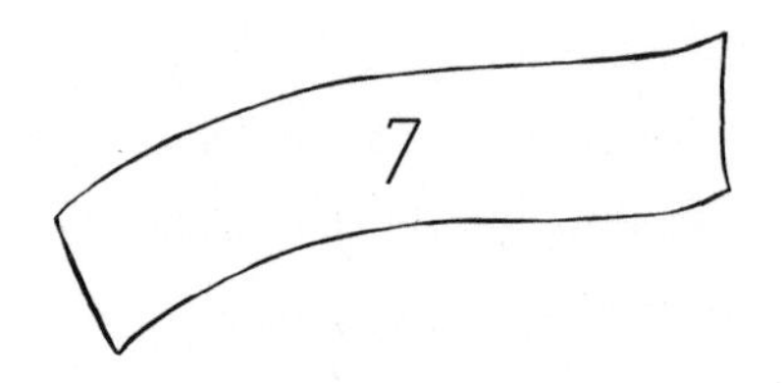

HIS USE OF THE PLURAL PRONOUN MADE ME VERY SUSPICIOUS

Dear Mr. Richard Gere,

There was a knock at the front door the other night, and when I answered, Father Hachette was looking up at me through his round glasses, the white of his priest collar illuminated by the porch light. He said, "I know he's in there."

"Who?" I said, because Father McNamee had instructed me to "play dumb" if Father Hachette should come looking for him. The night before, when Father McNamee was very drunk, he called Father Hachette "the one left behind" and "the man with no eyes to see nor ears to hear."

"I think you know exactly who I mean," Father Hachette said.

"Sorry," I said, and tried to shut the door.

"Okay, okay," Father Hachette said. "Will you at least come outside and speak with me?"

I hesitated for a second, but couldn't see the harm in speaking with him, so I went outside.

"Cigarette?" Father said to me as he lit up.

"No, thanks." He knows I don't smoke.

We both surveyed the street as he took a few puffs. It was cold, so no one was out on the stoops.

"Father McNamee is sick, Bartholomew."

I immediately pictured the squidlike cancer attacking his brain. But I didn't say anything, because I knew the probability of knowing two people with brain cancer was unlikely. Still, I couldn't help having some irrational fear.

"He has bipolar disorder. Always has. But he went off his meds right around the time your mother passed."

"He doesn't seem sick," I said.

"Do you know what bipolar disorder is?" he said, blowing smoke into the night.

"Yes."

"What is it, then?"

I didn't speak, because I wasn't exactly sure. I had a general idea. But I'm not a doctor.

"It's a chemical imbalance," Father Hachette said. "Bipolar people sometimes have too much of the happy chemicals in their brain—which makes them feel as though they can do anything. And this can lead to erratic, impulsive, and dangerous behavior."

I thought about Charles J. Guiteau killing President Garfield.

"These manic upswings are always followed by terrible downswings—fierce depressions. The bipolar person can become suicidal and dangerous. Do you understand what I mean?"

"Father McNamee is not depressed," I said. "I've known him for a long time, and I've never seen him dangerously sad."

"We took care of him when he wasn't feeling well, Bartholomew. Sent him on retreats. Listened to him rant, made sure he took his meds. It was a great responsibility—and a tiresome one. Often it was more work than any one of us could handle. We had many resources through the church. I say all of this to you because—frankly—I think you're in over your head. We are many, you are one."

He was wrong, of course, because I have you, Richard Gere.

"I enjoy Father McNamee's company," I said.

"So you admit that he's living here?" Father Hachette said and then laughed.

"I admit nothing," I said.

Moron! the little angry man inside me yelled.

Stay cool, you, Richard Gere, whispered in my ear, and I imagined I could see you standing next to me. You were translucent, like a ghost. But then you were gone.

A noise came from inside the house—it sounded like heavy footsteps.

Father Hachette turned around, and when I looked at the window, the curtains closed very quickly. Father McNamee had been spying on us, and I thought maybe he wanted Father Hachette to know I was hiding him, because he was not being very secretive.

"Since he's a grown man and he publicly defrocked himself, legally there is nothing we can do at this point," Father Hachette said. "But I wanted you to know that when Father

McNamee goes into a downswing—*and he most definitely will*—you're going to need help."

I nodded because that was the easiest thing to do.

"He'll see rain when there's only sun. He'll become suspicious of people. He'll be unbelievably gloomy and will start to yell at you, twist your own thoughts. That's when you'll know you're really in over your head."

"Okay," I said, although I didn't believe Father Hachette.

"I understand why you would be attracted to Father McNamee. His passion can be beautiful," Father Hachette said. "Extremely beautiful. John the Baptist beautiful. Elijah beautiful even."

"Beautiful?"

"Incredibly so. We've all been seduced by it over the years. Sometimes it even seems divine. And he can be quite prophetic—uncannily prophetic. We've all been attracted to his passion—pulled in."

I remembered Father McNamee's eyes sucking at me like whirlpools.

"Any questions, Bartholomew? This is a lot for you to swallow, I imagine."

"Do you think God has stopped talking to Father McNamee?" I asked. "Is that why he left the church?"

"God speaks to all of us, but He says more to some than others." Father Hachette flicked his cigarette butt onto the sidewalk and patted my chest again, like I was a Great Dane. "I've said all I needed to. You know where to find me, day or night. Right down the street at Saint Gabriel's. Tell Father McNamee we miss him, okay?"

"Okay."

We shook hands, and then he left.

As I watched him walk down the block I kept thinking that Father Hachette looked relieved—like he was floating, almost.

Why?

"What did the old man say about me?" Father McNamee said once I was inside, which was strange because he and Father Hachette looked about the same age.

"He said you have a bipolar disorder," I said.

"And I should be on meds, right?"

I nodded.

"What do you think?" he asked.

"About what?"

"Whether or not I should be medicated."

"I don't know."

"Do I seem crazy to you?"

"No," I said, because I knew that's what he wanted me to say. "But I'm not a doctor."

"You know Jesus was most likely bipolar," he said, nodding with great enthusiasm. "Preaching love your enemies one day and then flipping over the money changers' tables the next. Turn the other cheek, and then it's all swords and righteousness." Father raised his right hand and said, "'These things I have spoken to you, so that in Me you may have peace,' John 16:33. 'Do not think that I came to bring peace on the earth; I did not come to bring peace, but a sword!' Matthew 10:34. Seeking out multitudes to heal and feed and awe—and then escaping on boats to quiet places, praying alone in gardens. What if Jesus had been medicated?" He raked his fingers through his beard. "Do you think he would have been so eager to give his life for the world? That's not a reasonable, rational thing, after all. People don't volunteer for crucifixion when chemicals are placating their minds, hearts, and souls. No one would want Jesus taking mood-altering pills, right? And as Catholics we're supposed to live our lives as He did, right? *Right?*"

I nodded because what he was saying seemed logical.

Father McNamee nodded back once, said, "Besides, this is why God gave us whiskey," got on his knees in the living room, and continued praying.

I decided to skip Mass for the first time in my life, because I didn't want to see Father Hachette again. I didn't want to have another confusing conversation. And Father McNamee and I were having Communion on a daily basis—three times a day, at every meal. You, Richard Gere, appeared to me several times, ghostlike in the darkness of my bedroom, and you told me that it was okay to skip Mass, that I could pray and talk to God anywhere—but as you are a Buddhist, I'm not sure I can trust you on these matters.

Father McNamee prayed and prayed and prayed, and nothing else really happened until I went to the library on Monday morning. The Girlbrarian was working. I thought about the goals I had made with Wendy. How I wanted to have a beer at the bar with The Girlbrarian.

There is nothing I want more than to speak with The Girlbrarian.

I prayed for strength.

She was wearing black military-style boots, jeans, and a long white sweater that looked like a dress and covered everything from her shoulders to her knees. For an hour or so I watched her push her cart in and out of aisles as she returned the books to their homes according to the alphabet. She would study the spines of each through her long brown hair, and then she'd scan the shelves, her eyes zigzagging the rows.

Whenever she found the proper place she would nod once and push her lips together as if to say, "Yes, I do believe I have found your home, Mr. or Mrs. Book."

Then she would kneel or climb the little ladder attached to the cart before she made a space for the returned book. She'd slide the book back onto the shelf, make sure the spine was even with all of the other spines, and then give the top a little tap with her index finger, as if to say, "Perfect."

The whole time I watched The Girlbrarian I pretended that you were speaking to me, Richard Gere. You kept saying, *Look at her, Bartholomew. She's perfect for you. Go over and speak with her. Ask her what she likes to read. Ask if she likes looking at the river flow behind the art museum. Tell her you like her outfit. That she does her job with precision and efficiency, both of which you value highly. Ask her to have a beer with you. Why not? What do you have to lose? There she is. Go! It's as simple as walking fifty feet and saying ten words, big guy. Come on!*

When you spoke to me at the library, you kept calling me "big guy."

Come on, big guy. She's right there. And I'll be with you the whole time. I'll be telling you what to do in your mind. Come on, big guy! We can do this. Trust me.

It was nice to hear your voice in my mind—even if I was only pretending—especially since you are so confident and good with the opposite sex, both on and off the screen.

Each time The Girlbrarian climbed to the top of her ladder, I thought of that line you say to Julia Roberts at the end of *Pretty Woman.*

"What happens after he climbs up the tower and rescues her?" you ask.

And Julia Roberts says, "She rescues him right back."

I wondered if maybe The Girlbrarian and I would say something like that to each other after we had gone on so many dates, and in my mind you said, *Sure. Sure you will, big guy. It's easy. Just go over and say hi. Listen to what I tell you to do, and failure will be impossible.*

But I didn't listen to what you told me to do.

I didn't say hi.

I didn't do anything.

And I want to thank you for being patient with me, Richard Gere, because you never once yelled at me or called me a retard. You said only positive, encouraging things in my mind, and you were so nice, I almost wanted to cry. I understand why Mom loved and admired you so much, although the little man in my stomach was not amused. He kept yelling, *Hey, stupid! Richard Gere is not speaking to you! It's only your imagination! What type of a grown man pretends like this? Only retards!* With every sentence, he'd give a little kick or punch, and my insides started to feel sore.

But you ignored that little angry man in my stomach—you just kept encouraging me, Richard Gere.

You even appeared to me briefly in the library—just long enough to flash me a smile before your image evaporated.

Thank you.

I listened to you speak so sonorously in my mind for more than two hours until I realized that I had to leave and get something to eat before I attended my Surviving Grief meeting.

I ate a baked potato and a salad at Wendy's, because I was thinking about Wendy my grief counselor just as I was walking past that redheaded little girl's fast-food restaurant and was reminded of Jung's synchronicity, so I decided to go inside.

I smiled while eating at Wendy's—thinking about my grief counselor and the fact that there are no coincidences.

Thinking about Wendy at Wendy's.

Then I went to the address that Wendy gave me.

1012 Walnut Street
Third Floor

There was a coffee shop on the first floor, and when I asked for directions they told me to use a door that was in an alleyway. There was a buzzer and a black box with numbered buttons and a tiny hole you were supposed to speak into. Since I didn't know the entry code, I pushed the white circle call button and heard a *bzzzzzzz!*

A second later, a man's voice said, "Hello?"

"Um . . . I'm looking for group therapy. Grief management. Wendy sent me? Are you Arnold?"

"Are you Mr. Bartholomew Neil?"

"Yes."

"Wendy has said such nice things about you! Come on up! Third floor!"

I heard another buzzing noise and a click, so I tried the door and it opened.

I could smell the coffee shop—ground beans, steamed milk, warmth like breathing through a wool scarf on the coldest of days.

There was a narrow staircase and a wooden railing. The walls were painted a mint green.

I climbed.

When I reached the third floor there was a blond man with a well-groomed blond goatee waiting in the doorway. He was wearing a brown cardigan sweater with leather arm patches, moss green corduroy pants, and suede shoes that looked like a very expensive version of what you'd wear while bowling.

I glanced into his office and suddenly noticed that the entire room was yellow—yellow couch, yellow rug, yellow walls, and several abstract paintings of flowers that appeared to have been made by folding thin sheets of gold.

It was absolutely bizarre.

"Bartholomew!" he said and stuck out his hand, which I shook. His grip was perfect—not too hard, not too light. "Welcome to group therapy for the grieving! Come on in!"

I included all of the exciting punctuation marks because he was so enthusiastic. I was also a bit confused about "group" therapy, because there wasn't anybody else in the room.

"I'm Dr. Devine, but you may call me Arnie. I'm so glad you decided to join us. How are you today?"

His use of the plural pronoun made me very suspicious, since we were alone.

But Arnie's eyes struck me as sincere, and I felt as though he was really concerned—as though he wanted to listen to me. He seemed like a nice man, a good doctor.

"I'm fine," I said.

"Good. Good. Now, what has Wendy told you about us?"

"*Us?*" I said, not able to let it slide a third time.

"Max and me."

"Max?"

"She didn't tell you about Max?" Dr. Devine had a surprised look now that made me feel very anxious. Worry lines appeared on his forehead.

"She didn't really say anything at all—except that I would benefit from coming here," I lied. I didn't want to talk about Wendy's personal problems with her schooling, because I didn't want to gossip.

"Oh dear," Dr. Devine said. "Where to start? *Where. To. Start?*" he said to the floor. "Max and you have been grouped together for several reasons that I will explain shortly. But before he gets here—and I realize we don't have much time—I wanted to warn you about Max's . . . demeanor."

"What do you mean?"

"Well, Wendy really should have told you that—"

"What the fuck, hey?" a man said as he walked into the room from the stairwell. "Fuck this. Fuck *this!*"

"Hi, Max! Great to see you today! We were just talking

about you. This is Max, Bartholomew. He is also grieving. Bartholomew, this is—"

"Why the fuck is *he* here?" Max said, standing in the doorway.

"Now, Max," Arnie said. "We talked about this."

Max looked at me and then—a bit more softly—once more, he said, "What the fuck, hey?"

I was speechless.

"Should we all sit down?" Arnie said.

Max threw his hands in the air like it didn't matter and then plopped down at the far end of the yellow couch.

He looked to be about my age, but was wearing thick brown old-man glasses that made me wonder if he might be legally blind. Behind the heavy lenses, his pupils made me think of twin snails in adjacent bowls. Max had on black pants, black shoes, a purple button-up long-sleeve shirt, and a black vest—all of which reeked of stale popcorn. On the breast pocket was a gold name tag with his name printed on it.

MAX
HERE TO SERVE YOU!

When Arnie motioned to the other end of the couch, I sat down.

Arnie sat in a yellow leather armchair and crossed his legs.

"Bartholomew, the yellow room is a word fortress. Whatever words you let free in the yellow room stay in the yellow room. So feel free to speak freely. You are safe here. And in return, I must ask you to be a knight of confidence. A keeper of secrets. A sacred chalice for the truths Max may confide in you. And we shall be your word chalices. Can you help defend our castle, Bartholomew? Can you be a knight of confidence?"

"What the fuck, hey?" Max whispered before I could answer. When I looked over at him, he was shaking his head.

"Max, would you like to express something?"

"This ain't a fucking castle, Arnie. Give us a fucking break, hey."

"Okay, Max. Why don't you give Bartholomew an introduction? Welcome—"

"Introduction? *Fuck that!*" Max said.

"You will find that while Max has a gruff exterior, he's really a sweet man underneath of it all, which is why we've decided to match you two up."

I must have raised my eyebrows or something because Arnie said, "You look confused."

"What do we do here?" I said. "Is it like talking with Wendy?"

"Good question," Max said. "Great fucking question." He nodded like he meant it and wasn't making fun of me at all.

"Yes," Arnie said. "The yellow room is for talking. You are free to speak your mind. But the goal here tonight is to partner the two of you up, so that you might support each other through the grieving process."

Max blew air out between his lips.

"Max, would you please tell Bartholomew why you are grieving?"

Max blew even more air out between his lips.

"*Max?*"

Max looked up at the ceiling for a good fifteen seconds or so and squeezed his knees with his hands before he said, "Alice was my best friend, and now she's fucking gone."

"Yes, she is, Max. I'm very sorry about that."

"Did you fucking kill her, hey?"

"No, I did not," Arnie said.

"Then what the fuck are you sorry about?"

"I'm sorry for your loss. I'm sorry that you have to go through this grieving process. I'm sorry that Alice is no longer providing you with the comforts that you once had, and I hope that you will find a way to move on."

"I haven't missed any work, hey."

"Maybe you *should* take a few days off."

"Fuck that."

"Bartholomew, would you tell us please why you are grieving?"

"My mother died of cancer."

"Cancer?" Max said. He turned and faced me, eyes wide.

"Brain cancer. The doctors described it like a squid with tentacles, and—"

"Fuck cancer! That's what got my Alice too, hey. Fuck cancer. *Fuck.*"

Arnie said, "How do you feel about cancer, Bartholomew?"

"Um . . . I don't know. I don't *like* cancer. It killed my mother," I said.

"The yellow room is a *safe* room," Arnie said. "You can speak more forcefully about your feelings if you wish. You don't have to be polite, like you do outside of the yellow room, in the real world. Remember, this is a word fortress."

"Fuck cancer!" Max said.

I nodded in agreement.

"How's it been for you, Bartholomew? Since your mother died?" Arnie said.

"It's fucking hell, right?" Max said. "Fucking hell."

"Um . . . it's been *an adjustment*. I loved Mom. She was a good friend in addition to being my mother. But she wasn't right at the end. She changed."

"My Alice changed too," Max said. "She started to piss on everything. The bed. My clothes. The couch. Everywhere she was fucking pissing, which is how I knew she wasn't right. It was like she lost her fucking mind, hey."

"Mom was like that too. She had to wear a diaper."

"Fuck cancer."

"Yes," I said.

"Max, would you like to tell Bartholomew what you miss most about Alice?"

He looked at the ceiling, and I actually thought Max was going to cry.

Finally, he blew out another lungful of air between his teeth, like a leaky tire, pushed his clunky brown glasses up his nose, and then said, "I fucking miss having someone greet me when I come home from work after the late movie ends and my sister is fucking sleeping. Alice always waited up for me. Fucking always. I miss Alice sitting on my lap when I watched television. I miss the way she fucking purred when I scratched behind her fucking ears. I miss how she sat in the window all day, just enjoying the fucking sun."

"Wait . . . I don't understand," I said.

"What don't you understand?" Arnie said.

"Who are you talking about, Max?"

"Fucking Alice!"

"What relation was she to you?" I asked.

"She was my fucking everything. For fifteen fucking years."

"So she was . . . *your wife?*"

"What the fuck, hey?" Max said. His face turned bright red, like I had thrown boiling water on it. "Do you think I'm some sort of twisted fucking fuck?"

"It's okay, Max," Arnie said. "We never told Bartholomew that Alice was a cat."

"I said she sat in the fucking window, right?"

"People can sit in windows," I said.

Max dismissed my words with the wave of his hand and then said, "I fucking miss Alice and I'm not ashamed to say so—especially here in the yellow fucking room, where I'm supposed to fucking grieve openly, hey. She was a calico and more loyal than any fucking person has ever been to me—I don't give a shit if she was a cat or not. Fuck! I miss her. And I'll tell you what, hey!"

"Tell us," Arnie said. "Tell us everything. Let it out. We're listening. This is a safe place."

"You don't fucking care about my dead fucking cat! No one does!" Max said to me and then wiped his eyes. "What the fuck, hey?"

Richard Gere, you whispered in my ear—well, maybe I pretended you were whispering directly into my ear, thinking what would Richard Gere say and do?—*Tell him you want to hear about his cat. Lessen his pain. Be compassionate. Remember the Dalai Lama's teachings.*

I remembered a line I read in the Dalai Lama's book *A Profound Mind.* "It is important that we understand just how truly all-pervasive suffering is." I remembered the Dalai Lama saying it is easy to feel sorry for an elderly beggar, but it is much harder to feel sorry for a young rich man. He also said that all "conditioned existence is characterized by pain." And that all types of people are "enslaved" by "strong destructive emotions."

And so, heeding your spiritual leader's advice, I said to Max, "I'd like to hear about your cat. Alice. I really would."

He examined my face for a second or two, probably trying to decide if I meant it, and then said, "Alice was the best fucking cat that ever lived."

I began pretending again, and you, Richard Gere, in my imagination you whispered in my ear and said, *Look how his muscles are relaxing. Note the slope of his shoulders. Relaxed. He needs to talk. Listen. Ease his suffering. Be compassionate. And compassion will come back to you. Heed the words of the Dalai Lama.*

Max went on to talk about his cat for more than a half hour straight. He told me that he found her in a Dumpster in Worcester, Massachusetts, behind the movie theater where he used to work before he moved to Philadelphia to live with his sister. He was taking out the nightly trash when he heard a kitten crying. He had to tear open "a million fucking bags" before he found it. There were six other kittens inside but all of those were dead. "I wanted to kill the fucking scumbag who put kittens in a trash bag. What the fuck, hey? Who does that?" He was very worried that someone would find him standing next to the dead cats "with fucking trash and dead kittens all around my fucking feet" and accuse him of killing the cats, so he stuck the alive kitten into his coat and headed to the nearest convenience store so he could get some "fucking milk." It was late at night and the woman working the convenience store behind "thick fucking plastic glass" saw the kitten and excitedly exited her glass box to pet it. She made such a big deal over the kitten and was so nice to Max, showing him where the cat food was and letting him feed the kitten in her store, that Max decided to name the kitten after that convenience store worker. "What the fuck, hey? I thought," Max said. "So I asked what her fucking name was and she fucking said Alice. So that's what I fucking named my cat." Max went on to explain how—using a feather on a string and catnip—he trained his cat to meow on command and also run through an obstacle course full of hoops and mini-jumps "like what fucking horses jump, but smaller for baby cats." And he said that as Alice became an adult cat, he taught her how to speak to him.

"Really speak to you?" Arnie said. "Or were you only *pre-*

tending Alice could speak with you? Like most people do when they talk to their pets."

"Yeah, like fucking that, hey. Pretending," Max said.

I became very interested in Max at this point.

He talked a lot more about Alice, listing what types of food she liked—"Canned fucking tuna was her favorite!"—and how she liked to chase red dots of light that he projected onto the wall with "a fucking laser pointer" and how Alice "jumped and ran and pounced for fucking hours," how they both enjoyed watching the library's box-set DVDs of the original *Doctor Who* and how he thought about Alice whenever he was working, ripping "the fuck out of tickets" at the "fucking movies," because that was "his fucking job"—being a "fucking ticket fucking taker" at the "fucking movies," and it was "really fucking boring, hey!"

I told him that working at the movies seemed like an interesting job, especially since you could see movies for free, and Max said, "Going to the movies? Fuck that! You have to sit with fucking asshole strangers and you never know which one has a fucking cold or what fuck is going to bring a fucking crying baby. And working at the fucking movies fucking sucks. You end up watching *parts* of every fucking movie and then never seeing the rest. Fifteen minutes of this fucking film, fifteen minutes of that fucker. All the fucking parts get mixed up and make a never-fucking-ending Frankenstein film. You never get to see the whole thing start to fucking finish. Not fucking once. And you know what's the worst fucking part?"

"What?" I said.

"No cats allowed. What the fuck, hey? Alice loved movies! Why can't you bring your cat? *What the fuck?* That's why I always preferred watching fucking movies at home."

"Do you enjoy Richard Gere movies?" I asked.

"Richard Gere? *Richard fucking Gere?*" Max said. "*Fuck Richard Gere!* What the fuck, hey?"

"He's actually my favorite actor," I said, sticking up for you, even though you technically were one of *Mom*'s favorite actors. "And a brave humanitarian."

"Oh, I like Richard Gere," said Arnie, who had been listening to Max and me talk with a satisfied look on his face. "He was great in *Chicago*."

"Fuck Richard Gere," Max said once more. "Fuck going to the fucking movies. I miss Alice. I really fucking miss Alice. *Fuck!*"

There was a long silence here.

Max looked like he was melting.

You were compassionate, you, Richard Gere, whispered into my ear. *You let go of the self.*

Arnie looked at his watch, and then he said, "I'm afraid our time is almost up, gentlemen. Bartholomew, you'll be given more time to speak next week."

I nodded.

"Max, thanks for sharing all that you did tonight."

"What the fuck, hey?" he said and then shrugged, like sharing was no big deal.

"Can I ask a question?" I said.

"Certainly," Arnie said.

"Why is everything yellow in here?"

"Psychological research proves that the color yellow—bright yellow, that is—can make people feel more confident and optimistic. This, of course, helps with the grieving process. Ironically, pale yellow can have the opposite effect. So I go with bright yellow. It's all rather scientific. I am a doctor, you know," Arnie said and then winked at me.

"Oh," I said.

"Same time next week?"

Max blew air through his teeth, adjusted his big glasses, and then jumped up into a standing position. I stood, and Arnie walked us to the door. "It was a very good session, boys. I feel like we made great progress tonight. Be kind to yourselves this week. Grieve bravely and openly. Embrace the process. Good night."

Max and I walked down the steps and into the alley. I followed him to Walnut Street.

"Max?" I said.

"What the fuck, hey?"

"Do you say that to everyone—all the time?"

"What?"

" 'What the fuck, hey'?"

He nodded. "Except when I'm fucking working. They'd fire me. I just keep my fucking mouth shut and rip tickets at work."

"Could your cat really speak with her mind?"

"Fuck, yeah, she could! Arnie doesn't know. Arnie doesn't understand. He doesn't fucking believe me, but it's true. We used to talk all the fucking time—Alice and me."

"I believe you."

"You do?"

"Yes."

He reached into his jacket pocket and pulled out a pink circle of plastic. "This was her fucking collar." Max held it out to me. I took it.

There was a silver heart-shaped tag.

ALICE

"It's a very nice tag," I said.

Max took the collar back, wiped his eyes, and mumbled, "What the fuck, hey?"

We stood there looking at our shoelaces for a few minutes.

Then Max said, "Do you want to have a fucking beer somewhere?"

"Like—at a bar?"

"Fuck bars! Bars are where douche bags try to fuck each other. At a pub. A fucking beer at a proper fucking pub."

I thought about my goal of having a beer at a bar with an age-appropriate friend and decided a pub was even better, because I really didn't want to be near douche bags trying to copulate.

"How old are you?" I asked Max.

"I'm thirty-fucking-nine. Do you want a fucking beer or what?"

I am also thirty-nine, as you already know, Richard Gere.

Jung's synchronicity.

Unus mundus.

Unus mundus!

"Yes, I would very much like to have a beer at a pub with you."

"Okay, then. Fucking follow me."

Max walked very quickly and I trailed for maybe six or seven blocks before we entered a dark pub with railings around the bar and pictures of Ireland all over the walls.

We sat on stools and put our feet on brass rungs, just like on TV.

It was amazing.

The bartender was a frowning fat man. "What'll it be?"

"Two fucking beers," Max said.

The bartender tilted his head to one side, and his eyes narrowed. "What fucking kind?"

"What the fuck kind of beer do you like?" Max asked me.

"I don't know," I said, because I didn't often drink beer.

"Two fucking Guinness," Max said.

"O-fucking-kay," the bartender said and tossed two small cardboard circles onto the bar in front of us.

A TV hung over the shelved bottles of alcohol, and on it was some show where people had to run through an obstacle course. A foot-wide path separated a pool from a huge wall, out of which boxing gloves would pop and knock people into the water below if they weren't careful. We watched a few people try to cross and they were all knocked in. Every time someone fell, there were cartoon noises that sounded like springs being plucked or high-pitched whistles being blown. Then a giant of a woman shimmied across with her arms and legs spread wide like a spider and everyone in the bar cheered.

"Twelve-fucking-fifty," the bartender said when he placed the dark beers in front of us on the little cardboard circles.

"You owe him seven dollars," Max said. "This ain't a fucking date, hey."

I pulled out my wallet and gave the man seven dollars.

Max and I clinked our glasses, sipped our creamy beers, and watched men and women try to run across twelve or so balls that were floating on water—the goal being to end up on a platform of sorts. Every time someone fell into the lake, there were more cartoon noises, everyone in the pub would cheer and groan, and Max would snicker, raise his beer in the air, and yell, "What the fuck, hey?"

We didn't talk at all, which was okay with me. I was happy just to check off one of my life goals.

When he finished his beer, he said, "Bottoms fucking up. I have to go home and make sure my sister's okay."

I finished my beer and said, "Is there something wrong with your sister?"

"Nah," Max said. "Except she fucking doesn't miss Alice as much as I do. She's sort of fucking weird, but she's family."

Ask him, How *is your sister weird?* you, Richard Gere, whispered into my ear, so I did.

"Ah, she always has her fucking hair in her face. She works at the fucking library. She pretends to be real skittish, and she had some bad shit happen to her a few years ago. But she's okay now. Just a little fucking off. And she worries if she doesn't know where I am. I didn't tell her about having a beer with you because I didn't even know who the fuck you were before tonight."

It felt like all of my ribs had been crushed and my heart was on fire.

I had just drunk beer with The Girlbrarian's brother.

Father McNamee would have called it Communion.

"What the fuck is wrong with you?" Max said. "You look like you're taking a shit in your pants."

"I'm okay," I managed to say. "But I have to go."

"What the fucking fuck, hey?" Max said as I walked away from him and into the night. I walked quickly for an hour or so until I arrived home. Father McNamee was kneeling in the living room, praying.

"Father McNamee?" I said.

He opened one eye and said, "Yes, Bartholomew?"

"I have something to tell you. Something that will seem crazy."

"Sounds like it will require alcohol."

Father McNamee groaned as he stood, poured us whiskey, and we drank in the kitchen while I told him the entire story—everything I outlined above, letting him know that I was madly in love with The Girlbrarian, admitting that to someone for the first time, which felt surprisingly good.

When I finished, he smiled at me and said, "I'm happy for you. Love is a beautiful thing."

"What do you think it means?"

"What does *what* mean?"

"My being randomly paired up with The Girlbrarian's brother."

"Why do you call her The Girlbrarian?" Father said, sucking in his lips and squinting.

I didn't know why, so I said, "My just happening to be paired up with her brother. Do you think it means something?"

"I wouldn't know."

"Could it be divine intervention?"

"God and I aren't exactly on speaking terms these days. But again, I'm happy for you, Bartholomew. Cheers!" he said, raised his glass, and then took a rather large gulp of his whiskey.

We finished our drinks and had another round.

I felt like I was giving off light, I was so warm and happy, but Father McNamee seemed off.

I was a little buzzed when I went to bed.

I dreamed of my mother again, only this time she wasn't in any sort of danger.

Mom and I were sitting on the backyard patio, sipping her homemade tea brewed with the mint we grew in window boxes. It was a sticky summer evening. We could hear thunder in the distance and every once in a while we'd see a flash of heat lightning. We could taste the electricity in the air. Mom looked at me and said, "Why do you think Richard calls you 'big guy'?" She made air quotes around the words "big guy" and said them in a deep voice, like she was trying to imitate the way a man would speak, although she sounded nothing like you, Richard Gere. And by the look on her face, I could tell she did not like your nickname for me.

"It's better than 'retard,'" I said.

Mom slapped her knee and laughed until she couldn't catch her breath—until tears ran down her face.

Finally, after she calmed down, Mom said, "Who would ever think you were mentally challenged? You're more intelligent than most people, but most people don't measure intelligence the right way."

I looked away, and when I looked back, she had turned into a tiny yellow bird.

That bird sang to me for a minute or so, and then it flew up into the air, toward the heat lightning that was striking every few seconds, creating a strobe effect.

"Mom!" I screamed.

And then I woke up.

Your admiring fan,
Bartholomew Neil

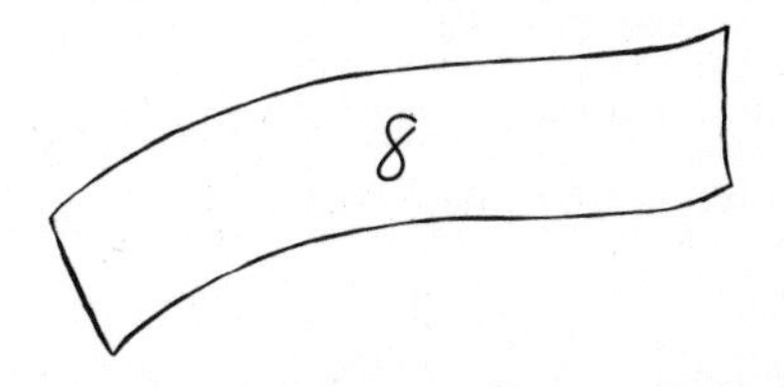

"TO THE POINT WHERE WE ARE UNABLE TO BEAR THE SIGHT OF THEIR MISERY"

Dear Mr. Richard Gere,

Wendy came to visit me wearing sunglasses.

They were rather large oval lenses that looked like eggs turned sideways (smaller sides pointing toward her ears, larger egg bottoms resting on the bridge of her nose). The frames were white. They covered most of her face, and made her nose look bunny-rabbit small.

"Hello, Father McNamee," Wendy said when we walked past him kneeling and praying in the living room.

He remained motionless, with his hands clasped tight, but then he opened one eye and tried to suck us in with it. It was like seeing the blowhole of a whale breach the water's surface. It sucked all the air out of the room.

Or maybe like looking into a well, and feeling the urge to step away, so you wouldn't fall in—and yet you lean in a little closer, anyway.

Then his eye snapped shut and he went back to praying, so Wendy and I made our way into the kitchen.

She sat down and removed her coat, but left her sunglasses on, which I thought was strange.

"How was group therapy?" she asked me. "Arnie said very nice things about you."

"It was okay. Better than I thought it would be." I smiled here, and you, Richard Gere, in my mind you whispered, *Go on. Tell her.* You sounded so proud of me. So I said, "And afterward, I accomplished one of my life goals."

"Really?" she said very loudly, enthusiastically, and then leaned in toward me. "Which one?"

I looked at her small knee—the left one; it was black because she was wearing leggings under her wool skirt—smiled, and said, "I had a beer with an age-appropriate friend at a pub. And after only one meeting with Arnie."

"*Bartholomew!* I'm so proud," she said, but it sounded too enthusiastic—fake—which depressed me. "Who was your lucky drinking partner?"

"Max."

Her orange eyebrows popped up from behind her white sunglasses. "Max from group therapy?"

"Are two people a group? I thought there would be more than one other person in group therapy," I said, because I did think that and had been wondering about why there were only two of us.

"We pair up people, like partners. Support buddies. We don't want to overwhelm people like Max and you with a larger group. You need to start with small steps."

"Max is grieving over a cat named Alice," I said, just stating a fact.

"People grieve for all sorts of reasons. It's probably best not to compare or try to measure."

I nodded in full agreement, thinking the Dalai Lama would also nod if he were here.

"What did you two have to drink?" Wendy asked.

"Guinness."

"Yum! I love Guinness! Guinness is good for you, they say. One of the healthier beers. Something about the dark color is good for your heart, I think. I read that somewhere. Makes me feel better about drinking beer when I do. So I always drink Guinness. Also, you can't drink as many. Too filling. So it's a safe beer too. I'm glad that you and Max—"

"Why are you wearing sunglasses?" I asked. It was a logical question. People don't often wear sunglasses indoors. Wendy had never before worn sunglasses during one of our meetings. And yet, as soon as the words jumped out of my mouth, I realized that the question was weighty and would change the nice, easy flow of the conversation. It was as if the power had shifted and I had become the counselor—or at least that's how it felt to me. I sort of sensed that I needed to become the counselor—like something needed to be done, and I was the one to do it.

Wendy paused and took a few seconds to think about her answer. In my mind I saw her eyes look up to the left, but I couldn't tell for sure because of the dark black lenses that were reflecting the circular light above, making two glowing circles out of one—twin robot moons.

Finally, Wendy said, "I was playing softball with my boyfriend and his buddies and I took a line drive to the face. Wanna see?"

I didn't say anything in response, but she took off her sunglasses, anyway. Her left eye was almost swollen shut. Iridescent yellow, purple, and green filled her eye socket like an oily puddle of gasoline rainbows.

"Based on the look you're giving me, I should probably put these back on," Wendy said, and then she was wearing her sunglasses again, smiling—yet her smile wasn't true, and harder to look at than the actual bruise.

Remember the bruise on her wrist last week? She wasn't playing softball, you whispered in my mind, Richard Gere. *She needs help. This woman needs saving.*

I looked at her wrist, and there was still a red mark, although it had faded considerably.

The angry man in my stomach was kicking and punching away.

Her trouble was so obvious.

I began to sweat.

"Bartholomew?" Wendy said. "Are you okay?"

I nodded and looked down at my brown shoelaces.

"You don't look so well."

I tried hard to keep my mouth shut like always.

"What's wrong?"

I knew that speaking my mind would only lead to trouble.

"Bartholomew?"

Something inside me was changing.

"You can talk to me. You're safe here. You can—"

I knew I had lost control when the words started to leave my mouth.

My mouth said, "Looking at your bruised eye—I could feel your pain. That happens to me sometimes." I said it before I could stop myself. I had not spoken this freely and openly for a long time. It was like you, Richard Gere, were speaking through me. It was like I was acting maybe. Saying the words in a script. And I knew from experience that saying such things made me lonely—left me friendless. I didn't want to say these things.

Moron! the tiny man in my stomach yelled.

(I have to say that everything seems to be unraveling lately. Or maybe it seems as though I am a flower myself, opening up to the world for the first time. I don't know why this is, and I'm not really in control of it either. Flowers do not think, Okay, it is now May, so I will reach up toward the sun and relax my fist of petals into an open hand. They do not think at all. Flowers just grow, and when it is time, they shoot colors out of their stems and become beautiful. I am no more beautiful than I was when Mom was alive, but I feel as though I am a fist opening, a flower blooming, a match ignited, a beautiful mane of hair loosened from a bun—that so many things previously impossible are now possible. And I have been wondering if that is the reason I did not cry and become upset when Mom died. Do the colorful flower petals cry and mourn when they are no longer contained within a green stem? I wonder if the first thirty-eight years of my life were spent within the stem of me—myself. I have been wondering about a lot of things, Richard Gere, and when I read about your life I get to thinking that you also have had similar thoughts, which is why you dropped out of college and did not become a farmer like your grandfather or an insurance salesman like your father. And it's also why so many people thought you were aloof, when you were only trying to be you. I read that you used to go to the movies by yourself when you were in college and you'd stay at the movie house for hours and hours studying the craft of acting and storytelling and moviemaking. You did all of this alone. This was maybe when you were in the stem—before you exploded into the bloom of internationally famous movie star Richard Gere. Such vivid colors you boast now! But it wasn't easy for you, I have been learning by researching your life. So much time spent acting on the stage. You lived in a New York City apartment without heat or water, one book reported. And then you made many movies before you became famous—always trying to beat out John Travolta for roles, and being paid so much less than him. But now you are Richard Gere. *Richard Gere!*)

"You're empathetic," Wendy said in this really flirty way, trying to distract me from what I was attempting to communicate—taking on the less relevant because the less relevant is always easier to take on. She said, "That's good. I like that about you. Women like empathy. Maybe this is a good place for us to begin working on your other life goal—having a drink at a bar with a woman."

She didn't understand what I meant when I said I could feel her pain, although you did, Richard Gere. You whispered in my ear, *I understand. You are seeing with your mind. You are putting together the facts. You can see him. His face. What he does to her when he gets angry. You see her trying to defend herself from his blows. Covering her face with her thin childlike arms, but he is big and strong and handsome and convincing and educated and cloaked in esteem and respectability. And you see her crying alone in a room for a long time before he comes back and she covers her head in defense, but this time he doesn't hit her. He says he is sorry. He says he doesn't know what came over him. And he cries even. He cries. He apologizes. He says he loves her. He says that he's trying hard not to lose his temper. He says he was beaten when he was a child, that he learned it from his father and is trying to break the cycle. He uses the words that she uses in her work. She thinks she can save him, which you admire. She thinks she is a failed therapist before she even begins, because she cannot solve the problems of her own life—so how can she help others? You see her alone at night, staring out her bedroom window, through her ghostlike reflection, trying not to see herself—trying desperately to see herself. Trying, failing, suffering. Bartholomew, you can see with your mind, and it is a great gift. You don't have to hide it from me. Although I understand why you hide it from the rest of the world. Why you waited this long to tell me about your gift and the problems it has caused you thus far in life. How you pretend that you don't see with your mind. How you try to be like everyone else, but can't. How you saw your mother's death coming a long time ago, and that is why you don't have to mourn now, because you mourned it while she was still alive. How you can read people when you allow your mind to work the way only your mind can work. How you know this is your time. Right now. That you were given a present long, long ago and have been waiting all these years to rip off the wrapping paper and take it from within the box.*

You read her mind. Or maybe you just sense it. Either way—you know her boyfriend's name is Adam, you whispered in my ear while Wendy was talking about how to impress a woman, saying something about listening, waving her hands around in front of her face, hiding behind her big sunglasses. *You think you're going crazy, Bartholomew. That is your worst fear. Well, test your mind. Say "Adam," and see how she reacts. Try it. Trust me. Just say the word "Adam" to Wendy, and then she will know that you have a gift. She has never mentioned his name to you. She will know that you can clearly see what is hurting her, and then she will not have to pretend for you anymore. Just like I have done for you, by bringing up your gift, you can do for her.*

I was afraid to test my mind, fearing that I was insane, fearing too that I wasn't insane, but had this strange power.

Which would be worse?

What would I do with such a power?

What would I do if I made a fool of myself in front of Wendy?

Idiot! the man in my stomach said, and then kicked and punched. *Anyone who talks to an imaginary Richard Gere is most definitely a* retard*! And if you blurt out "Adam," Wendy will surely think you are a retard too! You have no special gift. You have no powers. You are just a stupid moron who lived with his mother all his life until he became fat and ugly and backward and delusional as of late and . . .*

Wendy was waving her hands around more violently, talking about how every woman wants a gentle man—how gentle giants are sexy. Hiding behind her egg-shaped glasses. Pretending not to be broken and beaten and wounded and terrified. Pretending for me. Pretending for herself. And I knew that she was calling *me* a gentle giant.

Gentle giant is just another term for retard! the little angry man yelled.

It's time to trust your instincts, Bartholomew. I'm going to keep saying "Adam" in your mind until you say it, you, Richard Gere, whispered.

And then that's exactly what you did.

Adam. Adam. Adam. Adam. Adam. Adam. Adam. Adam. Adam. Adam. Adam.

Adam. Adam. Adam. Adam. Adam. Adam. Adam. Adam. Adam. Adam.

Adam. Adam. Adam. Adam. Adam. Adam. Adam. Adam. Adam.

Adam. Adam. Adam. Adam. Adam. Adam. Adam. Adam.

Adam. Adam. Adam. Adam. Adam. Adam. Adam.

Adam. Adam. Adam. Adam. Adam. Adam.

Adam. Adam. Adam. Adam. Adam.

Adam. Adam. Adam. Adam.

Adam. Adam. Adam.

Adam. Adam.

Adam.

Adam. Adam. Adam. Adam. Adam. Adam. Adam. Adam. Adam. Adam. Adam.

Adam. Adam. Adam. Adam. Adam. Adam. Adam. Adam. Adam. Adam.

Adam. Adam. Adam. Adam. Adam. Adam. Adam. Adam. Adam.

Adam. Adam. Adam. Adam. Adam. Adam. Adam. Adam.

Adam. Adam. Adam. Adam. Adam. Adam. Adam.

Adam. Adam. Adam. Adam. Adam. Adam.

Adam. Adam. Adam. Adam. Adam.

Adam. Adam. Adam. Adam.

Adam. Adam. Adam.

Adam. Adam.

Adam.

Adam. ADAM. ADAM. ADAM. ADAM. ADAM! ADAM! ADAM! ADAM!

"Adam," I said when I couldn't take it anymore.

Immediately, Wendy stopped speaking and her hands dropped to her sides.

It was as if giant invisible scissors had cut all of her lively dancing marionette strings.

Quick! Study her face! you said. *What do you see?*

Wendy's mouth was open slightly, and the color was rapidly draining from her complexion. It was like someone had pulled a white blind down over a sun-filled window.

"Why did you just say Adam?" Wendy said. Her voice was anxious. Gone was the kind, bubbly girl who wanted me to have drinks in a bar with age-appropriate friends.

See! you, Richard Gere, said excitedly. *See! This proves everything!*

"Adam did that to you, right?" I said—my confidence growing. "The bruise on your arm. The black eye."

See how she trembles! you said. *Ease her pain. Take away the secret. Practice compassion.*

Wendy opened her mouth to speak, but then she stood, grabbed her colorful trench coat, and headed for the front door with great haste.

"I'm sorry," I said, following her. "I'm sorry. Maybe I shouldn't have—"

"What's wrong?" Father McNamee said—still on his knees in the living room—as he watched Wendy exit. He looked at me and said, "What happened?"

Idiot! the angry man in my stomach yelled. *Retard!*

My underarms were damp, and my forehead felt moist. Nausea was overtaking me, and you were gone, Richard Gere.

Vanished.

I could hear myself breathing.

"It's okay, Bartholomew," Father McNamee said. "Let's go outside and get some air."

He opened the door, and I walked into the cold afternoon.

He followed.

I looked down the street, but Wendy was gone. She must have walked very quickly, and I began to wonder if she had run.

I tried to think—what did her reaction really mean?

What had I proved?

Richard Gere? I said with my mind, but you did not answer. It was like yelling into an empty cave and hearing only echoes.

"Breathe," Father McNamee said. "In. Out. In. Out. Do I need to get the whiskey?"

I shook my head.

"What happened?" he said.

I took a minute to think, and the cold air cooled my chest and calmed me down considerably.

Eventually, I told Father McNamee exactly what had transpired in the kitchen, except I didn't mention you, Richard Gere, for obvious reasons. Nor did I mention the angry man in my stomach, mostly because I didn't want to say the word *retard*.

When I got to the part about hearing the word *Adam* in my mind, Father McNamee squinted at me like I had slapped his face, but then he said, "Her wearing sunglasses indoors and the bruises on her arm—*anyone* could have deduced that our Wendy is in an abusive relationship. But knowing the man's name—now, *that's* something. If she had mentioned his name to you previously—if there had even been the slightest possibility—she wouldn't have rushed out of here as if we were demon possessed, now, would she have?"

"So what are you saying?" I asked.

"I don't know," Father McNamee said. "A few years ago, I would have easily said, 'Mysterious ways, Bartholomew, mysterious ways,' without giving it a second thought. But I can't do that anymore."

I looked into Father McNamee's eyes, and it looked like he had been broken into and robbed again.

He averted his gaze and said, "Are you well enough to go on a mission?"

"A mission?"

"Regardless of my crisis of faith, and your mysterious ability to name violent men you've never met, it's pretty clear that our friend Wendy is in need."

"What are we going to do?"

"What any decent human being would. Let's grab our

coats, shall we?" Father McNamee said, and then we were walking down the street.

Father McNamee was striding rapidly, and it was hard to keep up.

"Where are we going?" I asked.

"To the source," Father said.

"How did I know that Wendy's boyfriend was named Adam?" I asked.

"For most of my life I would have said something like this: 'You're thirty-nine years old,'" Father McNamee said. "'You've been a Catholic all those years. Do you really need me to explain where miraculous powers come from?' But I can't say that to you tonight, Bartholomew. I'm no longer your priest, and for good reason."

I thought about what he was implying, and I wished that you, Richard Gere, would speak to me, but you were not with us at this point. I missed you. And I wanted to know what the Dalai Lama would advise. I was curious about that. It was clear that I wouldn't be getting answers from Father McNamee anytime soon.

Father McNamee walked up three steps onto the porch of a row home and rang the doorbell. I stood behind him on the sidewalk. A middle-aged woman in a pink nightgown answered with her hair up in curlers. She was smoking a cigarette, and her naked shins were the light blue color of icebergs.

"Father McNamee!" she yelled and beamed. "What a surprise! Where have you been? We've all been worried sick about you! Father Hachette says you had a nervous breakdown! Are you okay?"

"I'm fine," Father McNamee said. "Well, I'm tired, truth be told. But that's not why we're here."

The woman glanced at me for a second and then said, "Do you want to come in?"

"You know Bartholomew Neil from Mass, I imagine," he said, ignoring the invitation. "Bartholomew, this is Wendy's mother, Edna." To Edna, he said, "Wendy has been counseling Bartholomew. It's part of her schooling."

I raised my hand and smiled.

Edna smiled back at me and said, "I recognize you from Saturday-evening Mass. I sit toward the front on the left."

I nodded, even though I did not recognize her and we had never once spoken. (I mostly look at the stained glass windows at Mass—never at the people around me.)

"We need Wendy's current address," Father McNamee said.

"Why? What happened?"

"We're not exactly sure yet," Father said.

Edna stared at Father again like she didn't understand what he had said, and then she said, "I've failed as a mother."

"I'm sure that's not—"

"It's true, all right. Wendy moved in with her boyfriend, an older man. I think he's a doctor," Edna said. Her eyes became red and glassy. "I haven't even met him, which makes me worry, especially since Wendy seems different. *Harder.* And I feel responsible, but how could I afford her schooling? I can barely afford our mortgage! I ask to meet him, and she changes the subject. It's like she's punishing me. And she seems sad all the time. Ever since she moved in with that man. Does that seem right to you, Father?"

"No, it doesn't."

"What kind of trouble is she in? Is he cruel to her?"

"We need the address. We're trying to help," Father said.

The woman shook her head, looked at her hands, and mumbled something—maybe a prayer—before she disappeared for a few minutes, but Father McNamee didn't turn around to look at me, which made me feel nervous.

When Edna returned, she handed Father McNamee a ripped-off piece of a cigarette carton with an address scribbled on the backside and said, "Wendy's a good girl. She has a good heart, but she's ambitious. I'm just another person in the neighborhood. Is that so horrible? Is that my fault?" Wendy's mother wiped her eyes and sniffled. "We haven't been granted many favors. Tell me once more you'll help her."

"I'll try," Father McNamee said, nodded reassuringly, and then gave the woman a hug. I watched her cigarette send up a tiny stream of smoke behind Father McNamee's head when she wrapped her arms around his neck.

"I know you're no longer a priest, but will you pray for me now?" she said when they released each other. "Just one short prayer?"

Father McNamee bowed his head and said, "Father, bless this woman, your daughter, and give her your promised peace in her heart. Be with us today, Jesus. See us through the riddles of our individual lives and help us see the beauty of our . . . perpetually stumped nature. Amen."

"Amen," the old woman echoed solemnly. She reached out, cupped Father McNamee's red cheeks, and said, "God bless you."

I could smell the lingering stale scent of old cigarette smoke as Father McNamee studied the address in his hand and mentally mapped a route, and then we were off again, walking quickly down the sidewalk.

"Do you really believe that there's beauty in our stumped nature?" I asked, wondering if I might be beautiful after all. I had definitely been stumped for decades.

"I do," Father McNamee answered.

"Like colorful flower petals are first hidden inside a stem?"

Father McNamee stopped walking, smiled at me through his beard, and said, "Beauty is within all of us, Bartholomew. It just hides sometimes. That's right."

Father McNamee walked on and on—and quickly enough to make me sweat, even though it was a cold evening.

Finally, we arrived at a trinity around the corner from South and Third Street. Father McNamee pushed the doorbell and held it for a long time. When he let go, we heard a man's voice say, "You don't have to ring forever."

"Adam?" Father McNamee said into the intercom speaker.

Silence.

"Who is this?"

"We are friends of Wendy. Will you please buzz us in?"

More silence.

Father McNamee rang the bell again.

"With whom am I speaking?" Adam said.

"Wendy's friends."

"What is your name?"

"Bartholomew Neil," Father McNamee said, which surprised me.

"Father McNamee?" Wendy said. I could tell it was her voice. I saw her orange eyebrows in my mind, her white, almost translucent skin.

"I am no longer a Father. I defrocked myself. Remember? But, yes."

A few seconds later the door opened and Wendy was standing there, wearing her egg-shaped sunglasses, black stretch pants, and a maroon Temple University sweatshirt that was much too large for her. "Come in," she said.

I followed Father McNamee into the first floor of the trinity, where there was a tan leather couch, a glass coffee table, a black rug that was shaggy like a dog, a large iron liquor cabinet filled with dozens of bottles, and a huge manly leather chair. This was the house of a wealthy person. I could tell instantly.

"How did you get this address?" Wendy said to Father McNamee.

"Your mother gave it to me."

"Why?"

"I asked her for it."

"Why?"

"We were concerned—Bartholomew and me. When you left so quickly—"

"I'm sorry. I wasn't feeling well earlier."

Father McNamee raised his bushy white eyebrows.

"Why don't you come upstairs and meet Adam," Wendy said.

"Adam, you say. That's the lucky guy's name? *Adam?*"

"It's really not such an unusual name, now, is it?" Wendy said, and then forced a laugh. "Come on up and meet him."

We followed her up an iron spiral staircase into a kitchen/dining room. A handsome man in sky-blue doctor's scrubs stood when he saw us. He looked like he was my age—at least ten years older than Wendy. On the table were two plates and two glasses of wine. They were eating red meat, radishes, and asparagus.

Adam had blue eyes, brownish hair cut respectable but shaggy like yours, Richard Gere. Wendy introduced us. When he shook my hand, he squeezed really hard, hurting me a little.

"I've heard a lot about you," he said. "Sorry about your mother."

I nodded and then stared at my brown shoelaces. I don't think Wendy was supposed to talk about our sessions with anyone else because it violates counselor-client privilege. I began to feel like I shouldn't have told Wendy anything about myself at all.

"Would you like a drink?" Adam said.

Soon we were seated at a large wooden table with wine-glasses in our hands.

I sipped and the wine tasted expensive, or maybe I assumed it did, since I know next to nothing about wine.

"So . . . to what do we owe this honor?" Adam asked, in a way that suggested he'd rather be eating his red meat and radishes, which is exactly what he started to do. "Don't want to let a good Kobe steak get cold," he added, as if he could read my mind. "If I'd known you were coming I'd have—"

"We're concerned about Wendy," Father McNamee said.

"Why?" Adam said as he chewed, looking completely nonchalant.

"Maybe because it looks like she went ten rounds with the current heavyweight champion," Father McNamee said, "whose name I cannot recall, but he must be able to smash up faces and make Wendy's look like it currently does."

"You know Wendy. Anything a man can do, she can do better—and don't tell her otherwise. No, she will play softball against all men, and that's that!" Adam said and then smiled at Wendy. "She's so competitive that she knocked down a line drive on the hot corner with her face. No ducking for her. *Admirable.* You have to admit."

Wendy smiled back but didn't say anything; she looked stiff as a cardboard cutout of herself.

Adam said "admirable" in a way that made me believe he was telling the truth. It was like watching a television program. He looked like the lead on the show—the good guy—like everything he said would be followed by a laugh track of hundreds who loved this man. He was that type of person—the kind who could make you want to believe in lies, the kind who makes you feel stupid and ugly and too tongue-tied to express your own ideas, no matter how sure you are that you are right and he is wrong.

Father McNamee stared at Adam for a long time—it was almost like Father McNamee had entered into a trance.

"Why are you looking at me like that?" Adam said to Father McNamee. "What are you doing?"

Father McNamee opened up the whirlpools in his eyes, and the whirlpools began to suck.

"Okay. Stop that. You're starting to freak me out."

You could feel the power.

I half expected the plates and silverware to begin sliding toward Father McNamee.

I averted my eyes.

"What's with these guys?" Adam said to Wendy, and then downed his wine.

Father McNamee kept staring into Adam's eyes.

The whirlpools were really starting to scare Adam, you could tell.

The whirlpools were sucking the color from his skin.

A giant pink elephant had filled the room and was crushing us against the walls, making it increasingly difficult to breathe.

"Stop staring at me," Adam said to Father McNamee.

Father McNamee leaned forward and kept staring.

"You told me the big guy was crazy, but you didn't say the priest was nuts too," Adam said to Wendy.

The angry man in my stomach started to rage with great fury.

"I never, ever used the words *crazy* or *nuts*!" Wendy said to me.

"Listen," Adam said. "Why are you staring at me?"

Father McNamee kept staring.

"Stop staring at me!" Adam said. "Stop it!"

Father McNamee stared so intently, he started to tremble a little.

"Horrible," Father McNamee said. "Horrible what must have happened to you when you were a boy. I've counseled many abusers, and they were all abused. You learn it, and you must *unlearn* it too."

"Get the hell out of my house!" Adam said.

"Horrible," Father McNamee said as he tilted his head. "You're broken."

Adam jumped out of his seat and made his way around the table, as if he were about to attack Father McNamee, but Wendy stood and put her hand on Adam's chest. "It's okay. They're leaving."

"I want them out of here!" Adam said, eyes wide, veins bulging.

"Okay," Wendy said, gently massaging his biceps now. "Just go upstairs. I'll make them leave."

"I swear if these two clowns aren't out of here by the time I—"

"I'll take care of it. You have more important things to worry about. Let me handle this. It's small stuff. Nothing. Don't worry."

Adam glared at us for an uncomfortable ten seconds and then yelled, "Out! I want you out of my house!" before stomping up the spiral staircase.

"You better go," Wendy said, trembling.

Father McNamee reached out and took her face in his hands. He removed her sunglasses, and her black eye looked even worse than it had earlier. The colors had dulled, but the damage appeared more pronounced and permanent—as if it had settled into her skin for good.

"You don't want to move back in with your mother, I know. You think that would be a step backward. I know she's depressed. Your mother can be oppressive. Adam provides a good life for you, financially. He pays for your schooling. He buys you nice things. He's handsome even. He looks like a shiny key to a better beautiful life. You think you can save him, but this is not how you save people."

"I got hurt playing softball," Wendy insisted, but she was crying now, and her words made her sound like a child.

"You can live with Bartholomew and me," Father McNamee said. "Leave with us now, and it will be easier for you. If you stay, he will beat you again when we leave. You know that. He can't help himself. He's sick. And make no mistake, you are part of that sickness now. You're keeping him sick. Continuing the cycle. You need to leave right away—for him, for you."

"It was a softball game. Third base. A line drive to my eye," Wendy said, but she was looking at her slippers now, and her words were quiet and light as plucked feathers.

"Our door is open to you any time, day or night," Father McNamee said, and then he hugged Wendy. "Let's go, Bartholomew."

We started to walk down the spiral staircase.

"How did you know his name was Adam?" Wendy said to me. She was leaning over the railing, watching us descend. She had put her sunglasses back on. Her angry words echoed in my head. *"How did you know that?"*

I couldn't think of the right way to tell her, so I just shrugged.

But then I thought of a line from the Dalai Lama's book *A Profound Mind*: " 'We should work toward cherishing the welfare of others to the point where we are unable to bear the sight of their misery.' The Dalai Lama said that. It's hard for me to look at your bruises. That's how we ended up here. That's all I can explain right now."

"Our home is open to you," Father McNamee yelled up the stairs, and then we left.

We didn't say anything to each other as we walked home.

I think we both knew what was happening to Wendy as we strolled—like our slow steps were prayers that could save her—and even though we had tried our best to protect her, there was nothing else we could do now.

Father McNamee seemed drained of energy, and I was too.

He got down on his knees and began to petition the Almighty just as soon as he arrived home, and he didn't stop until late in the night when our doorbell rang.

It was Wendy.

The entire left side of her face was swollen and bruised. Her teeth were coated red with blood. Her posture was defeated.

"I'm so stupid. I'm so weak," Wendy said, her voice sounding like a little kid's, and I felt for her—I wanted to take away her pain, mostly because she was saying the things the little angry man in my stomach says all the time, and I know how horrible it is to hear those sorts of words associated with yourself and to believe that it's all true.

She crumpled onto our couch and cried and moaned in Father McNamee's arms as he rubbed her back and I wrung my hands until they looked scalded.

When she had cried herself out, Father McNamee covered her with a blanket and whispered, "You're safe here, and you can stay as long as you like."

Wendy was asleep in the fetal position.

"She needs rest," Father McNamee whispered to me, and so I followed him upstairs.

He paused in the hallway and handed me his flask. It was silver and inscribed.

MAN OF GOD

We each took a few long pulls of whiskey. I felt my insides warm. When I handed the empty flask back to him, he lightly slapped my cheek twice and smiled at me.

"We've done good work tonight," he said.

"I didn't do anything."

"But you have," Father McNamee said, and his face looked so proud.

I opened my mouth to speak, but no words would come out.

I was confused.

"Good night, Bartholomew," Father finally said.

"Good night," I answered.

He went into Mom's room and closed the door.

I had cleaned out all of Mom's things, donating most to the local thrift store, but it was still her room—the place she had slept for many decades—so it was strange to think of our priest sleeping there now. And yet I felt like Mom would be okay with Father McNamee using her bed, because he was her favorite priest—a man she believed was all good.

I stood in the hallway wondering if I could take any credit for what Father McNamee had done to help Wendy. I couldn't decide.

So I went into my room and wrote you this letter.

Your admiring fan,
Bartholomew Neil

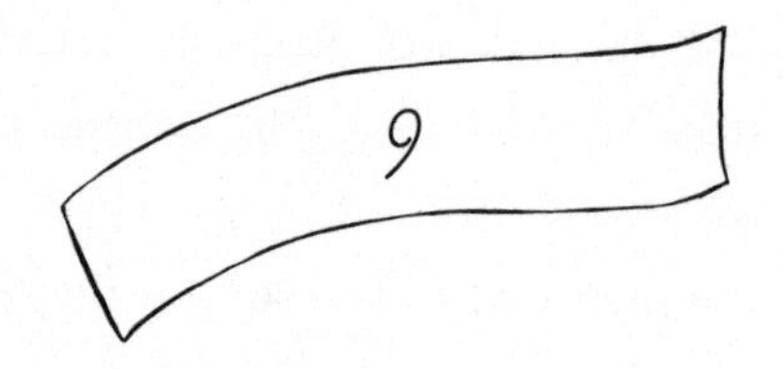

THERE WERE INDEED PATTERNS TO THE UNIVERSE

Dear Mr. Richard Gere,

Wendy didn't get up off our couch for three days, and the whole time Father McNamee prayed in Mom's room, which is becoming *his* room, and that hurts my brain a little.

The past few days have been a confusing time for me, as I'm not sure I enjoy having so many people in my mother's house—especially Wendy, who Mom never even met. It was starting to feel like Mom never lived here at all, and I don't like that one bit.

But I tried to remind myself of what the Dalai Lama says about compassion in *A Profound Mind*: "When our heart is full of empathy, a strong wish to remove their suffering will arise in us." Wendy was clearly suffering. I want my heart to be full of empathy; I want to be as much like you as I can. And so I'm trying.

Father McNamee brought Wendy buttered toast and orange juice, macaroni and cheese and coffee, but she left it untouched and mostly buried her face in the cushions of the couch. I heard her use the bathroom late at night and wondered how she held it all day long. The bruises on her face were transitioning from purple to yellow. Father McNamee said this meant Wendy was healing on the outside, but not yet on the inside. Father McNamee said Wendy was embarrassed, mostly because she'd "traded roles with me." I didn't understand what he meant at first, but after a day or so I figured he meant that I was the one trying to get Wendy through a difficult period when she was supposed to be helping me. I can understand why that would make her feel like a failure, and I began to wonder if she had a little woman in her stomach that yelled at her and called her names.

I've tried to speak with Wendy, or her curled-up blanket-covered body on the couch. At first I said I was sorry about what happened. I asked if we should report Adam to the police and offered to go with her, to hold her hand the whole time while she reported the violence her man had committed—I even told her how hard it was for me to be alone when I had to talk to the hospital people and social workers about the squid cancer that was eating Mom's brain, how I wish I had had someone to hold my hand and stay by my side—but Wendy did not respond; she didn't even make eye contact with me. Then I asked her if she wanted to counsel me about having a beer with a woman at the bar, thinking that maybe returning to our original roles would help her feel better and more normal. But Wendy didn't even pick up her head. Next I tried to talk to her about the weather and current events, which I had read about on the Internet at the library, but she didn't respond. She kept her head buried in the cushions of the couch. So I just listened to the tough (or lazy) birds outside the kitchen window, and I thought about how those little winged creatures sing on and on regardless of who dies or who gets beaten or who feels like a miserable failure.

The birds are steady as the sun.

Last night, I wanted to watch a movie, because I was feeling the need for some "movie magic," as Mom used to say, because she and I always watched a movie when one of us was down or when something bad happened in the world. "Movie magic is just the thing," Mom would say as she held up a VCR tape and shook it like a tambourine. So I picked out one of her favorite VCR tapes—*An Officer and a Gentleman*—shook it and said, "Movie magic!" as if those words and the shaking could heal Wendy, trying very hard to believe in the power of believing. Wendy was still stretched out with her head buried under throw pillows, her usual position, so I sat on the floor with my back up against the bottom of the couch, like I used to do when I was a teenager and Mom was lying down.

When Father McNamee heard the opening sequence of the movie, where you—as Zach Mayo—tell your drunk father that you want to join the navy and fly jets, my ex-priest began popping popcorn in the microwave, which surprised me, because he had been praying at the kitchen table for almost seven hours, so I thought he was deep in an effort to converse with Jesus.

Watching you on the TV screen after all of our many conversations was a bit surreal—especially because this was the first time I'd watched one of your movies since Mom died, and I had never watched any of your movies without her. I thought I would be sad, that I would miss her, but watching you this time around made me proud to know you, if that makes any sense. I had seen *An Officer and a Gentleman* a million times before, but this was the first time I watched it as your friend. It was an entirely different experience, which made me wonder if you, Richard Gere, can ever just watch a movie, as you probably know every actor in Hollywood by now, so every time you see a film, you aren't seeing strangers pretending, but people with whom you've worked and therefore have had conversations with and probably even drinks at the bar.

Father McNamee sat down on the floor next to me and placed a large bowl of popcorn between us. He was drinking his whiskey from a coffee cup, and I said, "No, thank you," when he offered me a swig, because I wanted to experience the movie fully conscious and whiskey sometimes makes me sleepy.

A few pieces of popcorn were perched in his beard.

We watched you train to become a pilot, Richard Gere, saw you make love, saw you make friends, saw you ride your motorcycle, saw you dance, saw you pretend to be a troubled, disturbed man. But when you were caught hiding extra shoes and belt buckles in the drop ceiling, and angry Louis Gossett Jr. tried to get you to quit the program—by making you do so many push-ups, squirting you in the face with a hose, and insulting you in numerous highly humiliating ways, while everyone else goes on leave—you'll remember that Mr. Angry Gossett Jr. says this to you: "Deep down inside you know that all these boys and girls are better than you. Isn't that right, Mayo?"

I sort of felt you and I were a lot alike at that point.

The little angry man in my stomach kicked and punched and yelled, *Fool! You are nothing like movie star Richard Gere, nor are you like the character he is playing in the film, which is an entirely different (and fictional!) entity! And* you *are just a stupid man who pretends he is unable to tell the difference because he has done nothing with his life, nor will he ever, and therefore favors fiction over reality. Here is your reality: everyone is better than you!* Everyone! *You couldn't even keep your mother alive, retard!* and as the little tiny man in my stomach kicked and punched and yelled, I started to think of him as a miniature Louis Gossett Jr. of my own.

In the movie, you screamed, "No, sir! No, sir!" as you well remember, and I realized that I had screamed that right along with you in real life, in Mom's living room, when Father McNamee looked at me and said, "You okay?"

I nodded. A few tears spilled down my cheek before I could wipe them away, and then we watched as angry Louis Gossett Jr. tried to get you to quit, made you do sit-ups, and finally got you to scream, "I got nowhere else to go! I got nothing else!"

I remember Mom always cried when you said those lines, and maybe it was because she'd had nothing but her house and me for so many years. She always wanted more. She wanted the fairy tale, but got brain cancer instead, even though she was a good woman who never did anything wrong, nor did she harm anyone, ever.

Father McNamee and I sat there until the film was over—only I just stared at the screen without allowing the pictures and sounds to enter into my mind.

I sort of retreated deep within some dark shadow inside my skull, hid in the dusty seldom-accessed attic of my mind, and I thought about Mom. How she is no longer here with me. Where she might be—what heaven might really be like.

I miss her.

I *really* miss her.

And even though I realize it's selfish, I wished she were with me watching the movie, scratching the top of my head even, instead of Wendy and Father McNamee. I wished nothing had changed. I wished life were fair. These thoughts made the angry man in my stomach dizzy and nauseated.

"Bartholomew?" Father McNamee said and nudged my arm.

I looked at him; he looked concerned.

"Are you okay?"

I nodded.

I glanced over my shoulder at Wendy, and her head was still buried under the pillows.

"I'm tired," I said.

"Maybe you should go to bed?"

I wanted to ask Father McNamee if we should be doing something more to help Wendy, if it was wrong to wish my mother were still here with me and not in heaven, what we were going to do next, and how I was going to move on with the rest of my life, but I knew he would say it would all be revealed in God's time and not our time—that we should simply wait for God to speak to me, for me to start hearing His voice, that we had to be patient. Or worse yet, he'd say he was no longer a priest and God no longer spoke to him. Since I already knew the gist of what my spiritual adviser would say either way, I decided that asking the questions was pointless.

So I went up to my room, turned off the lights, let go of consciousness, and drifted off quickly into the other world.

I dreamed about my mother again, and she came to sit on the edge of my bed.

"Mom!" I said in my dream, and immediately tried to hug her, but she was ghostlike and my arms went right through her body.

"Can we talk?"

She smiled and nodded.

Mom looked as she had at the end, although she had hair and no surgery scars.

She was herself—as she was before the squid cancer altered her.

"What should I do with the rest of my life?"

Mom shrugged.

"I don't even know what I want. I've never known. Let alone how to get it. I don't know anything at all, really!"

We looked at each other for a few moments.

When it was clear she wouldn't answer, I said, "I liked living with you, Mom. *A lot.* I miss you. I'm so lost."

But then she started to fade.

"Where are you going?" I yelled. "Don't leave me!"

She smiled once more before she blinked out of existence, and I woke up, sweating, to someone making a *shhhhhh* sound in my ear.

My heart began to pound, because I thought maybe Mom had come back for real, or that I had dreamed her death by cancer and was now waking up to live in the time before she died, but I couldn't see anything because the lights were out and the shades were drawn.

"Who's there?" I said finally.

"I don't have anywhere else to go," a woman said through the darkness, paraphrasing your most memorable line in *An Officer and a Gentleman,* one of Mom's absolute favorites. But it wasn't Mom, I could tell by the woman's smell—just a hint of apricot, lemon, and ginger wafting from her clothes.

After a few moments, I said, "Wendy?"

I could hear her breathing in the darkness.

"Do you think I'm a failure?" she said.

I tried to make out Wendy's face, but my eyes wouldn't focus. Finally, I said, "What?"

"Do—you—think—I—am—a—failure?"

"No."

"Yes, you do."

"Why would I?"

"Because I'm supposed to help people live healthy lives, and yet I let a man physically and psychologically abuse me because he has money, power, and influence."

"You were just trying to find your flock maybe," I said, remembering how much she liked talking about that. "Maybe you just fell in with a bad bird."

"A bad bird," she repeated, and then laughed. "Why did I do that—even accidentally—Bartholomew? Think about it."

"I don't know. Maybe because he's handsome and rich and persuasive? Maybe you were pretending, hiding things from yourself?"

She laughed in this very tiny way through the darkness—which made me feel uneasy.

"I'd have to drop out of school if I left Adam. That's the hard simple truth. And if I dropped out of school, my future would dim dramatically. It's statistically proven."

"Why would you have to drop out of school?"

"He pays my tuition. And provides food and a home and . . . everything I need."

"Maybe someone else will provide?" I said.

"I don't think so."

"You could get a job."

She laughed again in a way that made me feel I was simultaneously right and wrong.

"We don't want you to be abused by him," I said.

"You don't want anyone to be abused, do you?"

"No, I don't."

"And yet people will go on being abused forever and ever. Abuse has always existed since the beginning of time—and it always *will* exist, whether you care or not. You stay locked up in your mother's house and the library, so you won't have to care about everyone or *anyone.* You don't even play the game. It must be so easy for you."

Wendy's voice was cold now.

"I try to help everyone I know," I said. "I can't know everyone. You're right. I have limitations. But I know you. And I want to help you. I really do."

There was a long silence.

"Why?" Wendy said.

"Why what?"

"Why do you care about me? Why do you want to help me? Seriously. I want to know. Is it some religious thing?"

"Because you're a really nice person. You tried to—"

"I'm *not* a nice person."

"Sure you are."

Wendy laughed, and it felt like being hit in the face with an ice ball. "I lied to you about not doing well in school just to get you to see Arnie. I actually have a four-point-oh average. I'm top of my class. It was my plan to transition you to Arnie so I wouldn't have to work with you anymore."

Ha! I told you! Moron of the century! the little angry man yelled, and I began to feel sick.

"You lied to me. Why?" I said to Wendy.

"Because I'm not a very nice person."

The tiny man in my stomach pulled a fold of my innards into his mouth and began to gnaw with his sharp teeth as he dug his clawlike toenails into my intestines.

"Why don't you want to work with me? *Why?* I have to know the answer. I want to hear it straight from you."

Wendy didn't say anything in response, but the little man

in my stomach paused his chewing to say, *Because you are an idiot. The lowest of the low. A man only loved by his mother, who is dead. A retard! A collection of atoms that should be recycled into the universe. A fat pile of shit!*

I felt her lean in toward me, was warmed by her breath for a fraction of a second, and then her lips were on my left cheek and her hand was on my right.

"You're a better person than me," she whispered into my ear. "And I hate you for it."

She left my room, and I felt the warmth of her hand and lips on my face—her words burned in my ears for hours as I lay on my back and looked up into the darkness.

For some reason, it reminded me of the time when Tara Wilson tricked me and then rescued me from the high school basement, but never talked to me again after that morning. She pretended to be an evil and uninterested stranger whenever we passed in the hallway. Somehow I knew the same thing was going to happen with Wendy. History was repeating itself. There were indeed patterns to the universe.

When the sun came up, I went downstairs, and Wendy was gone.

She had left a note:

> *I'm going to work things out with Adam. Please don't get involved. I hereby resign as Bartholomew's grief counselor. Arnie will treat him for free if Bartholomew wishes to continue with his therapy, because Arnie has funding and Bartholomew is the*

right sort of test subject. I don't want to see either of you ever again. Please respect my wishes.

Wendy

Father McNamee read the note and stormed out of the house, not bothering to button up his coat. I followed him; it was hard to keep up, because he was moving so quickly.

I kept wondering what Wendy had meant by "test subject" and why I was the right sort. I didn't like the way that sounded, but I knew it wasn't a good time to ask Father McNamee, because his face was flushed and he was breathing heavily, like he does whenever he is extremely agitated.

We stopped at Wendy's mother's house, but Wendy hadn't been there. Father McNamee explained the situation—that we were trying to help Wendy, but she left us in the middle of the night—and Edna began to cry.

"I was never a good mother," she said.

"Pray," Father McNamee said. "Pray. Believe. Have faith."

Then Father McNamee bowed his head and said a silent prayer before he made the sign of the cross and turned to leave.

(I wondered if he was doing this instinctively, faking it, or if he had patched things up with Jesus.)

"Father?" the woman called as he walked away. "Father, wait! *Please!* I don't know what to do!"

I stood there on the sidewalk, wanting to comfort the woman, but not knowing how.

"What should I do?" the woman screamed.

It was obvious that Father McNamee wasn't coming back, so I caught up to him by jogging.

"Edna's really upset," I said.

He didn't answer.

After a few blocks, I realized we were headed for Adam's trinity. I did my best to keep up with Father McNamee, who was sweating profusely and breathing quite audibly.

When we arrived, Father banged his fist against the door, pressed the intercom button, and yelled, "Open up!"

"Wendy doesn't want to speak with you," Adam said through the intercom.

"She's just a girl, you bastard!" Father McNamee yelled into the gray speaker-looking square. "She's half your age!"

"You need to leave. She wants to be with me. Wendy's made her choice. And I'm calling the police if you don't vacate the premises immediately."

"*Wendy!*" Father McNamee yelled into the intercom, with a force that scared me. "He's not worth it! Run from this brute while you can, before he beats the best part of you dead and—"

"I'm calling the police now," Adam said. "If you're here when they arrive, I'll be reporting the bruises that Wendy returned with after being in your care."

"*Wendy!*" Father McNamee screamed like a madman.

People on the street had stopped to stare, and I could feel their eyes on us. One man had begun to film with the camera on his phone. I wondered if he would post Father McNamee's rage on the Internet.

Everything was happening too quickly.

The police were coming.

The little man was ice-picking his way through my intestines.

Adam was much more believable than Father McNamee and me. You could tell this just by looking at him. And he was a doctor too. Wendy would corroborate his story because she needed him to pay for her schooling. The cops would definitely believe him over us. I knew this. And the truth terrified me.

"We have to leave," I said to Father McNamee. "We have to go *now*."

He looked at me, and his eyes were no longer whirlpools sucking in everything around us—the pupils were smaller than two tiny black snowflakes. It looked like he was going blind.

His finger slipped off the intercom button.

I looked up and saw Wendy in the window above. We locked eyes before she turned away. She looked just as scared as I was.

"This isn't the way it's supposed to be," Father McNamee said, but it was like he was speaking to himself—like he was looking through me. "What's happening?"

"We have to go," I said, and then led him away by the arm.

Father allowed me to lead him—it was like he had become a scared little boy and I had become the father.

It all started to feel like déjà vu, for some reason—like I had done this before.

When we were six or seven blocks gone, he pulled out his flask and downed the whole thing, right there on the corner, until thin golden rivers spilled from the corners of his mouth.

Father McNamee was unraveling fast.

I remembered what Father Hachette had said about bipolar disorder.

Whenever I get depressed I go to the Water Works behind the art museum and watch the river flow, which helps.

I had some money in my pocket, so I hailed us a cab, stuffed Father McNamee in, pulled Father McNamee out, and we watched the river flow for a very long time, just looking at the water and listening to its roar.

Around noon, I broke the silence, saying, "Father, are you okay? I'm worried."

"Did God speak to you about Wendy?"

"No," I said, and it was true. I looked around for you, Richard Gere, but you were nowhere to be seen.

Father McNamee peered at the sun and said, "Maybe Wendy wasn't part of the plan after all. What do you think?"

"What plan?" I asked.

"God's plan. For you. For us. For right now. What your mother's death began. This. Right now. The cycle we are in. The tangent that has led us away from the past and into the now."

I didn't know what to say.

"Do you believe He has a plan for all of us, Bartholomew?"

Mom used to say that God had a plan for everyone, but I didn't respond, because I wasn't really comfortable answering Father McNamee's questions about God.

"What do you hear, Bartholomew?" Father McNamee asked me, cupping his ear and tilting his head. "Right now. Listen. Do you hear anything? What is it?"

"The river flowing?" I said, squinting.

He raised his ear a little higher before he said, "Is that the voice of God? I wonder."

"Is *what* the voice of God?"

"The river. What does the rush say?"

I shrugged.

"Could it be our burning bush, Bartholomew?"

I still didn't know what to say.

We listened for an hour, but only heard the constant roar of the river.

I felt like Father was waiting for me to say something profound, and the whole time the little man in my stomach was calling me a retard and telling me to keep my big fat mouth shut. I was stuck somewhere in the middle between Father's hopes and the little man's doubts.

"We're lost," Father McNamee finally said, and then began to walk.

I followed him in silence for hours, and it was dinnertime when we arrived home, but neither of us went to the kitchen.

Father McNamee dropped to his knees in the living room without even taking off his coat. He folded his hands and bowed his head, but then he said, "What's the use?" climbed the steps, and locked himself in Mom's bedroom.

I went to my room and wrote you this letter. I kept hoping that you would appear to me again so that we could talk, but you didn't.

Your admiring fan,
Bartholomew Neil

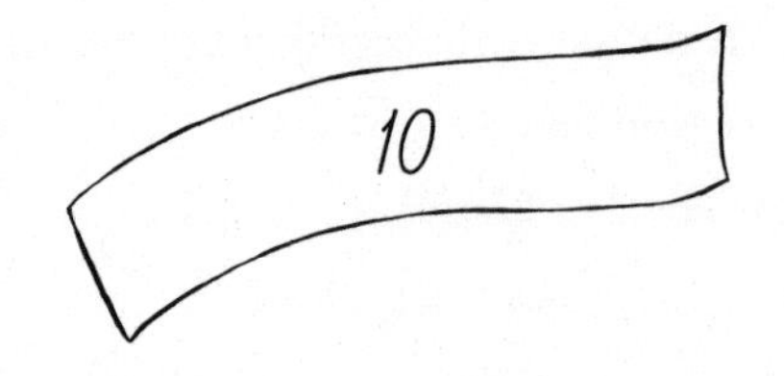

DID YOUR MOTHER TELL YOU ABOUT HER THEORY?

Dear Mr. Richard Gere,

Did you ever realize that Tibet's troubles with China escalated the year you were born?

1949.

The exact year you—Richard Gere, friend of the Dalai Lama and defender of Tibet—were born.

That's when China became a Communist country; they invaded Tibet shortly after, perhaps as you were speaking your first words.

What do you make of that fact?

Coincidence?

Synchronicity?

What would Jung say?

Do you believe in destiny?

Or that the universe has a rhythm?

You must if you believe in the Dalai Lama, who was reincarnated and destined to be a spiritual leader.

Two completely unrelated events—your birth, China's conversion to communism—that no one could have known would turn out to be linked in a very important and perhaps even fated way.

What does the Dalai Lama have to say about this? I wonder.

Have you ever asked him?

Back before she got sick, Mom always used to say, "For every bad thing that happens, a good thing happens too—and this was how the world stayed in harmony."

Whenever too many good things happened to us, Mom would say, "I feel sorry for whoever is getting screwed to balance all of this out," because she believed that our good meant that someone else somewhere in the world was experiencing bad. It actually depressed her when our luck was very good. Mom hated to think about others suffering so that we might enjoy life.

Do you believe that?

That in order for someone to win, someone else has to lose; and in order for someone to become rich, many others must stay poor; and in order for someone to be considered smart, many more people must be considered average or below average intelligence; and in order for someone to be considered extremely beautiful, there must be a plethora of regular-looking people and extremely ugly people as well; you can't have good without bad, fast without slow, hot without cold, up without down, light without dark, round without flat, life without death—and so you can't have lucky without unlucky either.

Maybe you cannot have Tibet without China?

Bartholomew Neil without Richard Gere?

Mom often used to say she was thankful when something bad happened to us, because it meant that someone else was experiencing good.

Like the time she lost her wallet and the week's food money with it, when the pension check was still several days away. She said, "Well, we're going to be a little hungry this week, Bartholomew, but whoever finds my wallet will eat well. Maybe they needed the money more than we did. Maybe the mother of a malnourished child will find our money, and the kid'll eat fresh fruit this week. Who knows?"

Or like the time when Mom and I were eating dinner at a seafood restaurant to celebrate her sixtieth birthday. She loved soft-shell crabs cooked with ginger, and so we would always splurge on special events—like milestone birthdays—making a night of it, getting dressed up in our best clothes, eating at an expensive restaurant, using our emergency credit card even, which we never did regularly, because we didn't have the funds and Mom always said that the interest rates could cost us our home if we weren't careful. But while we were dining, pretending to be rich for a night in the restaurant situated on an old-fashioned boat docked in the Delaware River, while we were pretending that life was grand and wonderful and posh, that we were rich important people who, without a second thought, could order waiters to bring us food originally found underwater, a pack of menacing, degenerate teenagers broke into our house. They spray-painted disgusting phrases and pornographic images on the walls—things like BIG HAIRY COCKS! next to a cartoon of a giant penis and testicles covered in pubic hair, and CUM-STAIN SHITBALL over Mom's headboard with an arrow pointing down to her bed, where one of these boys had done number two and then apparently ejaculated on top of his own feces.

It didn't make any sense.

It was perverse.

Disgusting.

Horrible.

Beyond imagination.

They also clogged up all of the sinks and left the water on so that each overflowed. And they smashed every mirror, dish, and glass we owned. Squirted mustard and ketchup all over the couch. Poured milk onto the carpets. Threw circles of lunch meat at the ceiling so that it was dotted with bologna and ham and salami, which rained down on us later. Dumped our crucifixes into the toilet and pissed on our Lord and Savior.

Why?

I remember coming home from dinner, seeing the edge of the wooden front doorframe splintered, the door slightly ajar, and knowing that something horrible had happened.

It was like looking down and seeing a gaping hole where your stomach used to be and knowing your legs were gone—like Mom and I had somehow each swallowed a live grenade.

Once we saw the damage, Mom simply sighed and called

the police, but they didn't come right away, and asked only a few general questions when they arrived hours later, before saying, "We'll file an official report." Father McNamee, however, arrived within minutes of Mom's calling him, armed with a phone book and several bottles of wine. He organized a dozen members of the church and a cleaning party began. The water was mopped up, the glass was swept away, the beds were washed and sanitized, and the walls were even painted over with paint and brushes someone miraculously found in our basement. Father McNamee washed our crucifixes in holy water, using a Q-tip to get in between Jesus' spine and the cross, saying, "Lord, I hope you like your back scratched!" I remember the men and women of the church working through the night—drinking wine the whole time, talking, singing even.

It was almost fun.

When the sun came up, Mom cooked breakfast for everyone, and one of the neighbors brought over plates for us to use. Before we ate, as we all held hands in a circle, Father McNamee prayed and thanked God for the chance to prove that people are good and often take care of each other when the right sort of chance arises; he asked God to burn this night into our memory as an example of what true disciples of Christ are and can be when called upon—people who help their neighbors with compassion in their hearts and wine in their bellies, ready and willing to overcome any sort of ugliness (no matter the magnitude of the tragedy)—and then we ate like a family.

Mom and I had never entertained so many people at once.

When everyone left, Mom said, "Wasn't that a beautiful birthday party!"

"How do we know it won't happen again?" I asked.

"Didn't you enjoy yourself, Bartholomew? I'd love to have another party like that. Such a treat having all those people here to celebrate my sixtieth birthday!"

"How do we know horrible thugs won't break into our home again?"

"We don't!" Mom said, almost like she wouldn't mind if they did—maybe like she even *wanted* it to happen again. "We don't know anything. But we can choose how we respond to whatever comes our way. We have a choice always. Remember that!"

I remember feeling scared—as if I couldn't be like Mom and never would be. That maybe I was a bad Catholic. A subpar human being, even. That maybe even Jesus thought I was a retard. Because I found it hard to celebrate what had happened to us. I didn't necessarily believe the clean-up party made up for the violation we were forced to endure.

"What have I been telling you since you were a boy? Whenever something bad happens to us," Mom said as she tucked me into my new bed, insisting that I needed some sleep after staying up all night, "something good happens—often to someone else. And that's The Good Luck of Right Now. We must believe it. We must. We must. We must."

She kissed me on the nose, pulled the blinds, and shut my door behind her.

I could smell the paint drying, and I couldn't sleep because I kept thinking about people breaking into my bedroom and urinating on my pillow.

Why would anyone do that?

How could Mom be so unaffected by it?

Would it happen again, even though Father McNamee promised to install a new door with a heavier deadbolt?

Was it my fault somehow—like maybe because I was in my midtwenties and I still hadn't managed to do anything with my life except live with Mom, I deserved to have my home raped? If I had a job, maybe we'd live in a better neighborhood. If I were a normal person, maybe I wouldn't attract negative energy and bad luck.

Was God punishing me?

These sorts of things happen only to morons! the little man in my stomach screamed. *Of course it's your fault! Smarter men don't have these sorts of problems!*

But then I decided to take Mom's advice, and so I thought about every single bad thing that had happened that night, breaking it down into individual acts.

1. Someone targeted our house.
2. Someone suggested a plan of action.
3. The door was kicked in.
4. Dozens of curse words were profanely spray-painted (each one counted as an individual bad thing).
5. More than a hundred pieces of glass and mirrors were smashed (each counted).
6. People went to the bathroom outside of the bathroom dozens of times (each movement counted).

7. Milk and condiments and lunch meat were wasted (each piece and ounce counted).
8. I'm sure they swore while doing all of the above (each cuss counted).
9. They ashed their cigarettes on the floor and left beer bottles all over the place (each drink and cigarette counted).
10. Pissing on Jesus must have counted as multiple bad acts, maybe one for every ounce of urine? (Also, maybe this counted as nudity?)

When I estimated the number of individual evil acts done by each person who trashed our house, the sum of bad things easily topped two hundred, and so maybe if Mom's theory was correct, it meant that more than two hundred good things had happened or would soon happen all over the world to strangers, or a few incredibly really lucky things (worth more than multiple bad things) had occurred or would eventually occur to even out the many terrible events that had happened in our home.

And I tried to think of what those good things might be: maybe a sick baby girl in Zimbabwe would receive donated medicine just before she was about to slip into a fatal coma; maybe a hungry beggar in San Francisco would find a warm steak in a trash can behind a five-star restaurant and dine under a full moon; maybe a young woman in Tokyo would meet the love of her life when she jogged into the driver's-side door of a slow-moving car because she was singing with her eyes closed and her future soul mate would be driving and feel so bad about the bizarre accident, he would ask her to have coffee; maybe an elementary school student in Paris would suddenly remember the mathematical formula he needed to pass a test, and therefore would avoid getting grounded for a bad grade; maybe a Russian woman in a Siberian prison would think of her kindly grandmother taking her sledding just before she was about to kill another prisoner by sticking a fork into a bulging neck vein and would have a change of heart; maybe a man in Argentina would find his lost car keys in the meadow where he was sunbathing and could therefore drive home in time to pick up his six-year-old son from soccer practice as a would-be kidnapper cruised the field for stray children; maybe a sun-sized asteroid headed for Earth would be pushed off course by an exploding star and would no longer end humankind seven thousand light-years from now . . .

I don't remember if these were the exact examples I came up with when I was in my twenties, but you get the idea—and as I sat in bed thinking of the many good things that had to happen all over the world in order to even out and nullify the horrible bad things that had happened to Mom and me, I started to see why Mom believed in The Good Luck of Right Now. Believing—or maybe even pretending—made you feel better about what had happened, regardless of what was true and what wasn't.

And what is reality, if it isn't how we feel about things?

What else matters at the end of the day when we lie in bed alone with our thoughts?

And isn't it true, statistically speaking—regardless of

whether we believe in luck or not—that good and bad must happen simultaneously all over the world?

Babies are born at the exact moment as people die; people cheat on their spouses, climaxing in sin, just as brides and grooms gaze lovingly into each other's eyes and say "I do"; people get hired while others get fired; a father takes his son to a ball game just as another man decides he will never return home to his son again and moves to another state without leaving a forwarding address; a man rescues a cat from certain suffocation, removing it from a plastic trash bag, just as another man halfway around the world tosses a sack of kittens into a river; a surgeon in Texas saves the life of a young boy who was hit by a car while a man in Africa kills a child soldier with a swarm of machine-gun bullets; a Chinese diplomat swims in the cool waters of a tropical sea while a Tibetan monk burns to death in political protest—all of these opposites will happen whether we believe in The Good Luck of Right Now or not.

But after our home had been raped, it was hard for me to believe and pretend happily like Mom—maybe because I have always been a skeptic, maybe because I am not as strong as she was, maybe because I am stupid, retarded, simple-minded, moronic.

The next day I felt very anxious, and so I went to Saint Gabriel's and found Father McNamee in his office writing personalized birthday cards to every church member born in the upcoming months.

I asked him to promise that no one would ever break into our house again.

"You know your mother's theory, right? The Good Luck of Right Now?" he said.

"Yes."

"Do you believe it's true?"

"I tried to pretend I did last night."

"And?"

"It helped. I admit it. For a few hours. But I still worry that—"

"Pray."

"For what?" I asked. "That our house will never be broken into again?"

"No. What happens to *things* is not important. Pray that your heart will be able to endure whatever happens to *you* in the future—your heart must continue to believe that the events in this world are not the be-all and end-all but simply transient unimportant variables. Beyond the everyday ins and outs of our lives, there is a greater purpose—a reason. Perhaps we don't yet see or understand the reason—maybe our human minds are incapable of understanding fully—yet it all leads us to something greater nonetheless."

"What do you mean, Father?"

He laughed in this good way, licked and sealed an envelope, and said, "Wasn't it nice seeing our flock rise to the occasion last night? They had other things to do, you know. But when they heard what happened to you, their hearts instructed them, and they immediately sprang into action and simply helped."

"So?" I said, wondering how that could protect me from future home invaders.

"You wanted to sleep in a urine-soaked bed last night, did you?"

"No."

"Well, those people made sure you didn't."

"I'm not sure I understand how—"

"That's also The Good Luck of Right Now. That's also part of your mother's philosophy."

"I don't get how it will protect us from future vandals," I said to Father.

"You're missing the point!" Father McNamee said, smiling and chuckling—like I was a young boy, like he was about to tousle my hair, even though I was a grown man.

"What *is* the point?"

"You'll understand it one day, Bartholomew. Without my needing to explain it to you. You will understand. I promise."

Richard Gere, I'm not sure I understand any better now than I did back then.

Even still, I've been wondering what good might have happened when Mom died to balance out the heavy bad of the hungry brain cancer squid ending her life. I've been trying to pretend that The Good Luck of Right Now produced something extremely beautiful when she passed, because Mom was full of love—enough to wipe out much, much bad. But I'm finding it hard to believe in her philosophy these days.

Father McNamee said nothing when I asked him about it on the beach the night after the funeral. And lately, given how manic he's been acting, I've been too afraid to ask him again, or even say "The Good Luck of Right Now" to Father McNamee, because I get the sense that he's having a hard time pretending himself, especially since he never brings up Mom's philosophy anymore.

And yet, your being born during the same year that China became a threat to Tibet gives me hope, because maybe you were really conceived to equal out the bad the Chinese government would do to Tibet. It seems like proof. Too significant to be coincidental. Jung would agree here.

And if you were a response to China's planning to invade Tibet, it helps me believe in Mom's philosophy, which gives me hope for my own postmother future and life in general.

I found this Dalai Lama quote on the library Internet: "Remember that not getting what you want is sometimes a wonderful stroke of luck." And it seems to agree with Mom's mantra.

I also found this other Dalai Lama quote: "There is a saying in Tibetan, 'Tragedy should be utilized as a source of strength.' No matter what sort of difficulties, how painful experience is, if we lose our hope, that's our real disaster."

What do you think?

Can we find some common ground here, Richard Gere?

Maybe our letter correspondence will be the good that comes of Mom's death?

Maybe you will help me move on to the "next phase of my life," like Wendy wanted me to do, when she was still around, before we figured out her secret?

Stranger things have happened, I suppose.

And this is the only hopeful outcome I have available to me at the present moment. So it's important for us to continue the pretending, even if we can't believe 100 percent.

Your admiring fan,
Bartholomew Neil

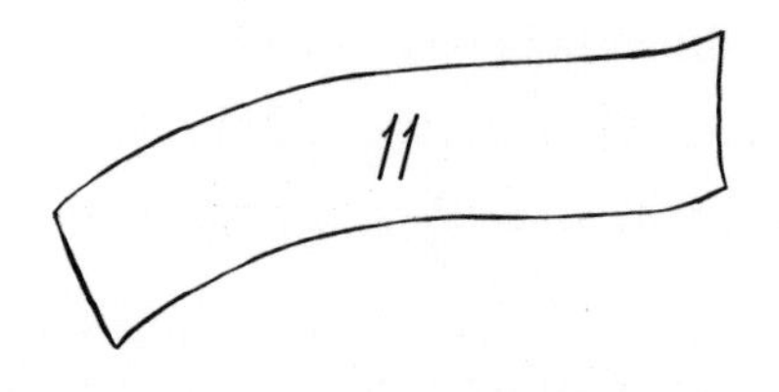

I DIDN'T UNDERSTAND WHAT TYPE OF MATH MAX WAS USING HERE, BUT HE SEEMED SO EXCITED THAT I DIDN'T INTERRUPT HIM

Dear Mr. Richard Gere,

After Wendy left, Father McNamee ceased praying and began drinking even more heavily than previously described.

Jameson straight from the bottle—about a bottle a day.

He called it his "Irish purification ritual."

Sometimes I'd hear him throwing up in the bathroom late at night, although he never left a mess. The toilet flushing over and over. And the retching reminded me of my mother at the end of her life, after the treatments—but, unfortunately, Mom hasn't visited my dreams at all lately, so I haven't been able to consult her.

I'd try to speak with Father McNamee through the locked bedroom door, asking if he needed assistance, but he only said, "I'm okay. Riding out the downswing. Just need to be alone."

Like when Wendy was on the couch, I attempted to take

care of Father McNamee the best I could, leaving grilled cheese sandwiches or ramen noodles by his door, which he sometimes ate in the middle of the night and sometimes left cold and untouched for me to take away in the morning.

I'd knock on his door before every meal and ask if he wanted to join me in the kitchen, but he would hold my eye for only the briefest of seconds before he looked away in silence. Sometimes he was in bed; other times he was standing, staring blankly out the window.

He wouldn't talk at night either or take a walk with me or even listen to the birds' symphony over morning coffee.

After a day or two of this, I began to worry.

I went to Saint Gabriel's to seek help from Father Hachette.

I found him in the church office, playing solitaire on the computer, looking rather bored. As soon as Father saw me, he said, "Why weren't you at Mass, Bartholomew? Your mother would be gravely disappointed in you."

(Do you think that his using the word *gravely* to describe my dead mother's theoretical disappointment was in poor taste?)

It's true that Mom would not want me to miss Mass, and since I didn't have a good answer for him, I tried to change the subject. "Father McNamee is not well."

"Edna told me about your attempt to save her daughter," Father Hachette said. "Quite dramatic. Quite dramatic *indeed*."

"Why are you smiling?" I asked.

"I'm not smiling," he said, even though he was clearly

grinning, as if he knew a secret and enjoyed keeping it from me.

His yellow teeth looked like petrified pieces of corn, and the way he was looking at me made the wrinkles in his face appear deeper than usual—so cavernous, I wondered if he had to clean them with a Q-tip.

The little angry man in my stomach woke up and got to work.

"Are you not worried about Wendy?" I asked.

"Actually, I've been to visit her and Adam. Edna came with me. The four of us had a very good talk just yesterday."

"You did?"

"I prayed with them. We had a productive back-and-forth. Wendy confessed to me afterward, here at the church. Let's just say, to ease your conscience, Bartholomew, things are looking up for our young mutual friend. So do not worry too much about her."

It was hard to believe Father Hachette was able to do what Father McNamee could not. Also, I knew he shouldn't have told me that Wendy confessed, because confessions are confidential. It was like he was bragging—like he wanted me to believe he was a better priest than Father McNamee. Father McNamee would never have bragged like that. Never. Nor would he have betrayed the confidence of a parishioner.

"Is she really okay?" I asked, thinking Adam should have been the one to confess, not Wendy, and wondering exactly what Wendy had told him. Did she mention the hurtful things she'd said the last night she stayed in our house? How much did Father Hachette *really* know?

"She's wrestling with her soul. Adam is too. They have a lot to sort out."

"He's evil, you know. He beats her. Didn't you see her bruises?"

"People are not evil or good. It's much more complicated than that. *Much.*"

"How could it be complicated when a man hits a woman repeatedly?"

Father Hachette looked down at his desk, took a cigarette out of a hard pack, tapped the filter twice, and lit up. "Why did you come here today, Bartholomew?"

I understood that he wasn't going to talk about Wendy—and to be fair, maybe this had to do with keeping what was confessed confidential—and so I said, "How can I help Father McNamee overcome his depression?"

Father Hachette frowned, blew smoke out the corner of his mouth, back over his left shoulder, and said, "You should come to Mass, Bartholomew. You should continue what you and your mother have always done. The routine of our shared faith will save you. In the end, the routines will save us all."

"Yes, I will. But what about Father McNamee?"

Father Hachette held my gaze for an awkward moment, and then he said, "Let me guess. He's drinking heavily. He's claiming God abandoned him. He's sulking alone in a room and emptying his guts into a toilet nightly? That's his ritual. Mountaintops and valleys. That is his pattern. And I bet he blames you for not hearing God's voice—for not providing him with divine instructions. Am I far off?"

He was not far off, as you know, Richard Gere, but it didn't seem like Father Hachette was going to help me today.

"I don't understand," I said. "You told me to come to you when I needed help. You came to my house specifically to offer your help. Was that a lie?"

"I'm glad you came, Bartholomew. Saint Gabriel's is your spiritual home. But you need to work on *yourself.* You need to grieve for your mother and then begin a new life without her. God can help you accomplish this task."

"But you don't want to help Father McNamee? You're not interested in his depression?"

"It's like trying to fight a hurricane with your bare hands—punching at wind and rain. Only a fool would try. You need to wait it out. Trust me. I have some experience with this. Father McNamee will right himself eventually. He always has in the past, anyway."

"Then why did you come to Mom's house and offer your help?"

"Honestly? It's *you* I'm worried about, Bartholomew. Not Father McNamee."

"Me?"

He nodded slowly behind a skinny finger of cigarette smoke that cut his face in half.

"Why?"

Father Hachette took a few more puffs of his cigarette, studied his hands like there was something written down on them, and then said, "You still don't know why Father McNamee came to live with you, do you?"

"To help me get over Mom's death—to help me move on with my life."

Father Hachette smiled, and I noticed how thin his neck looked wrapped in that black-and-white collar, like a fishing line leading up to a red-and-white bobber.

"And yet it's you who wants to help Father McNamee now. Things got flipped. You see?"

"Why are you talking to me like this?"

"Like what?"

"In riddles. Like I'm slow-minded. Too stupid for the honest truth."

Because you are a retard! the tiny angry man yelled.

"I'm sorry, Bartholomew. You see, I'm in an unfair position. I have an advantage, because I know more than you've been able to piece together. But it's not my place to tell you what you need to know." He stubbed his cigarette out in a bronze bowl full of butts. "Has he mentioned Montreal yet?"

The man in my stomach froze when I heard the word *Montreal*, because that's where my father supposedly was from.

"So he hasn't talked to you about that yet," Father Hachette said. "Hmmm."

I wanted to ask Father about Montreal's significance.

The little man in my stomach was screaming. *Use your words, idiot! He has information you need! And yet you sit here with your mouth shut, like a moron. Ask him about Montreal! Ask about your father!* He gave my spleen a few good digs with his clawlike toes.

But I couldn't make my mouth work, Richard Gere. I kept hoping you would appear to me, so that you might coach me through the situation, but you did not materialize, and I wondered if my being in a Catholic church had anything to do with it, since you are a Buddhist. Maybe Catholic churches limit your ability to appear to me—almost like a denominational force field.

"I can tell you this," Father Hachette said when he understood I wasn't going to open my mouth. "Father McNamee may not deserve your help, but he definitely needs it. He needs saving. That's why he came to live with you. The drama is all part of his spiritual process. He's a difficult man. But he is a man of God. To the best of his abilities, anyway."

"So what should I do?"

"Pray."

"Just pray?"

"And be patient."

"Should I be listening for God's voice?" I asked, hoping he would say that was delusional, ridiculous, thereby letting me off the hook.

Father Hachette smiled, tilted his head to the right, wagged his index finger at me three times, and said, "Always."

We looked at each other for what seemed like an hour. He seemed to pity me, and I started to hate him, even though it is a cardinal sin to hate a priest, one of the deadliest, I do believe.

The man in my stomach was wreaking havoc on my digestive system. He was absolutely furious.

"That's it?" I said to Father Hachette when the silence became too much to bear.

"Oh, I almost forgot. Try to get him to take these." Father reached into his drawer and pulled out a small orange bottle. He gave it a shake, and the pills inside sounded like an angry rattlesnake.

"What are these?" I said as I took the bottle from him.

"Mood stabilizers. Lithium. The directions are on the label."

I nodded.

"Tell Father McNamee that I miss him. I pray for him daily, and for you too, Bartholomew. I know you are unhappy with me, but I am serving you the best I can, given the unusual circumstances. I wish I could make it easier for you, but I can only offer my daily prayers at this point. You will understand soon enough."

"Thank you," I said, and then left.

Back home, I knocked on Mom's bedroom door and said, "Father Hachette is praying for you, Father McNamee. He sent medicine."

The door flew open.

Father McNamee's eyes were tiny black snowflakes again.

He grabbed the orange bottle out of my hand, stormed down the hall, dumped the pills in the toilet, flushed, and then returned to his room, locking the door behind him.

He had looked like an insane bull, charging through the hallway, storming toward some imaginary red cape.

It was like he'd become a completely different person.

"Why did you do that?" I said to the door.

"I'm not taking meds!"

"Why?"

"They make me piss all the time. They also make me fat—or fatter!"

After a mostly sleepless night, I attended morning Mass to make up for missing the previous Saturday night. Afterward, Father Hachette asked if I was able to get Father McNamee to take his pills, and when I told him what had happened, he just nodded and smiled and then chuckled knowingly. "I'll keep praying," he said.

Nothing much else happened until I went to group therapy with Arnie and Max, which is when I began to feel as though maybe God was really beginning to speak to me—if only circumstantially.

I arrived in the yellow room early, before Max. Arnie was dressed in a tie, vest, and matching pants—like he was just missing the jacket of a three-piece suit—and he seemed very happy to see me.

"So glad you decided to continue on with your therapy, Bartholomew," he said. "Please have a seat."

I sat on the yellow couch.

Arnie sat in his yellow chair.

"I hear that you are no longer working with Wendy," he said in a way that let me know he had heard much more.

I nodded.

"Things got a little too personal?" he asked, but nicely.

I nodded again, because it was the easiest thing to do.

"I'm sorry to hear that. Wendy is a *young* therapist. She's still learning."

"Is she okay?"

"Wendy?" he said, which was weird, because who else could I have possibly meant? "She's fine. But it's not your job to worry about her. Wendy's not your responsibility. She was supposed to be helping *you*, not the other way around. She's filled me in a little, regarding your treatment and progress, but maybe you'd like to tell me yourself."

"Tell you *what* exactly?"

"Where you left off with Wendy. What sort of things you were working on. Your interactions with her, you could describe those. How your grief counseling was progressing."

"Do you want to hear my life goal?" I said.

"Excuse me?"

"My life goal. Wendy said it was important to have those. Do you want to know what mine is?"

"Sure," Arnie said, bridging his hands over his knee.

"I want to have a drink at a pub with a woman my age—a woman who could one day be my wife. I believe that at the age of thirty-nine, I am ready to go on my first date—or I want to believe that, anyway. It's been a hard thing to believe in the past—especially when my mom was around. Do you think that this life goal is obtainable for me, even though I have never before gone on a date, nor am I well practiced at consuming alcohol recreationally with women?"

"Absolutely," Arnie said without the slightest hesitation. "It is a good, obtainable, age-appropriate, healthy, and extremely all-around positive life goal, which I encourage you to complete. How can I help you achieve this?"

I was excited to know that Arnie would help me woo The

Girlbrarian—so much that I was just about to tell him all about my secret crush when the door burst open.

"What the fuck, hey?" Max said as he entered the room.

"Welcome back to the word fortress, Max," Arnie said. "I'm so glad to see you here."

Max pointed at me and said, "I've come to rescue you. We need to get the fuck out of here *right fucking now!*"

"What?" I said. Max looked agitated and determined. I had never been rescued before, and I have to admit—even though I didn't yet understand what exactly I was being rescued *from*—that Max's ardent concern was flattering.

"Now, Max," Arnie said. "We talked about what happened. You don't have to participate in the study if you don't—"

Max grabbed my arm and pulled me to my feet. "Fucking trust me. Arnie is a liar. He's not even fucking human! He wants to lock us away in a room, take us far fucking far away, and film us. We need to get the fuck out of here. *Right fucking now!*"

"Allow me to explain, Bartholomew," Arnie said. "Max is perhaps being a bit unreasonable here."

"Fuck you, Arnie! Fuck your word fortress. Fuck the color yellow. I won't be your fucking lab rat. Pretending to care about us. You should be a-fucking-shamed of yourself. If you even fucking feel emotions! I trusted you! Told you everything! Even about Alice! *Fuck all of this!*"

Max grabbed my wrist, pulled hard, and I stumbled after him.

"Bartholomew, you aren't even going to entertain my side

of the story? Max is obviously agitated, and maybe he isn't the best person to trust at this point."

"Fuck you, Arnie! Fuck you!" Max pulled me out of the yellow room, down the steps, through the alley, and onto Walnut Street.

Arnie hurried after us, saying, "This is unfair. Don't I even get a chance to explain? Bartholomew, I can help you. You don't even know what happened yet. I can help you achieve your life goal."

Max just kept saying, "Fuck you, Arnie. Fuck you, Arnie. Fuck you, Arnie," over and over again, like it was a magical chant that could protect us while we escaped.

"Bartholomew," Arnie said. He grabbed my shoulder, spun me around, and looked into my eyes. "Don't you think you owe it to me to just listen? Don't you owe it to yourself?"

"He's a fucking liar!" Max yelled, grabbed my arm, and pulled me down Walnut Street. "Can't fucking trust him! No fucking way!"

Since he was The Girlbrarian's brother, and I had already had such a terrible time with Wendy and therapy in general, I decided to go with Max, thinking I could talk to Arnie later if need be, and that Max was much more likely to help me accomplish my life goal of having a beer with his sister, because they were kin.

"Sorry," I said to Arnie.

"Well, then. You know where to find me, Bartholomew. When you come to your senses," Arnie said, and then he finally stopped following us. "You need help. Help that Max can't possibly provide."

"Fuck you, Arnie!" Max yelled back over his shoulder.

I wondered how Arnie knew what I needed, when we had met only once before and had hardly even talked. Mostly we listened to Max talk. Arnie didn't really know me at all.

I had a funny thought—since Mom died, besides you, Richard Gere, no one really knows me. No one on the entire planet. Even Father McNamee doesn't know as much about me as you do. And there really isn't anyone else.

Do you find that strange?

Sad?

Pathetic?

Interesting?

"Where are we going?" I said to Max, once we were far enough away from Arnie.

"To the fucking pub."

"What happened between you and Arnie?"

"The fucking story of that requires the consumption of beer. *Much* fucking beer."

We ended up in the same pub Max took me to before, at a little table in an empty corner, drinking Guinness and looking at framed photographs of the extremely green, rocky, and often misty Irish countryside. Max downed an entire pint with one tilt of his wrist, pushed his big glasses to the top of his nose, belched loudly, and ordered two more Guinness, even though I hadn't even taken a sip.

"You'll fucking need another, once you hear this," Max said. "Trust me!"

I took a creamy sip and then listened to his tale.

According to Max, Arnie had called him on the phone

and asked if he'd like to be part of a study. "What's a fucking study?" Max asked, and Arnie explained that sometimes therapists put patients in a "controlled fucking environment" to study their behavior, advance our "fucking knowledge" of the "human fucking race," he said, and help the test subjects in the process. "Arnie hit me in my fucking weak spot, because he said there'd be a cat to pet, *and there fucking was too!*"

Apparently, Max was instructed to meet Arnie in West Philly at a "fancy fucking college," and when he did, he was taken into a "large fucking building that looked like a hospital but wasn't a fucking hospital, because Arnie called it a laboratory fucking facility," which creeped out Max for many reasons, which I will explain a bit further on.

Max was taken to an office and introduced to a man wearing "a white fucking lab coat" who inquired about the possibility of asking Max questions and "digital-fucking-recording" his answers, as the lab coat turned on the camera stationed on a "fucking tripod."

Max asked when he would be able to see the promised cat, and the doctor said that would be "the fucking dessert."

They asked Max all sorts of seemingly random questions, most of which he refused to answer because they were "way too fucking personal." Max said they asked him whether he had had sex with any men or women recently, and Max said, "Fucking whoa! That's a line crosser! What the fuck, hey?" And they didn't seem to mind that he hadn't answered the questions, which was "fucking weird" because they kept telling Max that he was doing fine, even though he was just getting mad and refusing to answer and sweating in his chair. "I don't fucking like this. Where the fuck is the cat?" Max kept asking, and they kept promising Max that he was very close to the part where he got to pet the cat. Max said they asked him even stranger questions next, like did he ever have "suicidal fucking thoughts," "extreme fucking reactions to criticism," "vivid fucking dreams," and "did he *really* believe in fucking aliens," which freaked him out because of what happened to his sister. The doctor said he was particularly interested in Max's belief that his cat Alice had been telepathic.

Max ordered another two beers, because he had finished his second.

I had only managed to drink half of mine, so I soon had two and a half pints of Guinness lined up on my side of the table.

"What happened to your sister?" I asked.

Just the mention of The Girlbrarian made my mouth dry—it felt like someone had poured hot sand down my throat.

"I'm not at that fucking part of the story yet. *Fuck!*" Max yelled. He then said they took him to the end of a "long fucking hallway" that had no windows or doors or anything at all—just white walls, ceilings, and lights overhead. At the end of the hall was a "weird fucking box" on the wall. The doctor touched the box with the tip of his right index finger, the box started to glow green, and then a voice said, "Recognized. Door opening. Hello, Dr. Biddington," as the door automatically unlocked and slid with a hissing noise, as if the inside atmosphere "were pressure fucking controlled, like a fucking airplane or a subma-fucking-rine." The doctor walked in. Arnie and Max followed. Inside there were no windows and no clocks and "no fucking TV." Everything was white—the chairs, the rugs, walls, the counters, "every-fucking-thing!" There were black balls in the ceilings of each room, and when Max asked about them, he was told there were cameras inside.

"Meow!" Max heard, and a medium-sized "short-fucking-haired calico" appeared and began to purr and rub up against Max's leg. The doctor said Max could name the cat "whatever the fuck he wanted" and she looked "a-fucking-lot like Alice—too fucking much like Alice!" She even had a black patch of "fucking fur" around her "fucking eye!" Max began to worry that they'd cloned his "dead fucking cat," which made him "sweat fucking buckets" because "what type of mind-fuckers go around cloning people's dead fucking cats? *What the fuck, hey?*" Then he began to worry that maybe he was on a spaceship, because the insides of spaceships are always "all fucking white." And the long hallway seemed like a "fucking entrance ramp," like "getting onto a fucking airplane." And if he were on a spaceship, he feared that Arnie and Dr. Biddington were not human—but aliens.

Max asked what they wanted, why had they brought him to this place.

The doctor said, "How would you like to live here with the cat for a few weeks—say . . . three weeks?"

Max said he "would fucking not!"

And then Arnie started to sweet-talk him, saying that they would pay him ten times the money he would make in an entire year working at "the fucking movies" and that he could keep the cat at the end and they would give him complimentary pills that would help ease his "fucking anxiety" and the food would be "gour-fucking-met" and all he had to do was stay in the room for twenty-one days with the cat, but without coming out or having any contact with the rest of "the fucking world."

"We would observe you," Arnie had said. "And ask you questions from time to time. But that's it. You wouldn't have to do a thing, except play with the cat."

I was amazed, and wondered if Max's story could possibly be true.

I said, "So they just wanted you to be in the room with the cat?"

"What the fuck, hey?" Max said, nodding, his eyes open wide. "Fucking weird, right?"

"Why would they pay you to play with a cat for three weeks?"

"I don't fucking know. But suddenly, while I was standing there fucking frozen, with the fucking clone of Alice purring at my fucking feet, I realized that the room was definitely a space-fucking-craft. Math. That's what I used to figure it out. Fucking math."

"Math?" I said.

"What the fuck, hey?" Max said, nodding confidently. "Three weeks was just enough time to travel to a different fucking galaxy if they put the craft in hyper-fucking-warp speed."

I didn't understand what type of math Max was using here, but he seemed so excited that I didn't interrupt him. Maybe you understand, Richard Gere, because you are so much smarter than I am.

"So it all made fucking sense. And that's when I fucking knew . . . that fucking Arnie . . . was a goddamn . . . fucking . . . alien," Max said, throwing in the pauses for dramatic effect. "A yellow-color-loving alien from outer-fucking-space. They're everywhere, you know. And I won't let you or me go through what my sister fucking went through. No fucking way. Not going to fucking happen. Not on my watch."

"Did you say *alien*?" I asked Max.

"Don't you fucking believe in aliens? The universe is so fucking huge. Probability is on the aliens' side. Those fuckers exist! How can you *not* fucking believe?"

"I don't know," I said. "I've never really thought about it much."

What I was really interested in was finding out more information about The Girlbrarian, so I said, "Max, have you ever read Jung? Have you ever read *Synchronicity*?"

"*Synchronicity*? Isn't that an album by the Police? 'King of Fucking Pain' is on that fucker, I think."

"No, it's a book written by Carl Jung. It's about coincidences and how there are none. *Unus mundus*."

"Unus-what-the-fuck-dus are you talking about here, hey? And what the fuck does it have to do with aliens? Or the fucking spaceship I almost ended up imprisoned in for three weeks?"

"Hear me out," I said. "Before we met, I saw your sister at the library. Many times. You might say I felt a certain connection with her. I've been watching her working in the library for years and—"

"My sister? Eliza-fucking-beth?"

"I had always wanted to speak with her, but I was too afraid."

"Why?"

"That's not the point," I said, because I didn't want to tell Max I was in love with his sister. I didn't know how he would take that information.

"What the fuck *is* the point, then?" Max said.

"My mother died a few weeks ago, which led to my having a grief counselor named Wendy, who recommended I see Arnie, who just so happened to pair me up with The Girlbrarian's brother. Think about it. *What are the odds?*"

"Who the fuck is The Girlbrarian?"

"The girl I have wanted to meet for years now! *Your sister!*"

"What the fuck, hey?"

"Synchronicity!"

"You want to fucking meet my sister?"

"More than anything in the world."

"You don't need synchro-fucking-nicity to meet my sister. I'll take you to meet her right fucking now. No problem. And she can fucking tell you about the aliens who abducted her. What the fuck, hey?"

Richard Gere, I couldn't believe my good luck.

It was hard not to think about my mother's philosophy—The Good Luck of Right Now.

More proof, as the bad of Mom's death would directly lead to the good of meeting The Girlbrarian for the first time.

Maybe Arnie *had* been an alien who tried to trick Max into boarding his spacecraft, but the good that balanced out the potential bad of his deception was surely taking place at that moment.

I had never been more certain of anything in my life.

I didn't care what The Girlbrarian said to me as long as I finally got to speak with her. She could have recited the Declaration of Independence seventy-six times in monotone and without making eye contact once, and my eyes would be riveted on her beautiful plump lips. And now I didn't have to worry too much about coming off as a freak or failing to say anything at all when I first met her, because Max would be with me.

Max is very talkative.

Max would explain why I was there, providing me with a legitimate reason to be in the same room with The Girlbrarian.

Max would provide a natural bridge for me—a cause for The Girlbrarian and me to speak, even if we ended up talking about aliens.

My fantasy was about to come true.

I was about to accomplish a life goal.

As I walked to The Girlbrarian's apartment, escorted by her very own flesh-and blood-brother—noticing the increasing amount of trash and broken glass on the concrete and the rising frequency of abandoned boarded-up homes—I thought about all of the random seemingly unrelated events that had to happen sequentially to put me in this very situation, this exact moment in space and time.

I wondered, Was there really math for this sort of thing?

Like maybe some secret division of the government had worked out an equation for people's lives—like you just plug in the variables of your existence and you get the guaranteed outcome.

fatherless + fat + jobless + ugly + Mom is your only friend x Mom dies – you are approaching 40 years of age

---

abused grief counselor + bipolar priest + in love with Girlbrarian x possible alien therapist + Guinness at Irish pub

Equals where I am right now!

Is that crazy?

I was never very good at math.

Regardless . . .

Who could deny The Good Luck of Right Now?

Who?

It was so obvious.

You appeared to me for a few strides and you smiled like you were proud. You gave me the thumbs-up, Richard Gere, and I could tell you were thrilled for me.

Just be yourself, you said, encouraging me. And then you laughed in this good Richard Gere movie-star way. *And be confident. Women love confidence. Remember that. Give her*

the fairy tale. What your mother wanted, but never got. Like in my movies, but this time—in real life. Don't overthink it. Trust your instincts. Break the cycle. I believe in you, Bartholomew Neil. Richard Gere believes in you! The Dalai Lama believes in you too. His Holiness told me himself.

I felt as though fate were finally on my side, and so I grew more and more confident with every step I took.

Thanks for being there, Richard Gere.

You are a true friend.

Your friendship makes me a better man.

And it's nice to share all this with someone.

Your admiring fan,
Bartholomew Neil

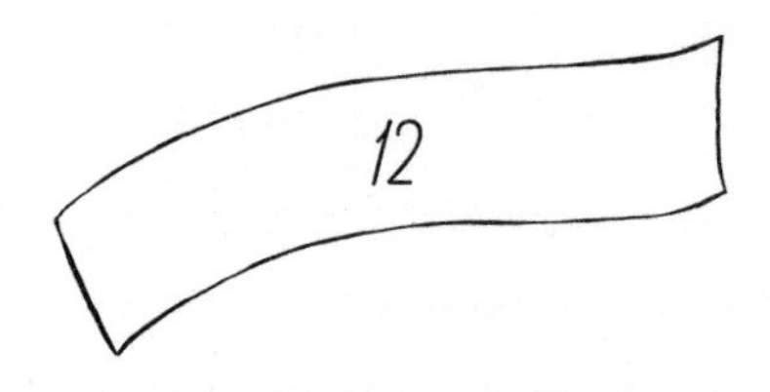

TEKTITE FORMED WHEN LARGER METEORITES CRASHED INTO EARTH'S SURFACE MILLIONS OF YEARS AGO, ACCORDING TO SCIENTISTS

Dear Mr. Richard Gere,

I bet you are wondering why my last letter didn't supply the details that collectively make up my first-contact story with The Girlbrarian, who shall be referred to from here on as Elizabeth because she does not like to be called The Girlbrarian.

"I'm a woman. Not a girl," Elizabeth said from behind that curtain of brown hair when she found out I called her The Girlbrarian. "And I am not an official librarian either."

Her voice was . . . reluctant and damaged and beautiful and maybe like a bird with a broken wing singing unfettered all alone in the wilderness when she thinks no one is listening, if that makes any sense, which it probably doesn't.

Turns out she was only volunteering at the library—perhaps waiting for a sign, but more on that later.

Well, I've been thinking a lot about what happened and

the fact is, it all seems sort of unbelievable—like if I told you exactly what transpired, you would call me a liar; you might even think I'd gone insane or was making the whole thing up to sound more important than I really am. And maybe you will choose to believe that I am lying in the end, when I am finished telling you everything, but there is nothing I can do about that.

I've been taking a few days to process, before I committed it to paper.

(I'm afraid you might not approve of my recent decisions, because you haven't appeared to me in days. Why? Are you shooting an important movie? Perhaps you are with the Dalai Lama? Planning one of your Free Tibet dinner fundraisers? Maybe you are visiting Tibetan monks who suffer in the burn wards of some faraway hospital after failed self-immolation attempts, and if so, please tell the burned and healing monks I hope their efforts will prove fruitful and they are not in too much pain.)

Regardless . . .

You're never going to believe what I'm about to say next, because I can hardly believe it myself: I'm writing you from upstate Vermont—although I don't know what town we are in.

Max and The Girlbrarian are in a motel room together, sleeping in twin beds—I know because Max asked the motel manager several times whether the room had two separate beds "with fucking space in between, hey, because this is my *sister*"—Father McNamee is in our room praying, and I'm sitting here shivering on a wooden chair outside in the parking lot ringed by snowbanks, writing you next to our rental car, under the billions and billions of stars that make up the Milky Way, which I only just noticed because the motel owners shut off the big sign that reads FRIENDLY FAMILY MOTEL REST STOP HOSPITALITY in giant outer-space-green neon letters.

Max insisted that I wear a shiny brownish gold "fucking tektite" crystal on a leather rope around my neck while I sit outside at night in the country, because it's supposed to protect me from alien abduction.

How, I cannot say exactly.

Max purchased it off a website called:

Fight Back! Protect Yourself from Aliens Now!

Apparently, your risk of being abducted by aliens increases swiftly the farther away you are from a major city, and so Max and Elizabeth are each wearing three tektite crystals of their own, but Max said you have to work your way up to three, and so I should start by wearing only one. Father McNamee said he would trust the Almighty to protect him and therefore is not wearing an anti-alien tektite crystal of his own.

Max also said that if I look up at the northern Vermont night sky long enough, I will definitely see a UFO at some point—"Look for lingering fucking orbs of lights that move too fucking rapidly across the sky and then stop on a fucking dime to hover," Max said before he left me out here to write you, saying he was "crazy fucking tired" and had seen enough "fucking UFOs" already—but I'm not really interested in space or extraterrestrial life-forms, especially since Max has told me such horrific stories about these beings from far, far away and their plans for us.

Father McNamee said that Jesus, God, the Holy Spirit, Satan, angels, and demons are all technically extraterrestrials, since they're not "of this world." But that's all he would say on the subject of aliens. Well, except that he also said it wasn't officially wrong for a Catholic to wear the special anti-alien tektite crystal, which is why I don't feel any guilt, even though Mom probably wouldn't have approved or understood the need. It was simply nice to receive a gift from a friend. If you can believe it, Richard Gere, this was the first present I have ever received from anyone except Mom. Life is really looking up.

I don't think Mom believed in aliens, but we never did have a conversation about that.

This is also the first time I have ever left the Philadelphia area (if you count the South Jersey Shore as the Philadelphia area, and most do), and while it is exciting to be traveling north, about to leave the country even, it is also a little terrifying, especially because I am finally going to meet my biological father, who is supposedly alive and living in Montreal. Father McNamee has been in touch with him, which I will tell you all about shortly.

It's been an overwhelming few days, and it's taken me this long to organize my thoughts before I could offer them to you in any sort of order that would make sense.

After I met The Girlbrarian—Elizabeth, I mean—I came

home that night and found Father McNamee kneeling in the living room, praying, which was an improvement, because he wasn't drunk in Mom's room or vomiting into our toilet.

When he opened his eye, it wasn't tiny like a black snowflake, but began to suck like a whale's blowhole again—and I knew that the storm in his mind had passed.

"I need a passport," I said.

"What?"

"I need a passport."

Father studied my face for a moment and then said, "How did you know we're going to Montreal?"

"Montreal?"

"Montreal," he said. "Yes. My hometown."

"I'm going to Ottawa, not Montreal."

"Ottawa?"

"Ottawa."

"No, surely you mean Montreal."

"Ottawa."

Father McNamee looked perplexed.

"How long does it take to get a passport?" I asked.

"You're not going to believe this, but . . ." Father McNamee reached into the pocket of his sweater and pulled out two passports.

"That's a passport for me?"

"And one for me too. Remember when we got our pictures taken at CVS?"

He had said the pictures were for the church's records. We went a few weeks before Mom died. I think I may have signed something too.

"Why do you want to go to Ottawa?" he said.

"Why did you get us passports?"

"It's time for you to meet your father. He lives in Montreal."

"My father was martyred," I said. "Killed by the Ku Klux Klan."

"That was just a placating bedtime story your mother told you so that you wouldn't have to think about why you didn't have a father all of these decades. That was her pretending with you. Protecting you. Your father is alive. And he's agreed to meet us at Saint Joseph's Oratory in Montreal in front of Saint Brother André's preserved heart, which is on display as a holy relic."

"What? Why?" I said. "My father is really alive? You've been in touch with him? There's a preserved human heart on display?"

I wasn't sure which one of those questions was more absurd.

"Yes, Brother André's heart is preserved and encased in glass, and your father is alive. We'll meet him there because Saint Brother André was a great healer. And you and your father need to heal."

I wasn't sure I believed Father McNamee. I didn't think my father was really alive. If he were, why wouldn't he have contacted me before? Why would Mom have lied to me?

Mom never lied.

Never.

Especially about something so important.

Even the little man in my stomach was on my side this

time—he didn't kick or claw or anything but crossed his arms smugly and used the bottom of my stomach as a hammock, because we both knew that Father McNamee was mistaken.

"Tell me how you came to believe you are supposed to go to Ottawa, Bartholomew," Father McNamee said.

I thought about Jung's synchronicity as I followed Father into the kitchen, where he poured us coffee.

"So?" Father McNamee said.

I told him everything I told you, Richard Gere, in my last letter.

Father McNamee smiled when I mentioned Max's theory about Arnie being an alien, and even though I could tell that Father didn't believe Arnie was an alien, he didn't say anything to the contrary or interrupt me in any way, which was nice.

(Polite listening skills really are rare, don't you think?)

Then I continued the story thusly:

"When we arrived at Max and Elizabeth's apartment, the first thing I noticed was the tint on the windows. They had put some sort of sticker sheet on every pane, so that each became a mirror and you couldn't see in," I told Father McNamee.

When I asked Max about the windows, he said, "Alien abduction protection one-oh-fucking-one."

He opened the door and yelled, "Elizabeth! I've got fucking company. He's been screened! You don't have to hide! Fucking trust me!"

We entered into a living room space. There was an old plaid couch with some rips in the fabric so that you could see the jaundiced stuffing poking out. In front of the couch was a scratched-up wooden coffee table, under which was a braided rug whose colors had long ago been vacuumed away. The TV was very old—not flat and streamlined, but a huge cumbersome cube.

"Stay right fucking here," Max said. "Have a seat."

I sat down on the couch.

Max went into the next room, which I guessed was a kitchen, because I could see the side of an avocado-green refrigerator that looked like it belonged in a museum of time-forgotten kitchen appliances.

"Elizabeth, what the fuck, hey? We have company!"

I heard whispering.

"He's not a fucking man in black. He doesn't even fucking wear the fucking color black fucking ever. I've had fucking beers with him fucking twice already! I saved him from Arnie, and if Arnie is an alien, and fucking Arnie wanted to capture Bartholomew, well then, do the math! It's pretty fucking safe to assume that Bartholomew is human. When the fuck did you ever hear of a fucking alien coming to fucking Earth to fucking capture another fucking alien? That's non-fucking-sensical!"

There was more whispering before Max said, "Fuck this!" and then dragged Elizabeth into the living room by her wrist. He sat her on the couch and said, "Bartholomew, my friend—fucking meet Elizabeth, my sister. Elizabeth, my sister—fucking meet Bartholomew, my friend."

Elizabeth rested her palms on her thighs and stared down at them, hiding her face behind her long brown hair. She was wearing tight red pants, a baggy brown sweater, and black military boots.

"You know Bartholomew from the fucking library," Max said. "He calls you The Girl-fucking-brarian."

"Just The Girlbrarian, actually," I said, using newfound Richard Gere confidence. Pretending.

Movie-star suave.

You'd think I'd be about to have a heart attack, but given all of the wild coincidences that had led to this exact moment in time, everything seemed fated, making my deficiencies irrelevant.

"Why?" she said. "What does that mean? The Girlbrarian?"

"It's just a nickname I made up," I said.

"I'm not a girl; I'm a woman. And I'm not a real librarian either. I'm just a volunteer."

"Jesus, Elizabeth. Be fucking nice, okay? This here is my *friend*. He wants to fucking meet you. When was the last time any-fucking-one wanted to fucking meet you?"

"Why do you want to meet me?" she said. "And please do call me Elizabeth."

"I—" I said, but I couldn't think of an answer that wouldn't make me sound like a pervert.

"He's wanted to fucking meet you for fucking years! What the fuck, hey?"

"Why?" she repeated.

I felt myself beginning to sweat. My temples felt moist, my underarms hot. And then it was like you, Richard Gere, possessed me and began to speak. "Well. I've noticed you. You seem special."

"I'm not special."

"But you are."

"How am I special, then?" Elizabeth asked. She had turned her back on me and was now looking at the wall with her shoulders slumped.

"Well, for starters, I like the way you put away the books so carefully—returning them to their proper places on the shelves. You're always gentle. You give each a little tap with your forefinger, like you're rewarding each book for providing a good reading experience to the library patron who had checked it out, encouraging the book to keep on being a great resource for everyone. And also how you don't just throw away old books, but inspect them to make absolutely sure that they aren't salvageable. You don't give up on them unnecessarily, and I think that's a beautiful and rare quality in a woman—*in a person*, I mean. Little things like that, I really admire. Most people don't take the time to do the little things, let alone savor them. My mother used to savor the little things, but she's dead now."

"You watch me do those things," she said, peeking back over her shoulder at me, through a straight curtain of brown hair.

"I do," I said. "It's the best part of my day, actually, whenever you're at the library. You're definitely the best librarian they have there."

"I told you already that I'm just a volunteer. They don't even pay me."

"It doesn't matter to me."

She stood up and darted into the kitchen.

"What the fuck, hey?" Max said and then followed her.

I heard them whispering in the kitchen.

When they returned, Elizabeth said, "Tell him about our troubles, Max."

"That's fucking personal, hey!"

"We're getting evicted," Elizabeth said. "Isn't that just grand?"

"What the fuck, hey? That's *family* business."

"What does it matter who knows?" Elizabeth said to Max. To me, she said, "We're broke."

"I'm so sorry to hear that," I said.

Max shook his head at me.

"What will you do?" I asked Elizabeth.

"We have just enough money to go to Ottawa," Elizabeth said. "So we'll go to Ottawa. As crazy as that sounds. We have no plan after that."

"We don't have to fucking go," Max said.

"I promised you," Elizabeth said. "And I never break a promise."

"What's in Ottawa?" I asked.

"Cat Fucking Parliament," Max said.

"What?" I said.

"It's the place where cats fucking roam free as they fucking please right next to what's essentially Canada's fucking White House. It is one of the best fucking places in the world, although I have only read about it. I've wanted to go for more than ten years now. It's my personal fucking dream."

"I promised I'd take Max to Cat Parliament for his fortieth birthday," Elizabeth said. "We've rented a car. We're leaving in a few days. Once we're officially evicted. And then we don't know what we'll do. Isn't that exciting?"

Elizabeth's sarcasm was frightening—she was like a cornered animal lashing out, her words like claws.

"Why are you getting evicted?" I asked.

"We fucking ran out of money saving up for this trip. We didn't pay the fucking rent."

"What if you did that study with Arnie? Didn't he offer you—"

"He's a fucking alien, remember?"

"Oh yeah," I said. "I forgot."

"We have just enough money to get to Cat Parliament," Elizabeth said. "We don't have any idea what will come after that."

Max looked at me nervously and raised his eyebrows. He covered his mouth and whispered, "*What the fuck, hey?*"

"Did my brother tell you about my . . . abduction?"

I didn't say anything.

"Do you believe in alien abduction, Bartholomew?"

I knew what they wanted me to say, so I said, "Yes." I didn't *not* believe in alien abduction, and I understood that it was important that I believe at this point—that this was a deal breaker for Max and Elizabeth. If she was ever going to be my girlfriend, I needed to give them this absolute right now.

"We can fucking trust him, Elizabeth. He's a good fucking person," Max said, which made me smile. "I screened him over Guinness. What the fuck, hey?"

"Okay, then. Why don't you tell him, Max?" Elizabeth said. "Tell him my story. Why not? See what he says. Maybe he can even save us, like Prince Charming. Why not?"

I swallowed hard, because Elizabeth was invoking fairy-tale language, Richard Gere, just like Vivian Ward in *Pretty Woman*.

Synchronicity.

Unus mundus.

"O-fucking-kay," Max said and went on to tell the story about how his sister was walking along the "Dela-fucking-ware River" one summer evening when over the water she saw a "white fucking ball of energy" that seemed to pulse and radiate—"like the most beautiful fucking star you have ever seen had floated down to earth gently as a fucking dandelion seed dancing in the fucking wind."

It was so "fucking mesmerizing" that she followed it thoughtlessly for hours, completely captivated by its beauty, but she never really seemed to get any closer to it—no matter how fast she walked, the "giant fucking orb of light" remained the same distance away from her. She walked for what seemed like an eternity without getting tired or thirsty. And then suddenly—"FUCKING POOF!"—she found herself at the exact place where she had first seen the bright light, as if she hadn't been walking at all. She looked at her "fucking cell phone" and realized that no time had passed. In fact, she was pretty sure it was five or so minutes *before* she had seen the light—which is when she suspected that she might be going "fucking crazy."

She couldn't sleep that night. Elizabeth kept trying to remember what had happened during that space of time when she followed the beautiful light in the sky, but the more she tried to remember, the more it receded into the dark forgotten part of her mind—almost like "a fucking dream" that is vivid in the morning, but completely forgotten by "fucking lunch." Try as she might, Elizabeth couldn't recall any of the details, and yet she suspected that so much more had happened to her than simply seeing a "fucking light in the fucking sky."

She became so anxious, the tightness in her chest became unbearable; Elizabeth began to worry that she was having a heart attack.

The next day she went to the emergency room, and after a few tests that proved nothing was wrong with her heart or her circulatory system, she took the medical advice she was given. She checked herself into a mental health facility, where they gave her medicine and bed rest and "fucking mandatory singing classes," and therapists conversed with her in "great fucking detail" about her childhood, teen years, and adulthood too.

After a few weeks in the mental health facility, she began to remember what really happened.

On that fated night she was pulled up into a UFO by a "fucking tractor beam" of sorts that teleported her from the river walk up into an all-white educational mind laboratory. There were space men with "elongated fucking heads" and "shiny black fucking eyes" and "tiny fucking bodies"—their arms and legs were thin as pepperoni sticks and their skin was lime green and spotted like that of "fucking frogs."

She was strapped down to an operating table by "ropes made of fucking electricity," and even though they experimented on her, she didn't feel any pain and was not afraid at the time. The aliens' mouths didn't move, but she heard their voices in her head, which were deep and "fucking sonorous." They said, "This will all be over soon. There is no use struggling. Just relax. We're doing this for the good of your species. You are what's known as a 'scientific hero' where we come from, because your brief discomfort will result in many great advancements that will benefit millions all over the galaxy. Do not worry. You will be returned to your planet shortly."

Max added a "What the fuck, hey?" here while opening his eyes extra wide and nodding enthusiastically.

I looked over at Elizabeth, and she seemed to be studying my reaction to the story, but when she caught my eye, she shrugged, which seemed odd.

Because she had missed so many weeks of work and hadn't bothered to tell her boss she was in a hospital recovering from "alien fucking abduction," her job at an advertising firm was no longer waiting for her, so she began to live off her savings and volunteer at the library, because she "always fucking loved stories."

"That's also when I moved here from fucking Worcester, hey!" Max said.

Elizabeth looked at me from behind that brown curtain of hair and said, "Crazy story, huh?"

Back in Mom's kitchen, I said to Father McNamee, "And that's when Max invited me to go to Cat Parliament with them in Ottawa. And Elizabeth said she didn't care if I went with them or not. What do you think it means, my having this experience and your already having the passports?"

"I have no idea," Father McNamee said. "But I want to meet these people. God doesn't do coincidences. You can bet your ass."

The next day I took Father McNamee to Max and Elizabeth's apartment. He told them about Saint Joseph's Oratory in Montreal and how he had planned on introducing me to my father at the very spot where Father McNamee first heard his calling to become a priest, back when he was a teenager. He explained very simply that God had ceased speaking to him and he believed that reuniting me with my father would please God and get Him speaking again. "Perhaps we should travel together," Father McNamee said.

"We're not really religious," Elizabeth explained, which was kind of awkward, because you could tell she and Max thought Father McNamee was absolutely crazy. "We're just going to see Cat Parliament, because Max loves cats. It's in Ottawa. Not Montreal."

"Cat Fucking Parliament!" Max interjected.

Perhaps sensing he was losing the battle, Father McNamee said, "Well, I have money to finance the trip," which surprised me, "and if you allow us to travel with you to Ottawa, and if you'll travel to Montreal with us—the cities are only two and a half hours apart by car—I'll share that money with you."

"How much money?" Elizabeth said.

"Enough to pay for the car rental, gas, hotels, and food for all four of us," Father said.

"Why would you pay for all that?" Elizabeth said.

"You're friends of Bartholomew. He likes you both very much. That's enough for me."

"I'm not his friend," Elizabeth said. "We just met yesterday."

"He's *my* fucking friend," Max said. "And higher numbers of people decrease the chance of alien abduction, Elizabeth. It's a proven fucking fact. Plus we're fucking broke. You said you didn't even fucking know if we had enough money to make it."

Elizabeth looked up at the ceiling of their living room and swallowed several times.

"Call it a hunch," Father McNamee said, "but I really think this is meant to be. And I do believe that Max and Bartholomew have already made up their minds. Don't you think it could be fun?"

"Fuck yeah!" Max said.

"It's your birthday," Elizabeth said to Max. "It's your present."

And then somehow—astonishingly—it was settled.

This morning we loaded up a Ford Focus rental car and headed north.

Elizabeth and Father McNamee took turns driving, because Max and I don't have driving licenses.

Like we were children and he was giving us a bedtime story, Father McNamee told us about the life of Saint Brother André Bessette, who was an orphan at the age of twelve, frail and often sick, uneducated, but a big believer in the power of Saint Joseph. Many came to believe that Brother André had healing powers, but Brother André always denied this—and even became incensed whenever people suggested he could work miracles. He said Saint Joseph worked the miracles. And yet, with the hope of being healed, people from all over still come to the oratory he built. "His heart is on display," Father McNamee said. "I was inspired by this story when I was young—still am."

"His real heart?" Elizabeth asked from behind her hair, completely ignoring Father's point.

"Yes."

"What the fuck, hey?" Max said and then gritted his teeth.

"It was stolen in the seventies, but then recovered."

"Why would someone steal his heart?" I asked.

"I really have no idea," Father McNamee said.

"How did they get it back?" Elizabeth asked.

"If I remember correctly, they found it in a basement," Father McNamee said.

Elizabeth remained silent in the front seat, hiding behind her hair, as I watched her in the side mirror, although I thought I heard her sigh quietly.

No one said anything for a long time.

We just drove north—all four of us looking out the windows at the dirty snow plowed and pushed up on the side of the highway, until we ended up tired and in great need of food and rest.

And that's how I ended up writing you from a motel parking lot in upstate Vermont, my breath silver in the air, and my hand red with cold.

I'm fingering my new crystal, looking up at the sky searching for hovering orbs of light, but I haven't seen one yet.

Max gave me the tektite crystal at dinner. We ate at a

diner called Green Mountains Food. He reached across the booth and put it around my neck for protection, as Elvis's "Don't Be Cruel" played on the jukebox.

Elizabeth said that tektite formed when larger meteorites crashed into Earth's surface millions of years ago, according to scientists.

"So this fucker," Max said, drawing disapproving stares from the surrounding diner patrons, "connects you to what's beyond Earth's fucking atmosphere, because it's been in contact with the great fucking unknown above." He pointed up and said, "Fucking impact theory. The meteors struck Earth so fucking hard, materials flew all the way up into fucking space and then rained down on our fucking planet like returning rock astronauts."

Max pounded the table with his fists to simulate the impact of meteors striking Earth.

"And the connection to fucking space means fucking protection," Max said, waving his plump index finger at me. "Fucking trust me. I know about these things—much more than your average fucking Joe."

I could tell that Max needed to pretend that this was true and that maybe Elizabeth was playing along—and so I quickly nodded and patted the shiny bronze-colored rock hanging around my neck.

"What the fuck, hey?" Max said, nodding. "Fucking protection."

I nodded back my agreement (or at least my acquiescence) at Max.

Then we ate dinner silently—but together, like a family.

I couldn't tell you the last time I ate dinner with more than two other people. Maybe it was after those teenagers broke into our house, trashed everything, and went to the bathroom on our beds.

It felt comforting, just having people around me—like being wrapped in a warm blanket with a cup of hot chocolate in your hands during a fierce winter night.

I wish you were there, Richard Gere. You would have really enjoyed the meal—well, the sharing of food, at least.

"Communion?" I said to Father McNamee when he snuck a sip from his whiskey flask.

"Indeed." He smiled at Max and Elizabeth.

And then it was just the sound of knives and forks on white plates and oldies music playing softly in the background and other patrons talking about the weather and local politics and sports and gossip and the quality of the food they were consuming.

Father McNamee kept humming "Don't Be Cruel" even after the song was over—he hummed it all the way to the motel as he drove the Ford Focus and is probably still humming it in our room as he lies in bed.

In our motel room, before I came out here to write you, Richard Gere, Father McNamee said my mom used to love Elvis, and she even saw him perform once before I was born.

He said "Don't Be Cruel" was one of her favorite songs.

I never knew that.

Your admiring fan,
Bartholomew Neil

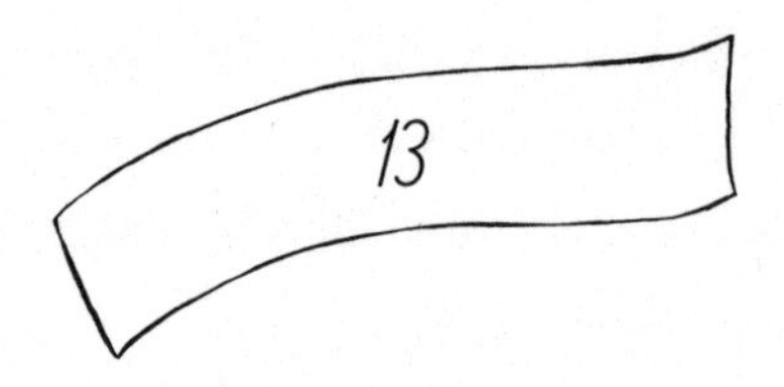

THEY LOVED LETTUCE MORE THAN CARROTS

Dear Mr. Richard Gere,

When we arrived at the Canadian border, we were made to wait in a queue and then stop our Ford Focus at the border patrol inspection booth. It looked like when you approach a bridge, only there was no gigantic metal structure connecting two pieces of land, nor was there any water—what I mean is that there were several lines of cars and little booths you had to drive through, only no toll to pay.

When we reached our booth, a mustache-wearing, tall man asked—in a deep, angry, gravelly voice—to see all of our passports.

Father McNamee handed them over, and the man looked at each for longer than seemed necessary, ducking down into Father's window at times, checking to make sure our faces matched the pictures. Our Canadian inspector wore an official-looking uniform and seemed to be disgruntled.

"Business or pleasure?" he said quickly, hardly even opening his mouth. The way his forehead wrinkled suggested there was definitely a wrong answer and he suspected that we would give it, which made me nervous.

"Depends on how you look at it, really," Father McNamee said.

Elizabeth was in the front passenger's seat, staring out her window, hiding her face from the inspector.

"What's wrong with her?" the inspector said.

"These sorts of things tend to make her uncomfortable, that's all," Father McNamee said.

"Where you headed?"

"Montreal and then Ottawa. Saint Joseph's Oratory is the main attraction."

"Cat Parliament," Max said from the backseat, managing to refrain from cursing. "Cat Fucking Parliament," he whispered almost inaudibly, but with an intense look in his eye.

"I used to be a priest," Father McNamee quickly added, which made me think he'd heard Max curse and was trying to curry favor with the border patrol inspector, since many Canadians are Catholic, according to Father McNamee, anyway.

"What is it you do for a living now?" Border Patrol said.

"I'm retired," Father McNamee said.

"Priests can retire?"

"Listen, I just need to take a quick trip into your good country. You could say it's a pilgrimage of sorts. A very necessary one."

The border patrolman looked at Father McNamee for a few seconds, pushing his lips together so hard, they began to turn white.

Father smiled back at him.

"What about you, miss?" he said. "*Miss?* Can you turn and face me, please?"

"What?" Elizabeth said without looking at the man.

"What do you do for a living?"

"I used to volunteer at the library."

"Now?"

Elizabeth remained quiet.

"Backseat?" he said, pointing his nose at me.

"Yes?" I said.

"What do you two do for a living?"

"I have always worked at the fucking movies," Max said, and I could hear the anger in his voice. He sounded very anxious. I could tell he was on edge. "What the fuck, hey?"

"No need for profanity, chief. Dial it down back there. You?"

I looked up and could feel the border patrolman looking at me from behind his mirrored sunglasses.

"I used to take care of my mother," I said, telling the truth.

"That's not a job," he said. "Is it?"

"It's all I ever did."

"What do you do now?"

I didn't know how to answer that, so I remained silent.

"Not a real job between the four of you," he finally said, and I could tell he hated us—that he thought we were all retards.

You are *a retard!* the little man in my stomach yelled.

"What kind of a *special* crew do you have with you, Father?" the man asked.

"A *very* special crew. The most special you can have! God's special children here. I can assure you."

The border patrolman's forehead was all wrinkles.

"Your mother's your primary source of income, Chief Two?" he said, and then pointed at me.

It took me a second to realize I was Chief Two, but when I did, I said, "She was my mother."

"You don't take care of her anymore?" he said. "What happened? Your mother fire you?"

"She just died of brain cancer," Father McNamee said. "And our trip is a bit of a memorial. You're being a tad insensitive, aren't you?"

The back of Father's neck was red, and I could tell he was angry.

I could see Father's eyes reflected in the man's sunglasses; Father's eyes were sucking again, like great whirlpools.

The patrolman tapped our passports on his palm a dozen or so times, like he was debating what to do with us.

Finally, he said, "Welcome to Canada," and handed Father McNamee our passports.

"Whew!" Father McNamee said as he rolled up his window and drove away. "I thought he was going to search us. And I have a half-dozen or so undeclared bottles of Jameson in the trunk!"

We drove for ten or so minutes in silence. I could tell that patrolman had made everyone feel extremely anxious. But we didn't talk about it; we just stared out our windows.

"What the fuck, *eh*?" Max said, finally breaking the tension, and then laughed at his own joke.

Elizabeth groaned.

When no one said anything, Max added, "We're in fucking Canada, *eh?*"

Father McNamee laughed like he finally got the joke, and when I asked what was so funny, Father said people in Canada often end their sentences with the word *eh?*

"That's a stereotype that will offend the locals," Elizabeth said.

"What the fuck, *eh?*" Max said again in a funny voice and elbowed me.

I laughed, even though I knew Elizabeth didn't want me to.

Then no one said anything for a long time.

"I didn't like that border patrolman," I said to my reflection in the window.

No one said anything in response.

As we drove through the bleak snow-covered flat countryside, passing so many silos with French names written on them, moving farther and farther up into our northern neighbor, it looked like the world wasn't really round, but an enormous tabletop that some giant had made into a diorama called Canada, and I kept thinking about the questions the border patrolman had asked.

Are those types of questions able to define us as people—measure our worth, our goodness, and whether or not we are safe visitors?

Where are you going?

What do you do for a living?

Business or pleasure?

Do the answers prove whether our lives matter, and whether we're worthy of being admitted into Canada?

If we're dangerous?

What was the point of asking any questions whatsoever, especially considering the fact that we could have easily lied and said anything that came to mind?

Any criminal worth his or her salt would be a proficient liar and could easily get through the border patrol stop, but—left to our own devices—people like me will fail every time.

I wish we had said we were doctors trying to cure brain cancer and were off to a secret underground laboratory in the northern territories—that we were on official world-saving business and didn't have time to answer petty and asinine questions.

"Stand aside, Border Patrol, for we are off to do great things that will amaze you," Father McNamee might have said, and we would have felt so proud. "Dare not stop us, for you do not want to block progress for all humankind!"

You, Richard Gere, would certainly have been able to act your way through that situation with ease and grace. You, Richard Gere, would have charmed the border patrol and had a much easier time. But the truth is this: you wouldn't have had to do any acting at all, because the border patrol would have instantly recognized you as a famous movie star—he would have welcomed you into Canada without asking a single question, except maybe a request for your autograph or for you to appear in a photograph with him, arms around each other's shoulders, smiling like you had been friends for decades.

Why is it that the people who are very good at answering difficult questions never get asked difficult questions, while people like me are always being forced to do things that are seemingly impossible?

The worst part was knowing this to be true: if Father McNamee wasn't with us, the border patrolman wouldn't have let us into Canada—he probably would have arrested us and thrown us into jail, because Max, Elizabeth, and I would have choked and freaked out during the question-asking part of the border-crossing experience, and the border patrolman would have not been able to understand why we were acting so—what he would call—strangely.

Idiot! the tiny man yelled, and I believed him this time.

Nothing else really happened until we arrived in Montreal.

Father McNamee had booked us into a fancy hotel where we parked underground and could swim on the roof, because there was a heated pool that was half outdoors and half indoors. Max and I scouted it out, but we didn't swim because I don't know how to swim—I'm actually terrified of water—and neither Max nor I had a bathing suit.

Standing on the roof deck, watching the heat rise up out of the pool and into the winter air, Max said, "How the fuck are we going to pay for this? Elizabeth and I are broke! This hotel has to cost a lot of fucking money! What the fuck, hey?"

"Father McNamee said God will provide," I said.

"You really fucking believe in God?" Max asked.

"Yes," I said. "Do you really believe in aliens?"

"Fuck, yes," Max said.

"What will you do after we visit Cat Parliament?"

"Don't fucking know," Max said. "We brought all our clothes. Left our fucking keys in the apartment. Skipped out on the last month's rent. We're fucking homeless."

"Aren't you worried?"

"*Fuck*," Max said, nodding and lifting his eyebrows.

"I'm worried too."

"Why are *you* fucking worried?"

"Because I don't know what to do without Mom. I'm not even sure how my bills are getting paid. Like electricity and water and cable and all of the other bills Mom used to take care of."

"You don't pay those fuckers?"

"No."

"Someone's paying those fuckers. Or they would have shut you down by now. Fucking nothing is free."

"Who would be paying?"

"How would I fucking know that?"

Every time I had thought about this in the past, my head started to hurt.

Just as soon as I knew who was paying my bills, I'd owe a real person money. Since I had no money, I wasn't exactly eager to end that mystery, truth be told.

I turned around and gazed out over the city of Montreal.

"It's pretty remarkable, our being here together. You have to admit," I said. "Extraordinary, even."

Max nodded.

"I never thought I'd see Canada."

"Me fucking neither."

We were standing on a shoveled concrete deck of sorts with our backs to the pool, looking over a five-foot wall.

"I guess for many normal, regular-type people, this wouldn't be any big deal," I said.

Max nodded again, and then he said, "Why the fuck do you think we ended up being so fucking different from everyone else? Do you ever fucking think about shit like that? People like you and me and Elizabeth—why do we even fucking exist?"

I thought about it and then—after searching my entire brain for the answer to Max's first question and finding none—I answered the second by saying, "All the time." After a minute or so I had a thought, and so I said, "Maybe the world needs people like us?"

"What the fuck for? We don't fucking do anything! I just rip tickets at the fucking movies! Anyone could do that!"

"Well, if there weren't weird, strange, and unusual people who did weird things or nothing at all, there couldn't be normal people who do normal, useful things, right?"

"What the fuck, hey?" Max squinted at me.

"The word *normal* would lose all of its meaning if it didn't have an opposite. And if there were no normal people, the world would probably fall apart—because it's normal people who take care of all the normal things like making sure there is food at the grocery store and delivering the mail and putting up traffic lights and making sure our toilets work properly and growing food on farms and flying airplanes safely and making sure the president of the United States has clean suits to wear and—"

"Little help?" a voice said. "It's too cold for me to hop out!"

When we turned around there was a beach ball at our feet.

A family must have swum out from under the glass divide and into the outdoor open-air water behind us.

"What the fuck, hey?" Max sort of whispered as he kicked the brightly colored ball toward the man.

The man caught the large ball between his two hands, lowered it so we could see his face, and said, "Thanks!"

He looked like a younger version of you, Richard Gere. Handsome, confident, many muscles in his stomach and chest and arms. Shaggy hair that—even though it was wet—looked like it cost a lot of money and effort to style and maintain. He also reminded me of those underwear models you see in the ads that fall out of the Sunday newspaper. His wife was wearing a green bikini, and while she was no Cindy Crawford, she was just as beautiful as Carey Lowell, which is pretty lovely, as you well know. They had a boy and a girl between them—maybe five and seven years old, both blond with pearly white teeth, the type of kids you see smiling a lot on TV while eating breakfast cereals—and they were all throwing the beach ball around, laughing and trying to catch snowflakes on their tongues, which was when I realized it was indeed snowing.

The steam that rose off their bare skin looked like their souls rising up and mingling above their heads in a playful harmonious dance that made my chest ache.

"What the fuck, hey?" Max whispered again as his index

finger pushed his huge glasses to the top of his nose, and it was like he was saying what I have thought many, many times: *What is wrong with us? Why are we so strange? Why does that—the normal family in the pool—seem so right, and what we have and are seem so wrong in comparison?*

Even though my mom and I had never gone swimming outside in the winter on a hotel roof that overlooked a foreign city, the scene made me miss Mom, and I said a quick prayer, asking God to let Mom appear to me in my dreams at least once more.

The man who looked like a younger version of you, Richard Gere—he kept glancing over at us, and it took me a few looks to realize that our staring was starting to make them feel uncomfortable.

Two misshapen, ugly, strange men in out-of-style boots and coats staring at anyone is a recipe for misinterpretation, right?

"Let's go," I said.

Max nodded and followed.

He didn't need an explanation.

Max knew what I knew—probably because he has lived the same sort of life as I have, even if his personal details were and are completely different.

Metaphorically, we—and our stories—are the same.

We went to our respective rooms, showered, and dressed for dinner.

Father McNamee took us to Old Montreal and we dined at a small fancy restaurant. Father asked if he could order for all of us, and when we agreed, he surprised me by ordering in French.

"What the fuck, *eh*, Frenchy?" Max said, eyes wide, nodding, impressed—like Father had done a magic trick—when the waiter left.

"I hope you will indulge me," Father McNamee said. "This is a last supper of sorts for us."

"What do you mean?" I asked.

"Everything will change when you meet your dad tomorrow," Father said, looking really uncomfortable. "Nothing will be the same afterward."

I nodded, just to be easy.

It was snowing outside, and we watched the flakes fall through the steamy window.

The waiter arrived with red wine and glasses. Father tasted, approved, and then the waiter poured glasses for all of us.

"To new beginnings, however strange they may be," Father McNamee said and then raised his glass.

We all clinked and drank.

Baguettes and French onion soup—small round brown bowls covered with bubbling cheese—came next.

Father broke a baguette into four pieces, handed one to each of us, and said, "We four are at pivotal points in our lives. To the miracle of our finding each other and being right here, right now together, which is indeed remarkable."

Elizabeth and Max didn't say anything, but bit their bread and began to chew.

"It's best when dipped into the soup," Father said and then poked the baguette through the cheese in his bowl until the bread turned brown and began to fall apart.

We all did the same.

"How do you feel about meeting your father, Bartholomew?" Father McNamee said, while examining his soup.

I didn't know how to answer.

In my mind and heart, my father had been dead for years, and there was a part of me, deep down inside where the tiny man lives, that wanted to keep it that way.

Another part of me still didn't believe that meeting my father was even a possibility, although Father McNamee seemed very confident, and he had never lied to me before.

"Cat Parliament in two fucking days, right?" Max said.

"Yes," Father said, nodded, and looked out the window at the heavily bundled people passing by on the sidewalk.

The waiter returned and said, "Lapin."

Four plates were put in front of us.

Meat covered in tan gravy, peas, and carrots.

"Bon appétit," the waiter said and then left.

We all began to eat, and the meat was tender and flavorful and seemed to melt like butter in my mouth.

"What is this?" Elizabeth asked after swallowing.

"Rabbit," Father said. "Do you like it?"

Elizabeth gagged, spit the food from her mouth, and ran out of the restaurant.

I chased after her.

She was retching over the mound of snow piled between the street and the sidewalk, so I held her hair and rubbed her back, just like Mom used to do for me whenever I was sick as a little boy. The entire restaurant watched us through the window.

Max and Father McNamee came out next, and Father said, "Are you okay?"

Elizabeth nodded and said, "I just need some air. Leave me alone, please. *Please!*"

When she began to walk down the street, Father said, "Follow her, Bartholomew!"

"Me?" I said.

"What the fuck, hey, Elizabeth!" Max yelled. "This is a free meal. Isn't it time you fucking got over this?"

Father smiled, winked, and said, "This is your big chance. Go."

It's snowing in Old Montreal. How beautiful! you, Richard Gere, said. Suddenly you were there, bundled up in a leather coat and a plaid scarf, smiling at me, your eyes twinkling like my new tektite crystal. *Use the charm of the moment! Step into the romance of now! You can make The Girlbrarian fall in love with you! Look around. This town is loaded with charm! Use it, big guy!*

"She doesn't like to be called The Girlbrarian," I said to you as I rushed after Elizabeth.

Doesn't matter, big guy. What matters is that you're going to be alone with the girl of your dreams in Old Montreal as the snow falls gently all around you. Love is imminent. You cannot fail. This is your moment. The Dalai Lama says be compassionate and all will work out for the best. Just be kind. It's time for love. This is the perfect moment. Give her the fairy tale!

"She's sick! She just threw up in a snowbank!"

That's The Good Luck of Right Now, right?

The bad that will lead to good!

The flip side of the same coin.

The universe is sending you a sign. The universe has put you in this exact position for a reason. Now is your moment, Bartholomew. The Good Luck of Right Now! Remember your mother's philosophy. What would she tell you? What would your mother tell us?

You looked so proud of me, Richard Gere, and I wondered how you found me in Canada—but then I remembered the letters I had written you, explaining where I was going. Your coming and helping me—especially knowing how busy you are with your acting and official Dalai Lama business—it means so, so much to me that I almost started to cry.

Thank you, Richard Gere.

Thank you one million times.

With a friend like you, I felt that I truly couldn't fail to impress Elizabeth now.

Cool tektite crystal, you said to me when you noticed it bouncing against my coat zipper as I ran down the sidewalk after Elizabeth, trying not to slip on ice.

"Thanks," I said.

You winked and nodded, gave me the thumbs-up with your expensive-looking leather glove—and then you vanished like a ghost.

When I caught up to Elizabeth, I could tell she was still upset, so I walked next to her for seven or so city blocks, catching my breath and allowing her to walk off her bad energy, like I had done before with Father McNamee.

I decided to wait until she spoke first, before saying anything.

When we reached the Saint Lawrence River, Elizabeth stopped and said, "Max wanted me to make sure you have your tektite crystal on at all times."

"Yes," I said, patting it with my glove. "I haven't taken it off since he gave it to me."

She pulled another leather necklace out of her coat pocket and said, "Max says put this one on too. You've worked up to it, wearing the first for more than twenty-four hours now, and my brother's research suggests that alien abductions increase near rivers. So you will benefit from extra protection, according to Max."

I took the extra tektite crystal and dutifully put it around my neck. It was hard to do with winter gloves on, but I managed.

We stood there silently for a time.

Then Elizabeth said, "You probably think I'm insane, acting the way I did back there."

"No," I said.

"Yes." She peered up at me from under her beautiful eyebrows, through her wispy curtain of brown hair that was now hanging down from within a homemade-looking purple knit hat.

I bit my bottom lip and shook my head.

We looked out over the river for what seemed like a half hour.

Finally, she said, "You may think this is a stupid sentimental explanation, but I used to keep rabbits when I was a little girl. My mom bought them to breed and sell, but the guy who sold them to us lied and we soon found out both of our rabbits were male. Mom quickly lost interest, like she always did, or was too lazy to find a female. She ignored them, began to pretend they didn't exist, probably because her pride kept her embarrassed about being duped. So I made the neglected rabbits into pets and loved them. Adored them. Talked to them. Even stole food for them from a nearby farm. Told them my secrets, whispering into their long, velvety ears for hours and hours."

I didn't know what to say, even though this obviously explained why she threw up.

It made me feel so sad.

"Max never loved them as much as I did," she said, and began to walk along the river.

I nodded and followed.

"Are you ever going to talk?" Elizabeth said.

"Yes."

"Say something."

"Something."

"Not funny."

I wasn't trying to be funny, so I felt ashamed. And then I could feel the little man in my stomach laughing at me, rolling around in my belly, crying tears of merriment even, because I was failing so horrifically.

We walked on for a block or so.

Then she said, "My rabbits' names were Pooky and Moo

Moo. They loved lettuce more than carrots. You'd think rabbits would love carrots best, but not these two. Maybe they were strange rabbits."

I didn't know what to say.

"Max, he loves cats," she said.

Somehow I found my voice and said, "Yes, he does. Was Alice a good cat?"

"She was a doll. But she was *Max*'s cat, not mine. Pooky and Moo Moo were mine. There will never be another Pooky or another Moo Moo."

"Mom was mine," I said before I could really think about what I meant. "There will never be another Mom for me either. She was one of a kind."

"You really loved your mother?"

"Yes. Did you love yours?"

"I hated her. I used to fantasize about killing her in her sleep. Slitting her throat with a steak knife—sometimes I'd imagine dragging the blade across her entire neck, making a huge red smile. And other times I'd just stab her jugular repeatedly. Sorry. I know that's pretty sick. But, oh, how I wanted to kill my mother when I was a little girl!"

"Why?"

"A million reasons. *Infinite reasons.*"

We walked for a few more blocks, gloved hands in pockets.

"My mother killed Pooky and Moo Moo and fed them to me when I was just a child."

I didn't know what to say to that.

"She told me what I was eating only after I had finished. Like she was delivering the punch line to a joke, she told me with a grin on her face. You cannot imagine the guilt. I felt Pooky and Moo Moo inside me, trying to hop out of my stomach, for months. She made keychains out of the feet and gave me one as a present the following Christmas. I screamed when I opened it and began to cry. She called me peculiar and ungrateful and spoiled and weak and silly. Then she laughed at me and told Max his sister was sentimental. She actually used that word. *Sentimental.* As if it were a character flaw. Like it was horrible to feel. To admit that you missed things. To care. To love even."

"How old were you?"

"Seven."

"Why did she kill your rabbits?"

"We were poor. Had no food. We couldn't really afford to feed them. My mother was a psychopath. I am prone to horrific luck. All of those things."

"Father McNamee didn't know that—"

"How could he?"

"I'm so sorry," I said.

"You didn't do anything wrong," Elizabeth said.

I felt as though I had failed horribly in the romance department, as all we had managed to talk about were Elizabeth's childhood traumas and her adolescent thoughts of matricide.

Hardly romantic banter.

"Tell me something nice," she said. Elizabeth stopped walking, faced me, and looked up into my eyes with frightening desperation. "Please! Anything. Tell me one nice thing. Something that makes me feel as though the world is not a terrible place. I'm at the end, Bartholomew. I don't care anymore. Tell me something that will make me care. Come on. Just tell me something good. One good and true thing. If you can do that, then maybe, just maybe . . ."

She didn't finish her sentence, but sighed, and I wondered what she was going to say.

Elizabeth kept searching my eyes, but I didn't have a clue as to what I was supposed to say here in response, and I hoped that you, Richard Gere, would show up to help me, because you always know what to say to women in these situations, in all of your movies, but you didn't materialize.

"Like what?" I said, stalling for time.

"Something nice about your mother maybe." She was choking up here, her eyes brimming with tears. "Something that will make me forget I just ate rabbit—that I have no place to live. That my life has been a cruel, sadistic joke—that everything is going to end shortly."

"*End?*" I said.

I hated to see her so sad, but wasn't sure what to do.

"Tell me something about your mother. Something nice," Elizabeth said, ignoring my question. "Really sweet. You seem like a sweet sort of man, Bartholomew. So please, please, please. Something sweet."

I thought about it—there were a million nice things to choose from when it came to memories of Mom.

"The first sweet thing that pops up in your head," she said. "Don't think about it. Just talk. *Please.* You must have nice memories of your mother if you love her so much. It should be easy for you! I need to hear something sweet—something *sentimental* even."

Suddenly I was talking without thinking—the words were flowing out of me like air—and I was utterly surprised to be saying so much. It was like she had found my hot and cold knobs and now words were suddenly gushing out of my spigot.

"When I was a little boy, my mother told me that if I wrote a letter to the mayor of Philadelphia—Mayor Frank Rizzo at first, and then it was Mayor William Green—asking for special permission to go to the top of City Hall, he might let me look out over Philadelphia from under the high dome atop of which William Penn stands. So I'd write a letter, and I'd take days to think up a persuasive argument justifying why I should be admitted. I'd write about how hard I was trying in school, what a good son I was, always completing all of my chores on time, doing what Mom told me to do, how I promised to vote in all of the elections when I was old enough—a promise I have religiously kept, as Mom taught me it was my patriotic duty as an American—and how I went to Mass every week and tried to be a good Catholic.

"Then I would write out the letter over and over until my penmanship was good enough to be read by a real officially elected mayor. Mom would read it, and as we dropped the letter into the neighborhood mailbox, we'd both cross our fingers and hope the mayor was moved enough to let us visit City Hall—that I had been a good enough boy.

"I'd always receive a personalized handwritten response a week or so later, saying I was a good boy and was allowed to visit City Hall. Mom and I would walk down Broad Street hand in hand, watching City Hall grow up from the street taller and taller, and we'd take the elevator up to the top of City Hall—which, incidentally, once was one of the tallest buildings in the world and was the tallest in Philadelphia until 1987—and we'd look out over the City of Brotherly Love, seeing how Philadelphia is mapped out in right angles, like a big grid constructed by the most anal of city planners determined to make sure no one would ever get lost, and I'd be so proud to be high in the sky looking down, knowing I'd earned it by being an exemplary boy."

I could see excitement in Elizabeth's eyes, and I hoped I was doing well here, because my heart was pounding and my gloves were soaked through with sweat.

"It wasn't until I was an adult that I figured out anyone and everyone is allowed to go to the top—regardless of whether they have been good or not—and that Mom had written the letters from the mayor, pretending.

"And so I visited the top of City Hall again as a man, took the same tour, but of course it wasn't as special anymore, because anyone could do it—I hadn't earned it. The building didn't rise as majestically from the asphalt when I walked down Broad Street, the elevator ride up didn't make my heart pound, the view wasn't as spectacular, the right angles of the city blocks didn't look as crisp, and I didn't even want to stay up there for very long, not without Mom."

"She sounds wonderful," Elizabeth said, and smiled.

"She was."

"You miss her."

"Very much."

"I'm sorry for your loss."

"I'm sorry you had to eat your pet rabbits and were abducted by aliens."

She sat down on a bench, and I sat next to her.

We watched the snow dance its way down from the sky and onto the river.

I thought Elizabeth would look up into the night, trying to spot UFOs, but she never lifted her chin even once.

She wasn't interested in UFOs that night—nor was she interested in talking about aliens.

From watching movies, I knew that this was the time to put my arm around Elizabeth, and my heart was about to explode, just thinking about the possibility of having my arm around another human being, our ribs touching through our coats.

But I didn't put my arm around her.

We just lingered next to each other on the bench until our hats were covered in white snow and our noses were red.

When she stood, I stood.

We walked back to the hotel in silence, leaving two sets of footprints that would shortly be covered by new accumulating snow and then shoveled away, erasing all evidence of our walk through Old Montreal together, and I thought about just how many millions of people had had significant small, quiet moments in the city of Montreal—moments that were so important to the people having them, but insignificant to everyone else who had ever lived.

Elizabeth opened her hotel room door with the plastic key card and then said, "Good night, Bartholomew."

"Good night," I said, standing in the hallway.

She looked up into my eyes for a long time, with her hand on the doorknob and the door slightly ajar.

Then she reached into her pocket and pulled out another tektite necklace.

When Elizabeth held up the leather loop, I lowered my head; she placed the necklace around my neck and nodded.

I nodded back.

"Max wanted you to have that, once you worked up to it. You have," she said and then went into her room.

It was funny because two tektite rocks didn't really feel like anything, but I noticed the weight of three.

Three wasn't too heavy, but palpable.

It was a tipping point.

I stood in the hallway for a time, wondering why—after spending the entire day with three people—I felt so much lonelier than I had ever before in my entire life, and yet I didn't want to go into the room with Father McNamee.

I wanted to be with Elizabeth—just to sit next to her silently for another five minutes would have been divine.

I also wanted to be by myself too, which was confusing.

Somehow I ended up all alone on the roof of the hotel, next to the steamy pool that was now lit, glowing blue and wondrous.

I looked out over the city and wondered if my biological father was really out there, somewhere in Montreal.

I looked up and wondered where Mom was.

I sat down on a chair and felt the cold on my face as I watched the snowflakes evaporate instantly, the moment they hit the warm, blue, chlorinated pool water—and I wondered if what I was witnessing could be a metaphor for our lives somehow, like we were all just little bits falling toward an inevitable dissolve, if that makes any sense at all.

I rested there by myself for what felt like hours, feeling like a snowflake the second it hits a heated pool—wondering if that could really be our whole life summed up in the grand scheme of the universe.

Even though she hadn't appeared to me, I talked to Mom for a time, telling her everything that had happened—asking her if my father could still possibly be alive—but the only answer I got was the noise of street traffic rising up from far, far below.

When I keyed into our hotel room, Father McNamee wasn't snoring, but sleeping peacefully, so I tried to be extra quiet and didn't turn on the light. The room reeked of whiskey, which meant Father McNamee would be hung over again in the morning.

I lay down in my bed and thought about how I was in Canada—how strange that seemed—as I stared at the ceiling.

Canada, eh?

It didn't seem real.

Like maybe it's just some unknown part of Philadelphia—or a known part dressed up as something else, like it was playing geographical Halloween, as crazy as that sounds.

Then, as Father slept, using the mini flashlight on my keychain, I wrote you this letter, trying to finish before it was time to go to Saint Joseph's Oratory, so that we might look at the preserved heart of a miracle worker and meet my biological father for the first time.

Your admiring fan,
Bartholomew Neil

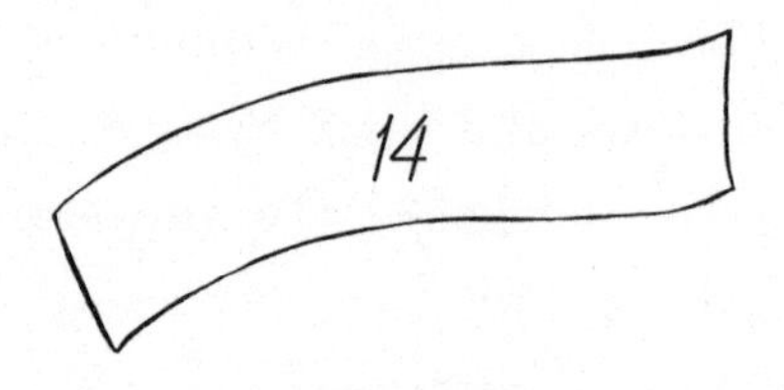

THAT IS THE MOST RATIONAL THING TO DO AT THIS MOMENT, GIVEN THE UNFORTUNATE CIRCUMSTANCES YOU HAVE INHERITED

Dear Mr. Richard Gere,

When I woke up on the day we were supposed to go to Saint Joseph's Oratory and meet my dad in front of Saint Brother André's preserved heart, Father McNamee was still sleeping, so I stared out our hotel window and admired the fresh snow cover that had fallen in the night. It looked like the city had been buried in fine white sand and was now pushing its way out again as various tides of morning commuters swept over the streets and sidewalks.

I smiled at my reflection superimposed onto the city in the window, felt a good lightness in my chest, took a shower, and then got dressed.

I let Father sleep for a time, as there were two empty whiskey bottles on the nightstand, although it was highly unusual for him to sleep past 6:30 a.m. no matter how much he had drunk the night before.

I was partly nervous to meet my biological father, but the larger part of me thought that my meeting him was completely impossible, and so I wasn't all *that* nervous, because how can you fear impossibility?

Father McNamee hadn't been acting very stable, and I didn't want to get my hopes up. I was pretty sure the idea of meeting my father in Montreal was just the product of Father McNamee's ongoing battle with madness. This was likely to turn out the same way our rescuing Wendy ended.

I did, however, allow myself to briefly think about the abstract possibility of meeting my father and decided that if this were ever to happen, say, in a parallel universe or something, I should probably be mad at him for leaving us, especially the boy me, who was quite impressionable and likely suffered more without a father than he would have if he had had a father—even a subpar father—and definitely for not giving my mom the fairy tale, because she deserved it; if any woman ever did, it was Mom.

Maybe I should be as angry as Elizabeth was with her mother—theoretically speaking—because what was worse, abandoning your son or making your daughter eat her pet rabbits? A tough call.

But in the real world that is my life, I wasn't mad.

How could I hate a stranger?

How could I be angry with a man I'd never met?

Max called our room and when I picked up the phone, he said, "We're ready. What the fuck, hey? Fucking breakfast? My stomach is fucking screaming, hey."

"Father McNamee is still sleeping," I whispered.

"Let's eat without him. There's a comple-fucking-mentary breakfast downstairs. Muffins and other breakfast items of that fucking nature. But there's a fucking time limit on that shit, hey. It says so in the fucking brochure they leave next to the bed. Time is of the essence when it comes to breakfast in Cana-fucking-da."

"Okay," I whispered.

I wrote Father a note, letting him know where we'd be, so he wouldn't wake up and be confused, and then Elizabeth, Max, and I had coffee and muffins downstairs in the fancy hotel lobby, sitting on Canadian-red leather seats.

"Today is the big day," Elizabeth said.

"Cat Fucking Parliament is the big day!" Max said. "Hey!"

I nodded, glanced at the clock hung on the wall, saw it was after ten, and said, "I better make sure Father McNamee is up."

In the hallway, outside our room, I knocked on the door loudly to let Father know I was coming in, and maybe to wake him up if he hadn't risen already. Then I entered.

He was still sleeping.

"Father?" I said. "Father, it's getting late."

He didn't wake up, so I shook his shoulder gently—and then it felt like I was suffocating.

Father McNamee was frozen.

It was as if he had turned to rock in the middle of the night, because he was cold and stiff and whiter than the freshly fallen snow outside.

Immediately, the rational part of me knew he was dead.

Part of my brain was sober and straight and functioning just fine.

But the irrational part of me took control and started to shake him more violently, yelling, "Father McNamee, wake up! We're going to Saint Joseph's Oratory today! Remember? You promised I'd meet my father in front of Saint Brother André Bessette's preserved heart! You promised me a miracle! Wake up! Wake up! Wake up! This isn't funny! *Wake up! Father!*"

But he didn't wake up, and the rational part of my brain still knew he wouldn't, but the problem was that the rational part was now losing to the irrational part of my mind, and it was beginning to seem like the battle was a lost cause. Rationality was getting slaughtered and was outnumbered ten irrational thoughts to one rational, at least. I began to shake and cry and feel as though I was going to black out and—

Then, Richard Gere, you materialized at that very moment, and I don't think I would have been able to get through that situation if you hadn't.

You came.

To rescue me from irrationality.

You came.

You were dressed in the red-and-yellow robe of a Buddhist monk, and your eyes twinkled extra hard.

Bartholomew, you, Richard Gere, said to me. *It was Father McNamee's time. This is the way of the universe. Our lives here on earth are transitory. This is all as it should be. Breathe. In. Out. Repeat. In. Out. Repeat.*

You demonstrated good breathing techniques here, elongating your spine, but I was too upset to breathe correctly.

"He was supposed to introduce me to my father today! Why would God bring us all the way up here to Montreal with the intention of introducing me to my father if He knew Father McNamee was going to die the night before he was to complete that task? It doesn't make any sense! This makes no sense whatsoever! Father McNamee must have left a note of some sort outlining what I'm supposed to do next. There must be a clue here that will explain everything."

I began searching the hotel room.

You will find no note, because there is none, you said confidently.

"How do you know?"

Richard Gere knows everything about your life, Bartholomew, because Richard Gere lives at the heart of your mind, deep within, at the center of your consciousness.

"I don't understand," I said as I continued searching for a note from Father McNamee—going through his suitcase, the drawers of the desk and dresser, running my arms and hands under the bed—and found none. "I don't understand! Why would God let Father die just a few hours before he was supposed to complete his mission? Before he was to introduce me to my real father? Why would God leave me all alone in Canada?"

You smiled the way Mom used to smile at me when I was a little boy and had asked her the type of question that puzzles children, but to which all adults know the answer—like, why do birds sing or why do trees look most beautiful when they are losing their leaves in the fall or why do we fight wars or why does eating ice cream give you a headache or why do people always laugh at me?

Are you alone? Are you not traveling with others?

I thought about what you were implying—that maybe it was all for a reason—but I didn't say anything.

Are you familiar with Buddhist koans? you, Richard Gere, said to me.

"No," I said, even though I vaguely remember reading something about this at the library once.

In the West, people often mistakenly think of koans as riddles, tests of one's intellect—something to solve. But a truer interpretation would be that koans are brief stories to meditate on—they have no answer. We cannot "solve" or "understand" these koans any more than we can solve or understand a shooting star or a lion's roar or the smell of fresh dew on roses or the feeling of warm sand between our toes. We can only ponder all of these things deeply, and revel in the mystery. It is a mistake to think there is a correct answer or solution, but it is good to ponder all the same. The Dalai Lama would agree here. Trust me. He and I are friends.

"What does any of that have to do with Father's McNamee's dying just hours before he was supposed to tell me who my biological father is?"

You smiled at me as if I were a child.

Are you asking me to solve the koan? There is no answer, Bartholomew. None. But it is good to reflect upon the question that lives at the heart of your current story. I suspect you will reflect on it for many years, and this will make you wiser—it will enhance your experience of this current reality.

"So you're saying that this story—what we are involved in right now—is a koan, something to meditate on, but it has no meaning?"

It has great meaning! It just has no answer.

"You're confusing me!"

No, you are confused completely independent of my influence.

"What am I going to do?"

You are going to call an ambulance, Bartholomew. That is the most rational thing to do at this moment, given the unfortunate circumstances you have inherited. But first, take the money and credit cards out of Father McNamee's wallet.

"What? Why?"

He wanted you to make this journey. You will need money to complete it. Trust me. This is completely acceptable. Father McNamee would want you to take the money and credit cards he had set aside for this journey and complete it in his honor. Search your heart, and you will discover that what I speak is the truth.

I searched my heart and it agreed with you, Richard Gere.

I saw Father's wallet on the table.

Do it, you, Richard Gere, told me, and I did, emptying his wallet, stuffing the money and credit cards into my pockets. And—

I saw something that made my heart leap, but also stunned me into a warm, deep calm.

Now hide the empty wallet in your suitcase so the police don't see it, said the voice in my head, but it was no longer yours, Richard Gere.

You were gone.

It wasn't my mother's voice or the angry little man's.

Was it my own?

Regardless, I did as the voice commanded me to do, slipping Father's wallet into an interior pocket of my suitcase that was somewhat hidden behind a stack of clean white underwear briefs.

Good, the voice said. *Now call the front desk and tell whomever answers that you need an ambulance sent immediately.*

It took about fifteen minutes—during which I sat calmly on the bed, my mind blank, shocked into submission.

Father McNamee was pronounced dead immediately.

Two large men struggled to put his solid round body on a stretcher, but—with much breath and sweat—they finally got him strapped down, at which point they covered him with a white sheet and took him away.

Next, two local policemen interviewed me in my hotel room. One was tall with a mole on the end of his nose and the other was short with long sideburns. They both had freshly sharpened pencils and spiral-bound notebooks the size of bread slices, in which they scribbled furiously whenever I spoke.

"We're sorry for your loss," Sideburns said.

"Unfortunately, we need to ask you a few questions," said the Mole.

"And we apologize in advance if any of the questions seem disrespectful, given the circumstances, but we have to do our job," Sideburns said.

I nodded.

"What were you doing in Canada with the deceased?" the Mole asked.

"We were on a pilgrimage to Saint Joseph's Oratory. We were planning to visit Cat Parliament afterward."

"*Cat Parliament?*" the Mole said, scribbling.

"In Ottawa," I said.

The cops exchanged a glance.

"Pardon my asking, but is that a peeler joint?" Sideburns said, scribbling.

"What?" I said.

"A . . . um . . . a gentleman's club. A place where you pay women to take off their clothes. Strippers."

"No, Cat Parliament's a place where feral cats can roam free. I think it's near the Parliament Buildings in Ottawa."

The police looked at each other again while raising their eyebrows and then continued to scribble.

"Were you drinking last night?" Sideburns asked and pointed the eraser on his pencil at the empty whiskey bottles.

"I wasn't. Father McNamee drank daily."

"You found him dead this morning? Dead in his bed?"

"Yes."

"Traveling with anyone else?"

"Max and Elizabeth are in the lobby. They don't yet know what's happened."

"Would you like me to get them for you?" the Mole said.

I looked up at him, not quite sure why he had asked me that.

"You seem to be in shock," Sideburns said. "Maybe you shouldn't be alone."

I nodded.

That sounded reasonable.

"Max and Elizabeth, you said? Those are the names I should call for?" said the Mole, and when I nodded, he said, "Got it," and left.

Sideburns walked over to the window and looked out.

"How do you think he died?" I asked.

"Don't know. Looks like a heart attack, most likely. Maybe alcohol poisoning. We'll have to wait for the autopsy results for the exact cause of death."

"Why do you think he died?" I let escape before I could censor myself.

"Come again?"

"Why do you think he died? We were so close. He brought me all this way."

"I don't understand," said the short cop with the sideburns, no longer scribbling my every word into his notebook.

I read his eyes and could tell he was worried, like maybe he was starting to become afraid of me—I'd seen that look many times before—so I didn't ask any further questions.

"These things are always difficult," he offered. "Maybe it's best to leave the bigger questions for another day. A counselor might be better equipped to help you with that sort of thing."

I thought he was probably right, even though I had failed so miserably with Wendy and Arnie, and when I looked at my brown shoelaces, the police officer looked out the window again.

A few minutes later the tall police officer returned with Elizabeth and Max.

"What the fuck, hey?"

"Oh my God. I can't believe it. Are you okay, Bartholomew?"

The police officers looked at each other once more, and then Sideburns said, "We're going to leave you alone now. But we'll need your names, passport numbers, and home addresses."

We told them our names and addresses—Elizabeth used their old address without explaining that they had been evicted, which I thought was smart fast thinking—and they dutifully copied down information from our passports before they gave us their cards and told us to contact them in twenty-four hours, after we had been in touch with Father McNamee's family at home, so that we could make the proper arrangements for the body to be shipped back to Philadelphia.

Then the police officers left.

"What the fucking fuck, hey?" Max said, and slapped the side of his head a few times like he was trying to get ketchup from a bottle.

"What happened?" Elizabeth said.

"I don't really know."

"How did he die?"

"I think he may have drunk himself to death last night. I found him dead in his bed."

"What are we going to do now?" she said.

"I don't know."

"I can't believe Father McNamee's really dead," Elizabeth said.

"Fuck."

Max and Elizabeth sat on my unmade bed, and we were all quiet for a long time—it was like we were having a moment of silence for Father McNamee. Wendy might have said we were "processing what had transpired, taking in the weighty information."

Finally, Elizabeth said, "Should we go to Saint Joseph's Oratory?"

"What for?" I asked.

"Father McNamee would want us to go," she said. "And maybe your father will be there?"

"Yeah! What the fuck, hey?"

"I don't think we'll be meeting my father today," I said.

"How do you know?"

I didn't tell Max and Elizabeth this at the time, but when I was emptying Father's wallet, I had found a picture of Mom, him, and me taken when I was a little boy; we were on the huge Ocean City Ferris wheel, spinning around in the sky, and—at the pinnacle of the ride—Father had held the camera out with his arm and snapped a photo of the three of us squished together. I looked terrified in the middle, but Mom and Father McNamee were smiling bookends and seemed so very happy, all alone in the sky with their arms around me. (The younger Father McNamee looks shockingly like I do right now, at the time of writing.) Finding this photo wouldn't have made me suspicious in and of itself, but then I saw Father McNamee's first name on his credit card and confirmed what I had seen when I gave the police his passport information.

His name was Richard.

Richard McNamee.

It's funny how I had known him my entire life, but had never before heard anyone say his first name, nor had I ever thought once to ask. He'd always been Father McNamee. Even Mom had called him Father McNamee. Or Father. I'd never heard anyone call him Richard before.

Or maybe I *had* heard it, but my brain just didn't register it.

Do you find that strange, Richard Gere?

Like maybe some part of my subconscious suspected and was protecting me—not allowing my mind to ever wonder what Father McNamee's first name might be?

Looking back now, I'm sure his entire name was listed on the weekly church bulletin, but who reads those?

Mom had called me Richard at the end of her life. I had assumed she meant you, Richard Gere, but now I'm pretty sure she had meant Richard McNamee, her great love—and I was also pretty sure I knew why Father ate so many dinners at our house throughout the years and why Mom would confess only to him and why he would always be so quick to help us when we were in need—like the time those teenagers trashed our home—and why he had dedicated so many masses to Mom right after she died, even though I hadn't filled out the proper card, and why he had cried on the beach after her funeral and why he had wanted to make a pilgrimage to Saint Joseph's Oratory with me—the place where miracles happened—because he most likely understood it would take a miracle for me to forgive his lifelong deception and the fact that I had grown up without a true father, even if I had an excellent religious leader in Father McNamee.

But then again, can a Catholic priest be an excellent religious leader if he had sex with your mom?

All of this was starting to make my head throb.

"*Bartholomew?*" Elizabeth said.

"Let's go to the Oratory," I said, thinking I could use a miracle right about now, thinking we came this far, we might as well see what Saint Joseph's Oratory had to offer us, if anything.

Then I picked up the keys to the Ford Focus, handed them to Elizabeth, and said, "Let's pack up our stuff and get out of here. It's already past checkout time."

"Are you okay?" Elizabeth said.

"Yeah. What the fuck, hey?"

Max and Elizabeth were visibly frightened.

I nodded, and then we were off.

Your admiring fan,
Bartholomew Neil

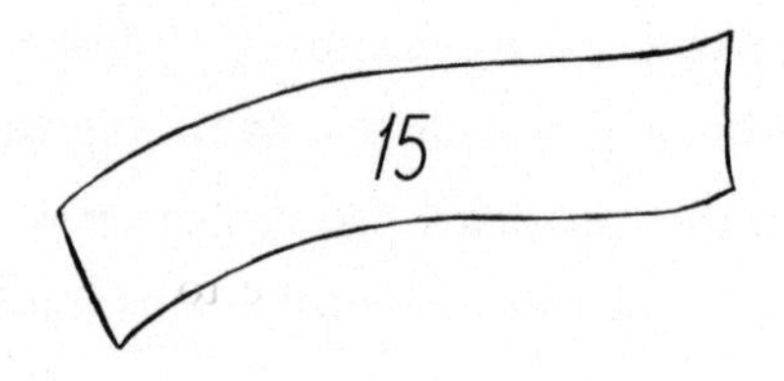

POOR, OBEDIENT, HUMBLE SERVANT

Dear Mr. Richard Gere,

Maybe you think I should have been more emotional over Father McNamee's passing?

Or maybe you even think I should feel guilty, because I let him drink an exorbitant amount of whiskey and never once suggested that he stop drinking to excess?

Maybe you think I should have protested when he said the rabbit dinner he ordered for us was our last supper?

Maybe you think I'm dim—retarded even—because I didn't figure out the mystery of my own father before now?

You could ask me a million different questions at this point in our letter correspondence—and I realize that you'd probably be justified, especially since I cannot give you the sorts of answers that would provide "normal people" any semblance of understanding, regarding the workings of my mind, but regardless of all that, I have so many questions for *you*, Richard Gere, friend of the Dalai Lama, ghost of my thoughts, pen pal, women-wooing mentor, and *supposed* friend.

If Father *Richard* McNamee was the "Richard" Mom was referring to while dying—if he really was my father, and I'm virtually certain now that he was—then why did you begin to appear to me and continue to do so for the past few weeks?

Was I making you up in my mind, like an imaginary friend?

Did I go mad and conjure you with my imagination—like a hallucination?

Or were you really appearing to me because you appear to many people who are in need—because that's just what you, Richard Gere, do when you are not making movies?

Maybe as part of your religious practice?

Could this be a Buddhist thing?

I know you'll probably just say that our case of mistaken identity and your appearing to me is just another koan, something to ponder deeply but never answer or solve.

The universe hiccups, and we poor fools try to figure out why.

I was tempted to cease writing you all together, especially since you haven't shown your face lately—and at a time when I need you most! But the truth is that I have come to depend on these letters. Recording all of this, emptying my mind of words, has proved quite therapeutic. It calms me in a way that nothing else can. Also, you are the only link I have to Mom now that Father McNamee, my true father, is dead.

Mom was your biggest fan.

She boycotted the Beijing Olympics for you.

At this point, there's no substitute for Richard Gere in my life, and therefore—regardless of how I feel about you right now—our letter correspondence will continue.

Do you think Father McNamee is in heaven?

Are priests who break their vows by sleeping with my mother welcomed through Saint Peter's pearly gates?

Does drinking yourself to death—especially when you declare a supper your last—constitute a suicide?

Do potentially suicidal adulterous priests go to purgatory?

Hell even?

Why am I asking a Buddhist these questions?

It's ridiculous.

I don't even think you believe in heaven, purgatory, or hell—do you?

To put it in your religious language, Father McNamee definitely didn't obtain nirvana, now did he, Richard Gere? Not in this lifetime, anyway. A man who drinks two bottles of Jameson and dies sleeping in his bed has usually not achieved nirvana, I would guess.

But he was a good man, overall. Yes, I think we can agree on that, if we decide to be objective, don't you think?

He was not proud of abandoning me, I can tell now in retrospect, looking back. And whatever happened between Father McNamee and Mom happened because of love. Lust is not dutiful, and Father never neglected us during my lifetime.

How conflicted must he have felt—following his religious calling and carrying around the picture of me and

Mom and him atop the Ocean City Ferris wheel, where he was free to put his arm around us, because no one could see us up there—he was unburdened from his vows and his calling.

We did actually go to Saint Joseph's Oratory—Max, Elizabeth, and me—if your interest hasn't faded, if you are even still reading, Richard Gere.

Elizabeth drove, and I used the GPS navigational system to find our way. A robotic woman's voice told us when to turn and how many miles we had until the next street would appear and there was a computer screen that showed us moving on a map, connecting us with a satellite above, in outer space, which is alien technology at work, Max explained, when I asked how the little machine in the car could possibly know where we were.

The voice that navigated was definitely that of a machine, and yet you could tell that the machine was a woman, which hurt my mind a little. How can machines have genders? The machine also had an American accent. How can machines have nationalities? This can't be a good idea, making machines talk like real people, can it? Giving machines humanoid identities?

The Oratory is on a hill—a great white building made up of steps and columns and turrets, with a giant copper-green dome on top.

Supposedly, pilgrims climb the many hard, cold steps that lead to the entrance on their knees—the pain providing penance. Do you find that strange, Richard Gere? No stranger than Buddhist monks dousing themselves with gasoline and lighting themselves on fire, you have to admit.

From the outside, Saint Joseph's Oratory is beautiful and impressive.

Breathtaking would not be an excessive adjective.

We looked up at it from the parking lot.

"What . . . the . . . fuck . . . hey?" Max said slowly, in a reserved tone, using his hand to shield his eyes from the frozen winter sun. And I could tell he was in awe.

"It's truly impressive, even from the standpoint of an atheist," said Elizabeth.

Mom would not want me to fall in love with an atheist, especially a self-proclaimed atheist, I knew that—nor would Father McNamee, most likely—but they were both gone, and I was making my way in the world alone, and so when I looked at Elizabeth that morning, I felt my heart reach for her, and I thought, Better be brave now, Bartholomew, because these people are all you have left, and you will need strength and courage to keep them by your side fighting the great dark loneliness that looms.

These were strange new times, and for whatever reason, Max and Elizabeth were here with me, helping me face the day, helping me grieve for Father McNamee, and so I chose right then and there to make our relationships work by overlooking our small differences. I didn't really believe in aliens, and yet I was willing to wear three tektite crystals around my neck. They didn't believe in God, but were willing to gaze at the preserved heart of a Catholic saint with me and hopefully light a candle for the recently deceased Father McNamee. Maybe they would even kneel with me while I prayed for Mom's and Father McNamee's souls.

"You think you'll find your fucking father in there?"

I smiled and shrugged. "Let's see."

I started to walk, but Elizabeth grabbed my shoulder and said, "Wait!"

When I turned to look at her, she pushed the hair from her face, so that I got a full, unobstructed view of her eyes, nose, and mouth. She was even more beautiful than I imagined. My heart was pounding.

"Maybe we should save this visit for later?" she said. "Considering what happened today—Father McNamee. That was already a horrific shock, Bartholomew. One we haven't fully absorbed yet. And I don't know what would be worse: if we actually find your father, or if we don't. Either might be too much for one day, and—"

"It's okay," I said, gazing into her eyes, which were the soft gray-brown color of mushroom pizza toppings.

I could see that Max was equally concerned.

Maybe this was also what Mom called The Good Luck of Right Now. The bad of Father McNamee's deception and death had led to the good of Max and Elizabeth taking care of me now. It certainly felt like Mom's philosophy was in effect once again—that she was even wiser than I had given her credit for when she was alive with me here on earth. And that's really saying something, because I gave Mom tons of credit.

To my concerned friends, Max and Elizabeth, I said, "My father won't be in there. Don't worry. I came to terms with this earlier this morning."

"How can you be so fucking sure?" Max said.

"Because Father McNamee was my biological father."

"What?" Elizabeth said.

"The fuck, hey?" Max finished.

Their eyebrows rose.

"My subconscious suspected this for many years, but I'm just finding out now."

"How do you know?" Elizabeth said.

"He told me," I said.

"When?" said Elizabeth.

"This morning," I said.

"But he was fucking *dead* this morning," Max said as a group of nuns in black habits exited a VW bus and began to stare at us.

"God bless you, Sisters!" I yelled at them, waving and smiling, because they looked offended by Max's excessive use of profanity, which had become customary to my ear, but still rankled others.

"Bless *you*!" a younger-looking nun yelled back, and then almost all of them waved.

"Father McNamee whispered the truth from beyond the grave," I said to Max and Elizabeth.

"Is this a Catholic thing?" Elizabeth said.

I laughed, and suddenly I felt light—like I had let go of a huge dark secret hidden inside of me for so, so very long.

I was still scared about the future—but I felt sort of free too, because the greatest mystery of my life was no more.

I wondered if I'd been subconsciously hiding the fact that I had known all along, maybe to protect Father McNamee. Even as a young boy I would have understood that Father's fathering me would cause a major scandal in our parish, and would have prevented Father McNamee from doing all the good he'd done as a priest since I was born—almost four entire decades of altruistic deeds he was able to do because Mom kept his secret. Maybe I was part of the whole cover-up too; maybe I just played along, pretending I didn't know, when really I did. I'm sure Mom would have gladly played this game with me—and, come to think of it, she did, telling me that my father had been murdered by the Ku Klux Klan, and therefore was a Catholic martyr.

We had all played the game together.

"Maybe it's a life thing," I said to Elizabeth, and then I led them into Saint Joseph's Oratory.

We took several escalators up to the main cathedral, called the basilica, which was gigantic and felt a little like heaven, if heaven were a modern-style cathedral.

"It looks like the inside of a fucking spaceship," Max whispered, and I could see what he meant, because the concrete rose up into great arches and domes, and there was even a decorative UFO-looking silver ring suspended over the altar.

I looked over at Elizabeth, and her fists were clenched.

There were also wooden carvings of all the disciples, depicted as long, stretched-out giants—like what you might see reflected in a fun-house mirror, only wearing robes and the hairstyles of biblical times. We found my namesake Bartholomew quite easily, although he is labeled by his other name, Nathaniel. He is holding some sort of leaf, and his left index and middle fingers make the peace sign, the fingertips of which rest on his chin.

"These fuckers look like aliens," Max whispered, and I had to agree, as they were elongated and skinny and otherworldly looking. "What the fuck does it mean? The disciples of Jesus carved to look like giant fucking aliens?"

"I don't know," I said.

"Father McNamee would have known," Elizabeth said.

"Perhaps," I whispered, and then we gazed at the other apostles, who all looked stern and stretched and wooden and dusty and even alien.

Yes, alien indeed.

I wondered how many prayers had been sent up from this building—up to heaven like we beam information up to our satellites now, when we are in our cars and need directions.

We wandered out of the basilica, down escalators, and into a great hallway of candles where you could pay money to light one for many various reasons, sending prayers up to Saint Joseph.

I made the requested donation, lit a white candle in a red glass cup for Father McNamee, and prayed to Saint Joseph, asking him to put in a good word with Saint Peter, petitioning to let Father through the pearly gates and into heaven, even though he had sex with my mother while he was a priest, drank himself to death, and never told me he was my father. Even still, he helped many members of our church over the years—and many nonmembers too.

Father McNamee was a good man, I prayed to Saint Joseph, and meant it too.

So many other people and pilgrims were lighting candles and praying; some were crying. It felt like a holy place, and even Max refrained from cursing for a time, which I interpreted as a great sign of respect.

We walked by walls on which hung hundreds of wooden crutches and canes donated by people who had supposedly been healed by Saint Brother André, a simple uneducated doorman who had dedicated his life to Saint Joseph and inexplicably became a miracle worker.

And then we went to Saint Brother André's final resting place.

His body is entombed in a shiny black marble box that sits under a brick archway. There is a painting of a red cross on the wall between the arch and the sarcophagus. In Latin, an inscription reads: "Poor, Obedient, Humble Servant of God."

But Saint Brother André's heart was not there.

I asked another pilgrim where I could see the heart, and she pointed me toward an information booth. The man there showed me where to go on a map that cost me two Canadian dollars.

We took another escalator up and climbed a flight of stairs to a room of dioramas—Brother André's bedroom, a mannequin of him standing in his office, a mannequin of him standing next to a chair, all behind glass.

"He was so short," Elizabeth said. "It's hard to believe such a fragile-looking man is responsible for all this."

"Yes," I said in full agreement. Saint Brother André didn't look like the type of man who accomplishes great things. He really didn't. He looked nothing like you, Richard Gere.

And then—when we turned around—we saw it.

The very place Father McNamee wanted me to go.

Where Father McNamee first heard the voice of God.

Opposite the dioramas was what looked like a vault fenced off by iron. Behind the gate stood a gray pillar, on top of which sat a square glass box, lined with ornately carved stone. There was a human heart inside this box. The lighting inside the vault was red, so it looked like you were peering inside a giant's chest—a giant wearing a great breastplate of armor that opened to reveal a heart encased in glass.

"What the fuck, hey?" Max said, ending his run of noncursing.

"Do you think it's real?" Elizabeth whispered.

"I do," I said.

"Who the fuck cut it out, I wonder?"

"I don't know," I said, trying not to think about the act of cutting a human heart out of a dead body—trying not to think about Charles J. Guiteau's dissected brain, preserved forever at the Mütter Museum.

"What do you think the aliens would think if they came down and saw this human heart on display?" I asked Elizabeth. "If they saw so many people worshipping around Saint Brother André's heart, lighting candles and praying to Saint Joseph?"

Elizabeth didn't answer, but squeezed my biceps through my coat and walked away.

Max nodded at me and followed his sister.

It was almost as if they knew I needed to be alone—and I understood this just as soon as they left me.

I stood and stared at Saint Brother André's heart for a long time, wondering who he had been.

They say a million people came to his funeral and walked past his casket in the freezing cold of Canadian winter.

How did that happen?

What separates men like him from people like Max, Elizabeth, and me?

From the rest of the world?

Father McNamee would have said Brother André had faith—he just believed more than other people.

And I wondered if faith were not a form of pretending.

I also wondered what Father McNamee would have said if he were standing there at that moment with me, in front of Brother André's heart—the place where he first heard his calling.

Would he have asked my forgiveness?

Would he have said he was sorry?

Would he have professed his love for me—his only son? Did he leave the church to finally claim me as a son and be my dad?

I'd never get the answers to these questions now, but standing there gazing at the heart of a miracle worker, I started to feel like it didn't matter—that I was going to be okay somehow, in spite of how uprooted my life had become.

I found Max and Elizabeth on a large balcony of sorts, looking out over Montreal, which was breathtaking, and not just because it was cold outside—cold enough to freeze you from the inside of your lungs out to your fingers and toes.

"Thanks for coming here with me," I said to Max and Elizabeth.

"No fucking problem," Max said.

Elizabeth smiled politely.

Then we looked out over snow-covered Montreal for another few minutes as our breath slipped in and out of us.

It kind of felt like we were supposed to be there in that time and place—almost like it was predestined. It just felt right somehow.

I don't know.

But maybe.

I thought about it and decided that I wasn't going to attempt to answer life's greater mysteries—especially given all I was dealing with presently—and so I figured it best to stick with the plan.

"Let's go to Cat Parliament," I said.

"Cat Fucking Parliament!" Max said, and then went back inside so he could exit the Oratory and hop into the Ford Focus.

"We can stay here as long as you'd like, Bartholomew," Elizabeth said. "If you need more time—"

"I'm ready to go," I said.

Elizabeth did something unexpected—she pulled a silver chain out of her coat pocket and put it around my neck.

"Another tektite necklace to protect me from aliens?" I asked.

"No. It's a Saint Brother André medal I purchased in the gift shop," she said, and then walked away.

I picked up the medal off my coat and studied it—Saint Brother André's tiny wrinkled face etched in silver.

I missed Father McNamee, but I knew he'd want me to carry on the best I could—I was certain of that.

And maybe that good moment on the oratory balcony with Elizabeth was an inheritance of sorts.

It was a nice thought.

So I ran after Elizabeth—feeling more alive than I have ever felt in my whole life—and we headed for Ottawa in the Ford Focus.

Your admiring fan,
Bartholomew Neil

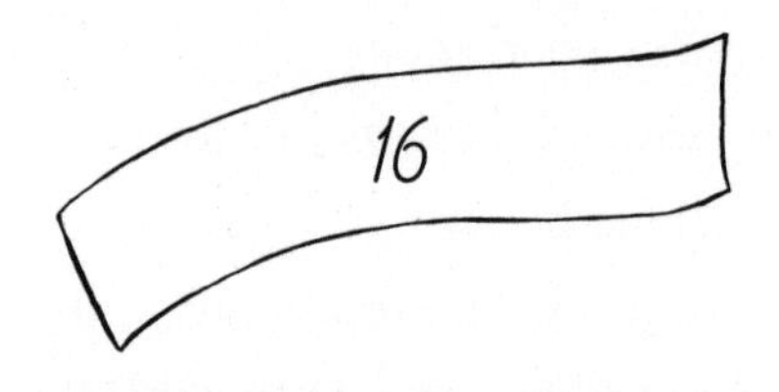

16

I UNDERSTOOD OUR FORTUNE COOKIE MESSAGES BETTER THAN I HAD ORIGINALLY THOUGHT

Dear Mr. Richard Gere,

While sitting in the backseat of the Ford Focus, listening to the robotic woman navigate and watching the flat, white, empty land pass by, I became very tired—too tired to think about all that had happened, let alone try to make sense of any of it.

Somehow—even though Max kept yelling, "Cat Fucking Parliament!" intermittently—I fell asleep.

In my dream, I woke up and I was in my bedroom, in Mom's house.

Mom and Father McNamee were standing next to my bed, holding hands.

"Is this a dream?" I said to them.

But they only smiled back, looking extremely proud.

"Are you two together in heaven?"

They just kept smiling.

"Why won't you talk to me?" I said. "Please. Say something. Let me know that you're okay, at least. Give me a sign."

Mom pulled Father McNamee in a little closer, they looked each other in the eyes, and then they simply blinked out of existence.

"*Mom?*" I yelled, and tried to get out of my bed, only to find that I couldn't. The blanket was strapping me down, binding my torso, wrapping me like a giant anaconda—I couldn't even free my arms. *"Father?"*

And then I was being shaken, so I opened my eyes and saw Max looking back at me from the passenger seat of the Ford Focus.

"What the fuck, hey?"

"You were dreaming," Elizabeth said as she drove. "You were yelling."

"I'm sorry," I said, and adjusted my seat belt.

"Elizabeth told me to fucking wake you up."

"Thank you."

No one said anything else, and I looked at my reflection in the window.

I felt so empty all of a sudden, so lonely—and I felt guilty, like maybe I hadn't been a good enough son to Mom or Father McNamee, like I should have told them I loved them more when they were here, or I should have done more things—or maybe just *one* thing—to make them proud. And I wondered if my being a fat, unemployed, friendless man made them feel terrible about themselves, like their love had created this monster of a son who embarrassed them endlessly. The worst thought was this: Even if I managed to do something worthwhile with my life in the future, even if the miraculous occurred and I finally got my act together in some small way, Mom and Father McNamee were no longer around to see it. They had died knowing the Bartholomew of the past, and I was not happy with the Bartholomew of the past—not one bit.

Also, now that I knew Father McNamee's first name was Richard, that I had misinterpreted Mom's calling me by your first name, that Richard was an identity double entendre of sorts—at least in my life—I was finding it harder and harder to pretend that you, Richard Gere, were my friend and confidant. And so even though I am still writing you letters, I feel as though I am now writing to a dead person or a figment of my imagination—a fictional character—which also makes me feel like a gigantic moron.

Writing you and talking with you when you appeared to me felt so right before that now it feels doubly bad—knowing that it was all fake, that I had been mistaken.

Regardless of all that, I feel like I should tell you the rest of the story, maybe just because I need to tell *someone*.

When we arrived in Ottawa, we asked the GPS system to find us a hotel, and she was able to do that no problem.

There was a valet service, and we used it, so they gave Elizabeth a small piece of paper in return for the keys to the Ford Focus.

Elizabeth told me I'd have to use my emergency credit card that Mom had given me long ago, because the receptionist might ask for my passport when we checked in at the desk, and it would need to match the name on the credit card, which seemed logical, so I did as she suggested. We rented one room for the three of us and said we'd stay two nights. The whole time Max paced behind us, because he was so eager to go to Cat Parliament in the morning that he had planned to go to bed as soon as possible so that the night would pass more quickly.

"You're all set, Mr. Neil," the receptionist said, and then handed me two rectangular room keys.

We keyed into our room on the fourth floor, and Max immediately began to get ready for bed by changing into his PJs—which were dotted with cat silhouettes and had these words blocked in red across the chest: THE CAT'S PAJAMAS—brushing his teeth, washing his face, and then diving into the bed closest to the widows. "Time to fucking sleep," he said.

"Max, it's only eight and we haven't eaten dinner yet," Elizabeth said, but he was snoring almost as soon as his head hit the pillow.

"Should we get dinner?" I asked, and Elizabeth nodded.

We bundled up and walked into the snowy city, feeling the sharp wind whip off the Ottawa River.

"It looks like England here," Elizabeth said as we strolled by the Parliament Buildings. "Clocks in high towers and whatnot."

"Have you been to England?"

"No. You?"

"Never."

"But wouldn't you say this looks like England?"

"I guess so."

We walked sort of aimlessly for a long time, taking in the city, feeling the cold on our cheeks, and it felt good to walk after driving from Montreal.

Elizabeth stopped in front of a window full of Chinese zodiac symbols, behind which a fat jade Buddha sat cross-legged, and she said, "Do you want to eat here?"

"Sure," I said, and we went in.

She ordered lo mein, so I did too, and we waited in silence for the food to come, while some sort of Asian-sounding melody played—high-pitched flutes and what sounded like a depressed music box.

I thought maybe lo mein would taste different in Canada, but it didn't.

When we finished eating, the fortune cookies came.

Elizabeth's read: THE ONLY THING WRONG WITH HARMONY IS THAT BY DEFINITION IT CANNOT LAST.

Mine read: A FRIEND IS A PRESENT YOU GIVE YOURSELF.

"What do they even mean?" Elizabeth said.

I didn't have a clue, so I shrugged.

We sat there for a time, drinking the rest of the green tea that came in a black kettle shaped to look like a dragon, which we poured into little white cups that had light blue Chinese symbols painted on them.

"Why do you think we're here together in Ottawa?" I said. "I mean, what are the odds?"

Elizabeth stared out the window at the passing traffic, and her face seemed to turn to stone.

When I had paid the bill, she stood, I followed her lead,

and we ambled around the snowy city of Ottawa for what seemed like hours.

Elizabeth kept her lips sealed, and so did I.

We just walked.

And walked.

And walked.

And even though I was very cold, I didn't say anything about that either, because I wanted to walk with Elizabeth forever and I didn't want to do or say anything that would prematurely end my being with her.

Elizabeth seemed to be deep in thought, and I somehow knew that it was best not to say anything—and so I didn't.

In the hotel lobby she asked if I'd like to have a drink with her at the bar, and I said yes before I even realized that I was about to fulfill my last remaining life goal.

Elizabeth ordered a dirty Ketel One martini on the rocks with extra olives, and even though I had no idea what that was, I said I'd have the same.

The drinks came, and I paid with Father McNamee's credit card.

We sat down in the fancy leather chairs, and the bartender put a bowl of trail mix next to our drinks on the little table that rested below our knees.

"Cheers," Elizabeth said, and lifted her martini glass.

Even though her voice wasn't all that cheery, I lifted mine and we touched rims, just like they do on TV.

When I sipped, it tasted mostly like salty olives; I enjoyed the burn.

I was having my first drink with a woman, but it didn't feel all that special—not like I thought it would.

I took a few tiny sips.

She took several gulps.

There was a long, uncomfortable silence, during which I could tell Elizabeth was having an argument with herself deep in her mind.

Suddenly she reached into her purse, produced an orange bottle of pills, and set it down on the table next to her drink.

"What are those?" I asked.

"These were my exit strategy," she said.

"I don't understand."

"Really?"

I shook my head.

"Max and I have no place to go. We have no home. No relatives. I promised my brother I'd take him to see Cat Parliament for his fortieth birthday. I'm going to deliver on that tomorrow. But then there's nothing left. No other options. And I'm tired, Bartholomew. I'm really tired."

It took me a second to understand what Elizabeth was saying, but when I did, I snatched the pill bottle off the table and said, "What if you came to live with me? Max can live there too. We could make a go of it. As a family."

"What type of family would we be?"

"The best kind," I said.

She smiled and looked at the floor. "You're just being nice."

"What's wrong with that? Maybe all of this, everything that has happened—my mom killed by cancer, Max and me meeting coincidentally, all of us needing to go to Canada, my seeing you at the library, noticing that you were different, and even Father McNamee dying—maybe all of it happened because the three of us are supposed to be together."

"You do realize how insane that sounds, right?"

"I don't know, does it? I mostly just listed everything that happened to us—facts—and then made my best guess."

I couldn't believe how confident I sounded, Richard Gere. You must have really rubbed off on me.

"I've never met anyone quite like you, Bartholomew," she said, swirling the olive-studded stick inside her glass. "I admire your willingness to offer kindness almost indiscriminately. But unfortunately, it takes a lot more than kindness to survive in this world."

I understood what she meant, but I also understood that Mom's philosophy was a powerful weapon, and I thought that maybe I could harness it here, so I said, "I'd love for you to live with me, Elizabeth. We can make it work. I choose to believe this because the alternative"—I shook her bottle of pills—"is so, so unattractive. Why not try to believe with me at this point? What do you have to lose? We can get a cat for Max! He could work at the movies, you could keep volunteering at the library, and I could . . ."

I didn't know what I could do, and that started to make me feel anxious. All I had ever done was take care of Mom and be her son. And yet here I was promising to be so much more than what I was—pretending again.

"I'm not well," Elizabeth said. "Neither is Max. We're damaged goods. We're problems—and nothing but. You do realize that by now, right? We're not easy."

"I'm damaged goods too! And I'm also problems! I'm a mess! It's perfect!"

"It's *not* perfect," she said in what was very close to a yelling voice. I could tell that she had been struggling for a long time—too long—and didn't have much left in her hope tank. "*None of this is perfect!* I'm not going to allow myself to hope for perfect. Perfect doesn't exist for people like us, Bartholomew. *Passable.* That's what I want. *Just simply passable.* If I could have a passable existence, I think I'd be very grateful." She shook her head and stared at her lap. I saw her lips moving behind her curtain of brown hair, and I could tell she was arguing with herself again. Then suddenly she looked up and said, "I don't think I could have ever executed my exit plan, anyway. I could never do that to Max. And now I'm putting my problems on you."

Elizabeth shook her head, looked up at the ceiling, and then stared at her lap again.

We were silent for some time, as we sipped our martinis.

And then I had an idea that seemed sort of weird, but I went with it anyway, because I felt like the moment required me to be something more than I usually am. "Pretend I'm you," I said to Elizabeth. "Here's how you would answer right now if we were in a movie—in response to my offer for you and Max to live with me in Mom's home like we were a family." Then using a girlie falsetto, overly dramatic Vivian Ward/Julia Roberts Hollywood voice, I said, "If we do take you up on your kind offer, do you actually think we could make it work, Bartholomew? Do you really? We wouldn't ask for much. We wouldn't dare. But do you think that maybe we could just exist together *passably*, because that's all I'd ever hope for—a passable existence." My voice started to quaver here. I wasn't sure why. "That's all I'd ever dare to ask. We're not greedy—but life, it really hasn't been generous to Max and me. So you have to be honest with me here, Bartholomew. Do you actually believe a passable existence is possible?"

Elizabeth drained her glass.

"I wasn't really abducted by aliens." She moved the hair away from her face. She was trembling. "The doctors called Max in Worcester when I was recovering in the hospital, because he was listed as my next of kin in my insurance information. He took a train to Philly that night and went crazy when he saw me. Max is simpleminded, but he has a huge heart. He really does. He doesn't understand that awful things happen every single day to people all over the world. Horrible things. Like being . . . like . . ." Elizabeth looked down at her lap, and the curtain of hair fell over her face once again. "They were drunk and subhuman and were never even brought to justice. Max's mind couldn't accept that, because how can you protect your sister from something so horribly random as being attacked near the Delaware River on the way home from an afterwork drink on a crisp fall Wednesday night? Attacked until your thighs are covered in blood. So Max and I made up the aliens story together in the hospital—almost like we were kids again—and I went along with it just to keep him calm. He insisted on moving in with me so that he could protect me from aliens, and it just escalated from there. But it's really kind of a beautiful brother-sister story if you can manage to look at it the right way, and . . ."

Elizabeth gave me a look that was half happy and half on the verge of tears.

When she forced a smile, I nodded, because I knew that's what was required of me even though I was terrified on the inside, and I didn't even know who was paying the bills associated with Mom's house, and maybe I never would, now that Father McNamee was dead, and I also wasn't sure a passable existence was actually possible for *me*, let alone the three of us together.

I didn't really know anything for certain at all.

But I believed I could pretend again for Elizabeth, pretend to be stronger than I really was, because that's what the moment required of me, and so I did. I pretended to be strong, and I tried to show Elizabeth compassion. As I did, I wondered if Father McNamee and Mom would be proud, Richard Gere. I'm pretty sure the Dalai Lama would be happy with my actions that night, because Elizabeth began to cry right there and then, not just little tears either, but she sobbed and sobbed until I reached out and held her in my arms, and then I began to cry too, because I missed Mom so much and Father McNamee was gone and I was just starting to understand the finality of it, that I would never get to have a father ever, that there was no mystery anymore, it was all solved and certain and over, and Elizabeth hadn't been abducted by aliens but had experienced something even more terrible than the teenagers who broke into Mom's house and pissed on my bed and shit on Mom's and put our Lord and Savior Jesus Christ in the toilet . . . and how did we end up in Canada, and why were our lives so much stranger than the lives of regular people?

Was there any hope for us?

As Elizabeth sobbed into my shoulder, I decided—whether it was true or not—to believe in The Good Luck of Right Now enough to take action, even to find a job if need be, so that I could give Elizabeth the fairy tale, like you did so many times in your movies, Richard Gere.

Mom would never have the fairy tale, but maybe Elizabeth could.

Maybe.

"Are you two okay?" the bartender asked, and when I looked up, a strand of Elizabeth's hair was caught in my mouth, and the several people in the hotel lobby bar were staring at us.

When she saw everyone looking, Elizabeth ran out of the bar, and I followed.

In the elevator, I didn't know what to do.

Elizabeth was still crying, but much more softly now—and yet I got the sense that she didn't want to be touched or comforted or spoken to.

Her face was bright red and snot was running out of both nostrils, even though she kept wiping it with the sleeve of her coat.

I kept my mouth shut.

When we arrived at the door to our room, she composed herself and said, "I don't want to wake up Max, okay? And I don't want him to know about any of this. Tomorrow is his big day. Let's make it beautiful for him. *Agreed?* It's what we have left. Let's make it beautiful for all of us. *Okay?*"

I nodded.

She put the card into the slot and the little rectangle turned green, but she didn't open the door.

"If we sleep on opposite sides of the bed, will you promise not to roll over? Will you promise to keep at least a foot of space between us at all times?"

"Okay," I said.

"Can we really live with you until we get our lives together?"

"Yes. I'd like that very much. And there's no time limit either."

"You promise? You won't change your mind?"

"Never."

Elizabeth nodded again and sort of winked both eyes at the same time, which I caught, even though she was hiding behind her hair again.

It was like she was maybe making a wish and sealing it with a double blink—or at least that's what I imagined.

We entered the room, but we didn't put the lights on.

She changed in the bathroom, and I slipped into my pajamas while the door was closed.

I dumped her bottle of pills in the toilet and flushed; I didn't want her to have an exit strategy.

She picked the right side of the bed, so I hugged the left edge all night long.

I didn't let myself sleep, because I wanted to keep my promise—I didn't want to risk accidentally rolling over and touching Elizabeth in the middle of the night.

So I listened to her and Max breathing and stared at the electric alien-green numbers of the alarm clock.

At 4:57 Elizabeth whispered, "Bartholomew?"

"Yes?" I whispered back.

"I'm sorry if I weirded you out tonight."

"You didn't."

"Really?"

"Really."

At 5:14 Elizabeth whispered, "Thank you."

"Thank you too," I said, and then we just lay there in the dark for two hours, until Max woke up, started jumping between us on our bed while screaming, "CAT FUCKING PARLIAMENT!" over and over.

I have to admit, in spite of all that had happened, Max's unbridled childlike enthusiasm lifted my spirits considerably.

It was nice to have friends.

And I started to think I understood our fortune cookie messages better than I had originally thought.

Your admiring fan,
Bartholomew Neil

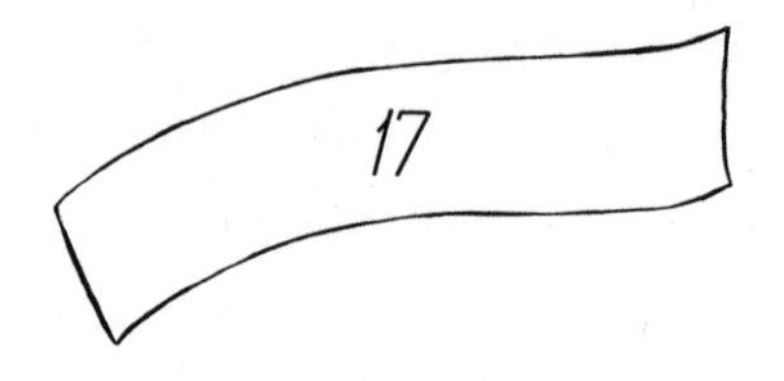

THE STRAY CATS OF PARLIAMENT HILL

Dear Mr. Richard Gere,

Max told us everything we needed to know about Cat Parliament as we walked through Ottawa to the main event.

According to local legend, the Parliament Buildings were kept rodent-free by a supremely talented colony of hunting cats until the 1950s, when poison became the preferred method of mouse and rat extermination. Out of the kindness of their hearts, people who took care of the Parliament Buildings and their surroundings continued to feed the cats for decades, and then some locals got together and created a special space for the stray cats of Parliament Hill to live together as a family—or a colony.

Now you can see two mini-houses lined by iron bars spaced wide enough apart for the inhabitants to sneak through as they please. The white mini-houses each have a shingled roof and four doorways under an awning of sorts, which doubles as a place for the cats to stretch and be lazy. A mini red-and-white Canadian flag flies from the top of the left house.

There is a boardwalk for the cats to strut across, and this is kept clear of snow—my guess is that the caretakers shovel it as necessary.

Bowls of cat food are placed at various spots around and on the mini-houses, and according to Max, volunteers take care of the colony on a daily basis.

The area around Parliament Hill really does look like England; I have decided it's true, even though I have never been, nor will I ever be likely to go, to England.

The back of the Parliament Buildings is round like a cathedral with many pointy spirals and also sort of looks like a spaceship, although I didn't say that to Max.

When we arrived early in the morning, the day after Father McNamee went to join Mom in heaven or purgatory, Max explained much of the above, and then he took off ahead of Elizabeth and me—he started running like an excited little boy just as soon as he saw his first cat in the distance.

"Cat Fucking Parliament!" he yelled, and skipped a few times as he ran. "Cat Fucking Parliament! I'm finally fucking here!"

"Have you ever been that happy?" Elizabeth asked me, and I honestly don't think I have ever once been that elated, never in my entire life.

Max grabbed the bars when he reached the cat sanctuary and he studied the few cats that were out in the morning sunlight.

Elizabeth stopped walking, and so I stood with her, maybe twenty or so feet away from Max, allowing him a private moment.

When we finally approached him, his cheeks were striped and tears were freezing to the bottom of his chin like a small beard.

His lips were trembling.

He kept sniffing and snorting.

"Are you okay?" Elizabeth asked Max.

"It's so fucking beautiful."

"The cats?" I asked.

"Fuck, yes! But also the fucking fact that people take care of stray cats. Cats! For all these fucking years. They feed them. They fucking give them shelter. They didn't forget about the cats when they no longer served a fucking function. These cats are completely useless to society now, but people feed them just because. Isn't that fucking beautiful? Isn't it just so fucking—*humane?* Do you even understand what I'm fucking talking about here, hey? Cat Fucking Parliament is the most beautiful place in the world, hey! You do see it, right? The fucking beauty?"

Elizabeth and I nodded as we watched a calico and a gray tabby eat breakfast, nibbling on tiny pieces of cat food.

"Look at them! Just fucking look. Beautiful! Fucking beautiful! *This exists!*"

After twenty minutes or so, Elizabeth and I retired to a nearby bench, and we watched Max enjoying his stay at Cat Parliament.

A few children accompanied by their mothers stopped to look at the cats, and as they stood next to Max, the juxtaposition was striking. For a man who said the word *fuck* at least once in almost every sentence he spoke—even the sentences that contained only two or three words—his heart was definitely childlike.

"It was my life goal to have a drink with you," I said to Elizabeth.

"Max told me," she said. "That's why I asked you to have a drink at the bar last night. To maybe help you feel better about losing Father McNamee so suddenly. I thought, at least you could cross off your life goal as completed. Sorry I ruined it by sharing my exit strategy. It wasn't a very good first date, was it?"

My heart leaped at the word *date*, but I played it Richard Gere cool and said, "You can share whatever you want with me. I mean it. Don't ever hold back. I think we need to be honest with each other, if we are going to help each other out."

"I agree. Thank you."

"I have a new life goal. Do you want to know what it is?"

"Sure."

"Someday—and it doesn't have to be soon, so please don't feel pressured—but I'd like to hold your hand for a short period of time. Maybe just a minute—and maybe behind the Philadelphia Museum of Art, near the Water Works, while we listen to the river flow. It's my favorite place in the world. You'd like it, if you've never been."

I couldn't believe I was saying this—my heart was pounding so hard.

But I was now extra Richard Gere cool on the outside.

Fairy-tale suave.

Elizabeth smiled and said, "Maybe someday we can hold

hands behind the Philadelphia Museum of Art, but not today, obviously, because we're in Ottawa. And it may have to be a long way in the future, if at all, because I have a lot to work through. I'm pretty sure all three of us need help, and I think we should get some when we return to Philadelphia. Okay?"

"I understand," I said, and I did. "We should get help. We *will* get help."

Elizabeth and I sat there silently for hours as Max admired the residents of Cat Parliament.

It was cold, but we weren't about to make Max leave, because we didn't know if he or any of us would ever make it back to Canada's capital city, let alone this very spot, and even if we did, somehow we knew it would never be the same as right then. There would be different variables, if we came back, a totally different equation made up of wildly different circumstances; it just couldn't be helped, because life was always evolving and changing, and therefore, no matter how much we'd like to, we would never, ever have that moment again—even if we tried with all our might to re-create it, going so far as wearing the same exact clothes even, we would fail, because you cannot beat time; you can only enjoy it whenever possible, as it zooms by endlessly.

At one point a big black cat began to curl around Max's legs, making the infinity sign. When Max bent down to pet it, the cat raised his head to greet Max's hand, so Max gave him a big scratch behind the ears. The cat closed his eyes in appreciation. Max did the same. And they seemed to be communicating. I wondered if Max was practicing his cat telepathy.

"Did you even fucking see that? How that cat picked *me* to fucking commune with?" Max yelled at us when the cat moved on. "What the fuck, hey?"

Elizabeth and I both smiled, because Max was so high.

Smiling didn't really make sense, considering the grander picture. No money, not a "real" job between us, and no idea what we would do when we returned to Philadelphia, nor who was even paying the bills that kept arriving at Mom's house marked paid in full—and to be frank, all three of us were a tragic mess emotionally.

But somehow just seeing a grown man enjoying the company of a feral cat on a cold winter's morning in Ottawa, to the wild degree that Max was living and fully appreciating that very moment—well, somehow it was enough for that time and place.

Enough to feel good about.

More than enough to make us smile.

And that's all I feel like sharing with you, Richard Gere, even though there is much more to the story—like how we got Father McNamee's body back into the United States; and how his family wouldn't speak to me at the funeral, even though we never told anyone the truth about him being my biological father; and how a tall man in an expensive-looking suit walked up to me, shook my hand firmly, and, while holding my shoulders and looking directly into my eyes, said, "Dicky was very proud of you," and when I failed to respond, he added, "We grew up together, eh? Best friends all through school. And where I come from, you take care of your best friends, so don't worry about anything—

just between you and me only, eh?" and then he winked and I double-winked back my promise to tell no one, not even Max and Elizabeth; and how Father Hachette helped the three of us find a therapist who would counsel us individually and also as a group, or what she called a "family unit," at a nominal cost we could afford; and how Elizabeth goes to Saturday-evening Mass with me now even though she still doesn't officially believe in God; and how Wendy broke down sobbing when, wearing her large sunglasses again, she applied for financial aid at Temple University, hoping to escape Adam once and for all, and a handsome financial aid adviser named Franklin consoled her, took her to dinner, and eventually put together a fantastic financial aid and loan package for her, winning her away from abusive Adam—I know all this because Franklin and Wendy now attend Saturday-night Mass at Saint Gabriel's, and sometimes we all double-date afterward at the local pizza place, where I inspect Wendy's face and arms happily, because bruises no longer appear on her skin; and how I got promoted to manager at my new job, working at the fast-food restaurant Wendy's downtown—synchronicity?—and Elizabeth was officially hired part-time by the Free Library of Philadelphia, and Max even got a raise at the "fucking movies," so we are now finally able to pay our bills without any help from my new well-dressed and tall Canadian friend who calls me every once in a while to say, "Dicky's looking down from heaven with a smile on his face, eh?" which always makes me feel good—like I'm finally a grown man capable of making his father proud.

As you know, there was a big gap between the first batch of letters and the last few, Richard Gere. I'm sorry my letters stopped so suddenly, but I got a little overwhelmed with all that happened in such a short period of time. It feels strange, to be honest, writing again—makes me feel a little crazy, or maybe it reminds me of how bubbling mad my mind got and maybe could become again if I'm not careful, if I don't take care of myself.

Our new therapist, whose name is Dr. Hanson—she's a tiny lady whose ballerina bun doubles as a pincushion for writing utensils—said it would be good for me to finish telling you my story, if only to say good-bye, to officially end the Richard Gere chapter of my life.

"Close the Richard Gere loop," she said. "It's very important to give your subconscious closure."

She also told me that it was necessary to tell you—and thereby admit to my subconscious—that I wasn't one hundred percent truthful in my letters, but embellished a bit from time to time to make things more interesting. Dr. Hanson says I did this because I was afraid I wasn't good enough to correspond with such a famous and important person as yourself, Richard Gere. But please know that—while that previous statement is technically true—metaphorically speaking, everything I wrote you was also one hundred percent equally true.

In some ways, I was more truthful with you than I've ever been with anyone else in my entire life, including Mom, so I hope you can be proud of that, Richard Gere.

I'm trying to hide less behind metaphor in my real life now.

Dr. Hanson says this is important.

I agree with her.

So does Elizabeth.

Dr. Hanson really is a gifted and healing person—maybe even a little like Saint Brother André, but in the modern world of here and right now, and not overtly religious.

I'm enjoying my new life.

I really am.

I'm living without Mom, and I'm okay.

Miracle?

Did we get one?

Maybe.

Regardless, I'm grateful.

One last thing—Elizabeth and I hold hands almost every day now.

It's true.

Are you proud of me, Richard Gere?

I'm trying very hard to give Elizabeth the fairy tale.

So—I think we're done corresponding at this point in time, right now.

I'm signing off for good.

There will not be another letter.

You can move on to your next assignment, or—if you were never real in the first place—you can just blink out of existence forever.

Regardless of whether you are just a figment of my imagination or not, I thank you for reading all of my words, even if we were both only pretending—thank you for being there when I didn't have anyone else, and for simply listening without judgment.

I wish you much luck with your struggles.

I trust you will free Tibet yet—and I will celebrate your accomplishment when it comes to be.

And please feel free to share Mom's philosophy with His Holiness, the Dalai Lama.

I'm going to miss you, but I really think this has to be my last letter.

Dr. Hanson's orders.

The you-me Richard Gere of pretending has run its course.

And there are real people here with me now—people who just might stick around.

Good-bye, Richard Gere.

Your admiring fan,
Bartholomew Neil

ACKNOWLEDGMENTS

Special thanks to my wife, Alicia Bessette; favorite European, Liz Jensen; and editors, American Jennifer Barth and Canadian Jennifer Lambert, for reading drafts and dramatically improving this book in every way possible; my agent, Doug Stewart, for ceaselessly believing in my work and me; the entire Sterling Lord Literistic crew and all of the foreign agents/scouts; the many foreign editors who have made this book available to readers around the globe; my film agent, Rich Green; Mom; Dad, for serendipitously telling me about President Garfield's assassination in great detail exactly when I needed to know, even though I didn't realize how valuable the information was to this project at the time (synchronicity?); Megan; Micah; Kelly; Aaron; Grandmom Dink; Pete; Barb and Peague, for allowing me to write in the Vermont house; Bill and Mo Rhoda; Mr. Canada (aka Scott Caldwell) and family for providing delicious and nutritious food, alcohol, BeaverTails, and shelter when we researched Cat Parliament in Ottawa; Dr. Len Altamura; Peruvian Scott Humfeld; Roland Merullo; Beth and Tim

Rayworth; Evan Roskos; Mark Wiltsey; Kent Green; all of the many people at HarperCollins (and at publishing houses around the world) who have worked tremendously hard to promote this book; every single fan who has ever said or written something nice about my work; and YOU, for reading *The Good Luck of Right Now* RIGHT NOW (synchronicity?). Thanks!!!

ABOUT THE AUTHOR

MATTHEW QUICK is the author of *The Silver Linings Playbook*, which was made into an Academy Award–winning film, and the young adult novels *Sorta Like a Rock Star*, *Boy21*, and *Forgive Me, Leonard Peacock*. He is married to the novelist-pianist Alicia Bessette.